CRITICAL ACCLAIM FOR
CATHERYNNE M. VALENTE'S
THE HABITATION OF THE BLESSED:
A DIRGE FOR PRESTER JOHN VOLUME ONE

"In this enchanting retelling of the [Prester John] legend, the first volume in a projected trilogy, Hugo nominee Valente (*Palimpsest*) imagines what might have been discovered by Rome's ambassadors if the letter had not been a hoax. Nothing is quite as fabulous as the prior presets had hoped. Prester John and St. Thomas the Twin married nonhuman women; the Fountain of Youth does not sparkle, but instead 'oozes thick and oily, gobbed with algae and the eggs of improbably mayflies'... Filled with lyrical pro̶ and fabled creatures, this languorous f̶ Prester John's original letter."

D0059498

"In *The Habitation of the Blessed*, Cat̶ her extravagant imagination loose on the 12th century legends of Prester John, the Nestorian Christian priest who set out from Constantinople to search for the tomb of Saint Thomas and ends up as the beloved ruler of Pentexore... The writing is luxuriant, as always, and the dialogue is often reminiscent of the delightful repartee found in Lewis Carroll's *Alice in Wonderland*."

—Kat Hooper, *FantasyLiterature.com*

"Catherynne Valente's *The Habitation of the Blessed* is in a word, sublime. I have never read anything like this before. Intimate, evocative, and powerful, the price paid to experience it is that one can never again come to it with innocence, never again read it for the first time."

—*Little Red Reviewer*

"When I picked up *Habitation*, I really had no idea what I was getting into. I just saw that Catherynne M. Valente published something new and I slammed my money down… This book is haunting. It tells a story that stays. Let it visit and stay with you."

—Michael Phillips, *LithiumCreations.com*

"*The Habitation of the Blessed* tells an imaginative story brimming with beautiful imagery."

—*FantasyBookCafe.com*

"Valente is skilled at showing age-old legends in a new light. [...] The intersecting, yet distinct, narratives explore the story from different angles and give the reader multiple viewpoints [...] but trying to boil the story down that way doesn't really do it justice. The author's prose is lyrical and dream-like, like poetry conformed to a novel format."

—Slade Grayson, *Bookgasm*

"Basically, if you're a fan of Cat's work, you're going to want this. And if you're not a fan, then buy it and become one."

—Stephanie Gunn, author and reviewer

"Valente has the uncanny gift of taking the mightiest words and stringing them into the loveliest thing[s]."

—*Books I Done Read*

"This is not the type of whiz-bang magic that feels cheap and flashy. This is real magic…strange, dark, gritty, and completely mesmerizing. If other books are a pencil drawing then Valente's work is a masterpiece of oils. Valente is an artist and her words are her medium…I really have no clue what's going to happen next or what the end goal will be. And you know what, I don't care. All I know is that I'll be there for every step of the journey."

—*Elitist Book Reviews*

"Folks, Cat Valente is one of my favorite people, and she's a hell of a writer, and her new book *The Habitation of the Blessed* is very cool."

—John Scalzi, author of *Old Man's War* and *Fuzzy Nation*

THE
FOLDED WORLD

A DIRGE FOR PRESTER JOHN
VOLUME TWO

WITHDRAWN

OTHER BOOKS BY
CATHERYNNE M. VALENTE

THE
FOLDED WORLD

A DIRGE FOR PRESTER JOHN
VOLUME TWO

CATHERYNNE M. VALENTE

SAN DIEGO PUBLIC LIBRARY
NORTH PARK BRANCH

NIGHT SHADE BOOKS
SAN FRANCISCO

The Folded World
© 2011 by Catherynne M. Valente
This edition of *The Folded World*
© 2011 by Night Shade Books

Edited by Juliet Ulman
Cover art by Rebecca Guay
Cover design by Cody Tilson
Map by Tim Piotrowski
Interior layout and design by Amy Popovich

All rights reserved

First Edition

ISBN: 978-1-59780-203-1

Night Shade Books
http://www.nightshadebooks.com

For Deborah Schwartz and Kat Howard,
my medievalist darlings, the invisible audience
for all my subtle clevernesses, stalwart
and mighty women who see the world so clear.

And for my tribe, all those for whom
the world is worth folding in half, in quarters,
in eighths, and more.

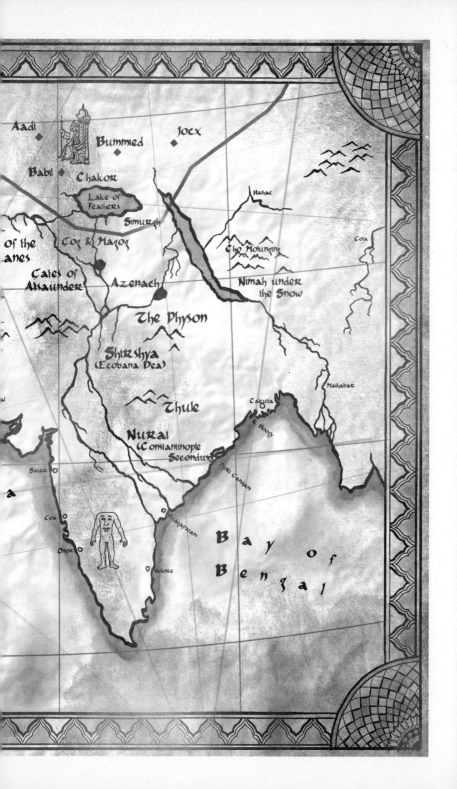

Those who were strangers are now natives; and he who was a sojourner now has become a resident...for those who were poor there, here God makes rich. Those who had few coins, here possess countless besants; and those who had not had a villa, here, by the gift of God, already possess a city. Therefore why should one who has found the East so favorable return to the West? God does not wish those to suffer want who, carrying their crosses, have vowed to follow Him, nay even unto the end.

—The Chronicle of Fulcher of Chartres, 1099

Enjoy the scent of the ox-eye plant of Najd, for after this evening it will come no more.

—A tutor in the Egyptian court of
Salah ad-Din Yusuf ibn Ayyubi

THE CONFESSIONS

I have felt it necessary to remove the name of my master from these documents, as, if he is not dead he is certainly not living, and confessions are the province of living men. It is rightly to be called ours now, and not merely his, our confessions, our book, our unsettling and unbearable tale. I look on these pages, their hasty script, their untidy gaps, and they seem to me like a fierce and unruly child of whom Hiob had the raising, and I had the troubled marriage. Yet it does not feel correct to give it my own name. These are not the Confessions of Alaric of Rouen, they are only a confession, at no kind of altar. As exemplars of their kind, they are mostly a disaster of poor choices made in the dark, and miserable happenings that might have been avoided if someone or other were less of an idiot than he proved to be.

I expected to return home more quickly than has proved possible. The passage through the mountains surrounding Lava-puri clotted up with mud driven by heavy rains, and of course Hiob himself has become something more like a relic we will soon be forced to bear homeward in a lovely box than the venerable leader of our mission. For my brother suffers still the effects of his rather unwise ingestion of a lurid blossom which rose up from the rotting fruit of the book-tree that grows still in a distant part of this province. I am often angry with him for playing the fool and the glutton, though it is unworthy of me to allow my mind to wallow in such judgments, for I cannot understand how such a wise man could think no ill effects would befall him if he but ate some alien plant he knew nothing about. As I write Brother Hiob lies like the princess of the country tale, on a hard bier wrapped in flowers and vines and thorns. The blossom continued to grow out of his mouth after he fell into his current swoon, and now its orange and red flowers open up in many places on his body, and I cannot tell if they are rooted in his flesh or if they all spring from the vine that wedges open his withered throat, around which I each day pour water and a mash of the local grain, proper fruits, and milk. As of late I have had to massage the corners of his lips to open wider in order to feed him, for the emerald stem has swelled fat and healthy in such pious and fertile soil as my brother. The whole business is enormously unpleasant and not a little obscene. The tendrils of the thing have wound around his fingers like rings, and a curtain of pollen drifts round him day and night, blowsy and golden. It makes me sneeze; I cannot abide unruly life.

Hiob, my brother, you have left me, and I am alone. How could you be so thoughtless?

And then, of course, there is always the woman in yellow, called Theotokos though I will never call her so, haunting my steps and tending to Hiob as though he were her own son, and never leaving me though I would have her gone, I *would* have her gone, for she torments my heart and my mind altogether, and I am not so young that these two organs sit surely in my body, but rather in her presence rattle around like old teeth. She lifts his withered arms to wash him, his legs, and her hands on his insensate flesh lead my thoughts in spirals whose center points I dare not even consider.

I am not in the main troubled by women as many of my brothers are. God made them, and while it is true He also made serpents and scorpions and sharks, I am quite certain that in the kingdom of sharks there is a morality, a virtue, a justice, no less than in our own. It is only that we cannot effectively communicate with the shark save by extremely significant bite or equally emphatic harpoon, and so debates on the nature of selachian philosophy are rare. So it is that the outline of the woman in yellow when the sun moves behind her chills me in the same fashion as the outline of a shark in clear water would do—I see in it a clear presage of my own demise.

And yet even as I lay out argument, I recall the metaphor of Prester John, and how he called Christ a shark, and the Logos a lamprey affixed to its side. I thought I saw some truth in this unlovely image, though undoubtedly it is a heresy, and perhaps both women and God can be called creatures of the deep. And having thought of those former books, my heart comes round again to Hiob and his situation, and sinks once more into a dark and freezing tide whose ebb I cannot hope for.

With the permission of all concerned, I began the building of an anchorhold some fortnight ago. The boughs of the great tree bend over it, and I intend there to continue my brother Hiob's work for two reasons. Firstly, I have no reason to think he will ever awake, yet no reason to think he will not, and between the two of them I believe this work must fall to someone, and I say without pride it is obvious I am best suited. If he did awake, I confess I would have not the first idea how to remove the plant matter from his body. I try not to think about it. My own throat itches in sympathy.

Secondly, there is little enough else to do here.

It is a simple affair: I hewed a good measure of camphor wood, whose fragrance pierces my mind, and with fastening and burying their stumps much like a puzzle, wedged them firmly one against the other until a structure quite humble but serviceable emerged. Its roof I thatched from fragrant leaves, slick and wide and green. I sweat profusely, for the heat is unbearable in this place, and there is not an inch of my dwelling which does not bear my sweat or my blood. That is as it should be. A bed of rushes I have, and a desk of piled extraneous wood, broad enough to serve my purposes. A stool the woman in yellow allowed me to take from her, but asked me for a curious exchange.

I will give you a chair, she said to me, *and more books besides, for surely you have not forgotten that they are not yours to take but mine to give, but you must spend a night with me.*

I am chaste, I protested, but my heart—no, something deeper than my heart, some dark, squamous knot of viscera—leapt up.

She gave me a pitying look, as one gives to a child who has interrupted his teacher to give the answer before the question is asked and thus blurted out that Jerusalem was the chief city of Russia.

I do not desire you. I do desire that a man who demands so much of us, our treasure, our food, our goodwill, our chairs, give to me whatever I ask, and I ask for a night. I want to know who you are, Alaric of Rouen, and who Hiob is, and how you dare appear as if out of a dream and put your hands around us, squeezing until you have all you desire. Of course you speak to me of desire, desire is all you are made of. And though you may not trespass the bounds of my body, you will certainly trespass anywhere else you please, and yet have the temerity to call yourself chaste while you thrust against my world.

Women and sharks both flay one alive, but only women can shame a man while they slice out his heart.

I agreed; it is a small price. The boredom of the contemplative life will give her a meager coin—I doubt she will be able to stay awake through my accounts of learning to read Latin and assisting Brother Vridel in the herbiary. The life cycle of fennel is such a fascinating subject. But what night she would ask of me she kept to herself as all other things, and allowed me to chose once more from the tree. However, I would not make

Hiob's mistake. I do not have his pride, and I did not care if I were the one to read the tree's strange fruit first. Before I took my first steps towards the orchard, I drew together two of the younger novices, Brother Reinolt and Brother Goswin, neither of whom I cared for personally (thus I would not be weakened by affection, but have the strength to be cruel to them). Each of them had an elegant hand and an obedient enough ear, and both showed signs of a dangerous sort of boredom. Their eyes had become canine, tracking the young women of the village as they went about their livelihoods. Novices, until they have burst their last pimple, are consistently engorged and constantly besieged with temptation. Best to put them to work.

Copy as quickly as you can. Do not make mistakes. Do not put your head in your hand and read dreamily. These books will rot and you must beat them at the race, to take their tales before they puff out in a cloud of spores. If you feel your heart moved by the story, your mind drifting to distant lands all full of fantastical creatures, think on Hiob, and how that vine will feel in your own mouth, cracking your teeth.

The choice was mine this time. It sat heavily with me; Hiob chose so well I cannot believe it was anything other than Providence. What if I should chose nothing specially of interest to us, some chronologue of tree sap and yearly rainfall? What if I should fail and spoil all my preparation? Why could there not be some kind-hearted librarian cloistered away in the village, with a reliable catalogue of all the books the tree could be relied upon to produce? How I should like to meet that man; all would be made clear and easy. Instead I was made to stand at the doubled-up root of the devilish tree, looking up into its boughs, terribly full and bright, the afternoon sun impossibly golden, filtering through the scarlet leaves and full, ripe fruit: in squares and scrolls, in red and green and blue and violet and silver, a hundred books and more in which I was meant to discover the fate of the Kingdom of Prester John, and ransom Hiob from his insensate and rapturous sleep.

In the end it seemed better to chose at random and trust in God than try to somehow apply strategy to such a great mystery. I climbed a little, shut my eyes, thrust out my hand, climbed a little more, did much the same, and tumbled back down the tree with three books clutched to my chest, out of breath, their perfume pulling at me with dusky fingers. Only then did I dare to look at my catch, my net of strange fish hooked out of the sky.

The first was deep blue, and on its cover a wing had been embossed, its feathers spread open like fingers.

The second was leafed in silver, glistening dully, and on its surface I saw a hand, and in the palm of the hand there was a monstrous mouth, open as if to speak.

The last was black, heavy and solid, and it crackled slightly as I touched it, as if it had once been burnt. On it was figured a creature with a dozen arms, arranged around its body like the spokes of a wheel.

I shuddered and flushed all together, and I felt as I did once long ago, when a girl came to my window all bright with the night, her eyes full of stars, her lips dark and trembling with the January cold and the very nearness of sin. The image of her rose so fiercely in me; I felt towards those books the same anticipation as when she stood quite still at the threshold of my house and my body, and I suppose I was as helpless before each of them as the other. All my plans fled before me. I wanted to open them all, for everything to be open and plain and naked before me.

The books were warm and alive in my hands. Yet the moment passed, and I could not see that lost girl in my memory any longer, nor the darkness of her lips. The day was bleeding out, and so much work to be done.

Saturn, Cold and Dry

The palace in which our Supereminency resides is built after the pattern of the castle built by the apostle Thomas the Twin for the Indian king Gundoforus. Ceilings joints and architrave are of sethym wood, the roof ebony, which can never catch fire. Over the gable of the palace are, at the extremities, two golden apples, in each of which are two carbuncles, so that the gold may shine by day and the carbuncles by night. The greater gates of the palace are of sardius with the horn of the horned snake inwrought so that no one can bring poison within. The other portals are of ebony; the windows are of crystal; the tables are partly of gold, partly of amethyst; the columns supporting the tables are partly of ivory, partly of amethyst. The court in which we watch the jousting is floored with onyx in order to increase the courage of the combatants. In the palace at night, nothing is burned for light, but wicks supplied with balsam...

Before our palace stands a mirror, the ascent to which consists of five and twenty steps of porphyry and serpentine. This mirror is guarded day and night by three thousand men. We look therein and behold all that is taking place in every province and region.

Seven kings wait upon us monthly, in turn, with sixty-two dukes, two hundred and fifty-six counts and marquises. Twelve archbishops sit at table with us on our right and twenty bishops on the left, besides the patriarch of St. Thomas, the Sarmatian Protopope, and the Archpope of Susa...our high lord steward is a primate and king, our cup-bearer is an archbishop and king, our chamberlain a bishop and king, and our marshal a king and abbot.

—The Letter of Prester John,
1165

THE BOOK
OF THE RUBY

Being an Account of the Winning and Losing of a Great War, composed by Hagia of the Blemmyae Despite Protestation, as Her Daughter Anglitora, who Commanded the Forces of Her Nation, There Being No One Else About Who Knew a Damned Bit About the Business of Fighting, God Save Them All, Never Learned Her Letters.

This is not my tale to tell.

I am but a reluctant author—that thick, deep root which storytellers tap and from which they suck up all their strength is not mine. I have no map to it. Perhaps one day I shall have the muscular fortitude to write in truth for myself, to tell the tale of how I was born, how I lived and worked, how I drank from the Fountain and loved my mother. Of John's coming to our country, and how I met and first loved him. How we made our child between us like a strange machine. It seems, to be frank, a gargantuan task and I am tired. When I think of the great number of words that would have to be piled upon themselves in order even to begin the long fable of his rule, my heart stills and wishes only to sleep. What a heap of useless, glittering gems those words would be! And such work to build them up, only to lose the lot if just one ruby were misplaced. No, I could not do it. It is too much. When I am older; when I have wisdom like holes where my teeth used to be, wisdom where anger and need used to be, then I will tell that tale.

And yet here I sit, in a tent of black silk with silver stars stitched into it, the war over and everything sour, I sit and scratch parchment in the country of the cranes, hiding here, hoping not to be found. Dawn on the Rimal is a lonely thing. It is a line the sun crosses. One moment you can only see black and the next a kind of hard, sharp whiteness cuts neatly across the sand, as quiet as shears, slicing away the wool of the night. All that's left is skin. The bald, peeled skin of the sun and the sand, mating endlessly across the expanse of the Rimal. And in the dim light the girl at my side glares at me with her black eyes with golden sparks stitched into them. She says:

Why are you making excuses? Just say what happened. It doesn't have to be pretty. It's just that someone has to say it. Or else who will remember? All our friends are dead.

The girl is my daughter. And as she sees me write this she puts out her soft pale wingtip to touch my hand so tenderly, as a daughter touches her mother when they have both been through so much, when they have hurt together like two wet ropes pulling in opposite directions, when they have fought with their shoulder blades pressed together like one flesh. This is how she touches me, but she says:

I am not your daughter. I love you like a hard, hot knot, but you have to tell the truth. You have to write that I am John's get but not yours, and how it hurt you, and how my real mother sounded when she spoke, and how you first met me, and what I brought to you that day, and how you didn't forgive me for a long time. I can't write it, so you have to. I know you can. You owe me the best words you can think of. It doesn't have to be pretty but it has to be true.

She brought a helmet. And I still haven't forgiven her.

Children can be so difficult.

In all of the stories from John's country, the great concern is: who should be king? Will it be this young, earnest prince or that cruel, decadent duke? Will it be the correct boy, who has lineage, father to father, or this upstart who has not paid his genealogical dues? It seems to me that in that place where John is not unusual, where he is home and hearth and an everyday sort of man, kingmaking must be a kind of sport. All the people of his nation must come to see it happen, to make bets on the players, to wear the colors of their preferred champion and cheer when the lesser contenders fall down in the dust with their heads sliced off or poison dribbling from their lips. It must be very exciting—but the stories usually end with someone being king. That's the whole purpose of the story. The next tale picks up with another throne, another young, pure-hearted knight robbed of his birthright, another black-greaved usurper. For all that they love to make kings, John's folk seem to have little interest in the actual business of ruling anything. They like to become, they do not like to be.

John insists that I do not understand these stories. That is probably true. I tell him pointedly it is no one's fault who their father is. One can neither blame nor credit them for the habits of the creature who flopped about on their mother. John enjoys, I think, being shocked by me. He would not admit it, but he likes the blows I give his heart. He says Christ is king, and all earthly kings strive to be like him, and thus, as Christ's tale is one of rising from lowly beginnings to take His rightful place at His Father's hand, of course the histories follow this natural course.

It is hard to understand what foreigners mean, even when they have been so kind as to learn the local language. But now John is king, and it is with some dry amusement that I note how his world gave him only tools to want a crown, not to wear one.

The girl is not my daughter. But she is mine. Her name is Anglitora. I should have said that at the first. I told her that this was her story, but if she had been my daughter she would not be so hopeless when it came to letters. I would have taught her to write her own history, how writing is like giving birth to yourself—no one can do it for you without making a mess. I have tried to give her her letters, and she knows enough to disapprove of my progress. Enough to scowl at me, her long, muscled neck shining bronze in the candlelight. She cannot help her father or mother either, she hoots when she is upset and passes a hand over her eyes and oh, how like John she looks when she does it:

You must get to the point. If you do not get to the point quickly, people will get confused. The point is the war, not that father was foolish when he was young. The point is how I came to the al-Qasr and the sun was so bright it bounced off the helmet in my arms and father winced, and so did you, and all the birds cried out because they are birds of omen and you cannot be made of omen without knowing the future. Just say: one day a man named John came to Pentexore, and he was a stranger but you were all kind to him anyway, and when the Abir rolled up like a great stone he became king and you became his wife, but you already loved him, so that was all right. It's easy, really. It only starts to get interesting when I come across the desert.

I laugh in the dark, and it is the first time I have laughed in so long. She is still such a child, hardly even forty, and this is what children think: the story only begins once they enter the action. Nothing came before them and what came after is only distant, indistinct, seen through a haze and a veil. I'm sure I think this way as well, though I seem virtuous to myself, in that I believe the story of Prester John began when I found him lying face down in a pepper-field. This is a mountain in the path of the story—you cannot assail it or walk around it. We discovered him and brought him home. Myself and Hadulph the red lion and Fortunatus the gryphon and two pygmies whose names I have forgotten. That was how it started.

Anglitora disagrees—it began with a crane, obviously.

But I have said it is her tale, and I only have the telling of it. I bow to her will.

I do recall that it was morning. A pure light fell down through the banana leaves and papaya trees, turning the sun and shadows green at the edges, turning the air clear and sweet, and we had not yet opened the court for the day's doings—John ate his breakfast of red rice and blackbulb, conferring with one of his advisors, whom he called a proto-pope and who was truly called Vidyut, a vaguely confused but well-spoken orangutan with a passion for philosophy. John called Grisalba, my dear friend and a lamia, an archbishop, and she liked that very fine. I was queen; everyone called me so, though it never sat right with me. A queen should be more than I was in those days: just holding on, to John, to Hadulph (whom John called an abbot), to Fortunatus (a cup-bearer) and Qaspiel (a cardinal) and all I loved, and to my poor child who wept so bitterly and could not make herself understood, even as she howled on her mother's throne. For I had a child, a princess for our kingmaking tale, before Anglitora came.

I must stop for a moment. To speak of my child strangles my heart, which is already throttled half to death. If another woman were writing this, she would say: *Queen Hagia had two daughters, one fair and one monstrous.* But I am writing it, and the fair one puts her warm human hand on my knee and her cool crane's wing over my hair and whispers:

How fares my sister, do you think, with all of us gone? I remember how you loved her, then. I remember how she laughed at my arm.

Do not ask me. I cannot know. It was morning, I know it was morning, that is all I remember. It was morning when she came, striding up to the door and the court like you belonged there, like you knew us all so well and even despised us a little. I remember how you looked, how tall and strong, the muscles in your legs and your good arm, this girl with long blue-black hair and skin the color of the Rimal at sunset and a gaze that cut us so deeply we understood you without any need to speak. That arm spoke so loudly: a girl in amber armor, her breastplate full of golden veins and bubbles, one arm strong and human, one arm a long, pale wing, a crane's wing, its longest feathers grazing her knee. And in her arms like a child: a bronze helmet. And the sun hit it like a blow, glancing off and hitting us each with a closed, glowing fist.

Yes, that's how it was. That's it.

John's face moved horribly—continents of memory drifted there, and I watched him work out the lineage involved, how her jaw looked so like his, her nose, and how that wing, that tell-tale wing called out his sin and could not be denied.

"Kukyk," he whispered, and that was Anglitora's mother's name. I am her stepmother, but if the crane had the rearing of the child, I had the rearing of the woman. Perhaps it is truer to say that the crane-girl had two mothers and no father to speak of.

It's no one's fault who their father is.

I cannot say if I was hurt. I was not jealous—John had told me the tale of the crane and how he made love to her while the nation of birds fought and mated with the nation of pygmies in the valley below them. I thought it was a beautiful story, one which made sense, had a good beginning, a logical progression of events and a satisfying conclusion, unlike his endless parade of paladins becoming king to no good end. I did not think of a child. I did not think of an epilogue. John and his crane-maid did not battle, they only mated. But the crane must win that fight, to determine whether the bird or the pygmy owns the get. Without blood drawn, their offspring could never be one or the other, human or crane, but both, confused, in one body. How hard her life must have been. I do not think I was hurt, not in the way women are hurt in John's stories when their men mate with others. I had had a husband before him. We all have our histories. I think I only looked on her and envied her strength and beauty, for my own child fell into one of her convulsions even as her crane-sister set the helmet before us.

This is what Anglitora of the Gharaniq said to us:

"Never mind how embarrassing this must be for the king. I am here to embarrass. Take it, fold it up in your pocket, and consider it later. Pay attention now. I have brought this thing and it is a war helmet. I have taken the skull out of it to make this business cleaner. In the teeth of the skull was a letter. I have brought them both so that you will not think I am lying. For a year now this bronze flotsam, and iron too, have washed up on the shore of the Rimal, in my mother's country. Sometimes heads are still stuck in them, and breasts in breastplates. Our beaches are clotted with them. There can only be one conclusion—something is happening on the other side of the great sand sea, and it is ugly and bloody and full of death. The drakes determined that I was best suited to deliver this news, to shame you, if I needed to, into considering how full of danger and blackness this single helmet is. It *brims*, my father, it spills over. How long before living men come piling up, living men who also want to be king, who are like the men Alisaunder and Didymus Tau'ma spoke of? How long before the Rimal is not an ocean but a road?"

And we quailed, all of us. We thought of every tale we had heard of John's world. And I, I thought of the mirror I had shown him, the mirror of the phoenix, and all those domes burning, all those palm fronds red with flame. I thought of the unspooling of grief within him, and how it had undone much of what love had sewn up.

My father had gone mad, you mean to say.

No, not mad. Let us say he had come apart, and one half of him was my husband, and one half of him was his former self, and the two did not enjoy their own company. Like the Word and the Flesh of his unfortunate, torn-apart god, and I wish I could say which of them I had to mate. If only I could have simply destroyed the man from Constantinople and kept for myself his better parts, his kindness and his big, round laugh, his curiosity about each of us, his excitement concerning the birth of our child. But where his two parts met stood the mirror, the glass showing all the darknesses of his former life, lit with fire and shouting for help.

Each day John sat at the phoenix's mirror, watching a city burn, a city I did not know, could never know, with domes and spires and crosses and crescents. As he watched, the city burned over and over. His face grew ruddy with the flames, his eyes empty as he listened to the screaming and the thundering of horses on city streets, yet he would not let it be. Perhaps a phoenix's mirror only shows that which burns, I tried to argue, but he could not hear me. Cross-legged before the high glass he strove with his great work, a rewriting of his Bible that could include us, all of us, without breaking the Word of God over his knee.

And in the beginning God created Heaven and Earth, he wrote. *And between the two a land where the Heaven could embrace the Earth and merge with it, as man with woman and beast with beast. And the Earth was without form, and void, and the Heaven was without end and border, and darkness was on the face of the deep, and the Spirit of God moved upon the face of the sea of sand. And God said let there be light, and there was light and the light was the word and the word had form.*

"It's this part that I can't work out," he said once, before the mirror kindled his brain. "Where dominion comes into it. I can keep God blessing us and saying be fruitful and multiply, that's all right, but if He gives man dominion over all the beasts and the fish of the sea and the fowl of the air and every living thing, where does that leave Fortunatus and Qaspiel and little Hajji? Where does it leave you?"

"Not long ago you would have said 'under your dominion' and been satisfied," I mused, and stretched my arms above my shoulders.

John seemed discomfited, as the part of him that loved me warred with the part of him that had come over the Rimal seeking God.

"But *someone* has to have dominion, do they not? We cannot simply have no dominion at all, and moving on the face of the deep and the water and the sand and everything with no hierarchy, no sure knowledge of the natural order. Perhaps speaking things can have dominion over things which do not speak. That seems reasonable. After all, you eat beef and mutton and do not ask their permission."

"Is that what dominion means? The privilege of eating things without asking first?"

Hagia, you are digressing. Are you not glad I am here to marshal you and march you straight?

Of course. I am too easily caught in remembering. John never finished the work; what is unfinished cannot be important.

The crane-girl put the helmet down on the purple stones of the al-Qasr. It clanged and my child began to weep. Well she might.

The crane went on: "You may blame me, if you like. You'll find it easier, to blame me for bothering you with the troubles of the cranes. I will take that blame. She who tells a truth must take responsibility for it. She owns the life of that truth, and must see to the caring and feeding of it, the rearing of it, the use of it. And she must see it through to the end. Say what you like—I will not abandon this thing I brought with me over the waste. I will stay by its side, to the very and most bitter last."

And so began the war, which had ended and yet not ended,

was won and yet bitterly lost, upon us yet far off. She brought it to us, but we took it from her, and how it blossomed in our hands.

I am sorry. Perhaps if we had closed our eyes and refused to treat with that war we would have stayed secret and safe. But I became the creature I was made to be: half my mother and half my father, screeching to the moon and striding over the sand. I was determined before I was born. I was always going to be Anglitora, forever meant to be her, unable to be any other one, even if I wanted to be. When I face the west I am my father's daughter, and there is blood everywhere that I cannot staunch, and there is gold and myrrh too, the stuff of life and death, and secrets and buried things. When I face the east I am my mother's child, and I am free, and I do not care whom I hurt, for pain and joy come walking hand in hand together across the desert, and I cannot tell them apart.

And when you face straight ahead, Gli? When you face the dawn on the Rimal with me, when you face the sun and the long days ahead?

Then, Hagia, then I am yours.

THE CONFESSIONS

T he bones of my back popped and stretched—but I confess that it was a pleasure to find I had done well in choosing my book off the great tree. Hagia's voice looped and wrote neatly upon my brain once more, and I felt I had come to know her a little, as one comes to know a cousin one did not grow up with, but discovered as a grown man and found to be pleasant company. Yet it could not escape my notice that this was a younger Hagia, one full of sadness and anger, instead of the intelligent and melancholic matron Hiob and I had encountered in the scarlet book with those searching eyes embossed on its cover. Yet there was a pleasure in that too, to witness this other Hagia, not so resigned to her life and her husband's death—not even yet aware of his death. It was something akin to meeting one's mother as a girl. Knowing all that would happen to her, but unable to tell her. And the child, the child haunting the margins of that wiser, gentler Hagia's tale, the full belly of the blemmye's last rotting chapters, now born and broken and hidden away.

I shuddered; a cold shadow had come on me.

Brothers Reinolt and Goswin bent their heads over their pages; I could see their pates gleaming like eggs in the nests of their hair. What wonders were they reading? I crushed this thought in me—I would not go Hiob's way, I would not be jealous of the texts; they were not mine to be jealous of. Yet my resistance had less resilience than I'd hoped—I called out and asked them at least the authors of their books. They could not help but absorb that much, even if I had instructed them not to read for pleasure but for the work of copying.

"I believe it is some sort of lion," said Brother Reinolt. "There is much concerning a deformed child."

"I could not possibly say," sighed Brother Goswin with some irritation. "He has not identified himself as of yet save as a knight of St. Albans, and it all appears to be some sort of encyclopedia. I cannot make heads nor tails of it, Brother Alaric, if I am an honest man."

So sated, I ate some small scrap of bread and availed myself of water. Not for the first time I praised Hiob in my heart, for scribe's work is hard on all the parts of a man's body, yet he seemed never to tire. I have always been the lazier of us—but I keep my laziness in a box at the bottom of my heart, and dance with vigor to distract anyone from seeing that weak boy at the core of me who wants only to dream and rest. When I was a youth in the abbey I used to dream out of the cloister window at the chestnut trees in the courtyard, how white their blossoms or how rich-looking their nuts, depending on the season, wishing for any diversion but the illuminated page before me, wishing to do any work but writing out one more word with my cramped and aching hand. Of course now those days seem sweet to me, when I was but learning my Greek and my Aramaic, when Brother Hiob was a junior in our ranks and ruddy of face, insisting upon exercising in the yard each morning to keep himself hale though no wrinkle had yet marked his face. *Alaric*, he said, *if you do not serve your flesh it will never serve you. It is no honor to God to absent your attention from his greatest gift. Eat, but do not indulge, be strong, but not proud, and for the Lord's love sit up straight at your podium or I shall whip your calves.*

It is possible I ought to have listened more intently. He was in a real sense my father, as Anglitora, whatever her matrilineal unsavoriness, was Hagia's daughter. A child of the heart. My true father thought little of giving me up to the abbey at Luzern and writing me but never; of my mother I know only that she was whispered to be a witch, capable of healing a cough or cursing cattle merely by pulling some herb with her right hand or her left. She was said to be beautiful, but likely with some southern blood in her, this accounting for my own olive skin and dark eyes. She died—put to death or perished in some other wise. My father did not keep me long enough to say and on the subject my memory is silent. Hiob was my parent, and later my brother. His was the only soul who stood guard for mine, and spoke well of it to Heaven.

And I see now that I already speak of him as though he were gone, and believe it, would prefer it to the idea that one day he might wake with that flowered vine in his mouth. I would have him spared that knowledge, that pain, if the sparing of pain were mine to give and not Our Lord's. His bier stood silent near us, the scratching of our work and the reedy breathing of our brother sawing in time to one another. It was a terrible thing to have so near, but I wanted him close and safe—and well it might serve as a warning and stauncher of passion should these books too, inevitably, begin their foul blooming.

And thus I did not, could not hear, when Hiob's withered, beleaguered hand began to move, whispering over the petals of a blue and violet flower, his finger moving in swirling patterns while we, yet unsensing, wrote on into the eve.

The Left-Hand Mouth, the Right-Hand Eye

Being the Works and Days of Vyala the White Lion, who was Hadulph's Mother, and also Guardian to Sefalet, the Royal Child, During the War which took the King and Queen to Far Off Places. Written Afterward with the Help of Qaspiel the Anthropteron, as Claws are Poor Claspers of Quills.

L ove is a practice. It is a yogic stance; it is lying upon nails; it is walking over coals, or water. It comes naturally to no one, though that is a great secret. One who is learned might say: does not a babe in her mother's arms love? From her first breath does she not know how to love as surely as her mouth can find the breast? And I would respond: have you ever met a child? A cub may find the breast but not latch upon it, she may bite her mother, or become sick with her milk. So too, the utter dependence of a tiny and helpless thing upon those who feed and warm her is not love. It is fierce and needful; it has a power all its own and that power is terrible, but it is not love. Love can come only with time and sentience. We learn it as we learn language—and some never learn it well. Love is like a tool, though it is not a tool; something strange and wonderful to use, difficult to master, and mysterious in its provenance.

If love were not all of this, I would not have devoted my mind, which is large and generous and certainly could have done much else, to it for all these centuries.

If love were not all of this, I would never have known that wretched, radiant little girl, nor let her learn her teeth on my heart, which children can find with more sureness than ever they could clasp the breast, and latch upon it, and bite, and become sick, and make ill, and all the worst of the six ails of loving, which are to lose it, to find it, to break it, to outlive it, to vanish inside it, and to see it through to the end.

First I should say that I had no desire to raise another child. Hadulph was my joy, red in chest and mane, and he was enough. As a cub he was all-demanding, his redness a smear of blood against my fur, and when he slept his tail made patterns in the snow of Nimat. His father had been red, too, and sometimes I think all the brightnesses of my life have been banners of scarlet in the winter. Hatha was the father of Hadulph, and though there is little breeding among the white and red lions, he came to Nimat-Under-the-Snow lean and bold, and when he bit the scruff of my neck I was pleased. That is not love, either, not the child suckling nor the sire biting, but oh, it is sweet, and Hatha told me afterward the sutra of Yiwa, his antelope goddess, and among his words were: *we are all devoured by the world. Everything we want consumes us in turn, and we drown in wanting forever.* That was almost as good as the son he gave me, though I was as surprised as any to bear a single cat and not a litter. Perhaps the heart of Hadulph was so hungry he drank up all his possible brothers and sisters. My heart is like that.

When I was born my mother said: *well, you're alive. What will you do about it?* And that was all she taught me of the world. That is a cat's education—a bit of leonine milk and a short introduction to killing things weaker than oneself and off you go, kitten, into the snow, into the mountains, into the pine barrens and a forest of hearts and weeping. You see, perhaps, how I came to the notion that love is learned, not inborn. My sire was not much better—a big strapping fellow with a cream-colored tuft on the end of his tail, he gave me my name, Vyala, and said: *if you want to be cuddled, find a panoti. The world is a toothed place, and I am busy.*

I am not resentful. We all move and speak according to the dictates of our blood, our quiet, unalterable drives, and if a lion is gruff with his children, that is because his gruffness was so deep etched he could not erase it if he wished too. Perhaps the folk of the warm valleys are right about their Abir; perhaps my mother and father would have learned gentler thoughts if they had changed their lives like gowns. But the white lions abstain from the great lottery, and I am only myself, only Vyala, for all time, and they were only themselves, and all of us together could summon about a mouthful of feeling for each other, no more.

I think I was waiting, in those early years. Love can be spent out, spooled onto the earth and lost. I was saving up my capacities. For Hadulph, for all those who came to sleep in the curve of my ribs and be eased of their sorrows, for the royal child to come. They asked so much of me. I had to be alone for a century or two, just to store up fat against the love they would claim. Still, even still, I have that core of feline hardness that is my birthright, and if I do not wish to be moved, I am not moved. I often think that is the only power in the world, to chose whether one's own soul is swayed or stands stony and unwavering.

And so when my son came to me in my frozen cave and told me what he would have of me, I stretched my paws and yawned and chuckled. Why should I care that the queen had had a broken child? She should have thought better of letting a human breed her. It was never going to go well, a blemmye and a man. They took their chances and came up with a monster—too bad, none of my concern.

"Don't be cold," he said to me, and I laughed again. His friends were not my friends. "War is coming. Someone must stay behind."

I would stay, but not to be a nursemaid to whatever the creature was that ran stumbling down the halls of the al-Qasr. I did not want to know about men over the Rimal, I did not want to see what the mirror had shown. We do not live on the Axle of Heaven because we wish to be part of the affairs of Nural. Those who live in the heat have no delicate feelings; the sun burns it out of them. They think their own destinies are the destinies of all.

"Come and see her," he said. "Come and see her and decide then."

My son had spent too long at court, where no one speaks their desires. Where they coax and wheedle instead of wearing their hearts before them like a white blaze on red fur. He had forgotten how to speak to me, how to tell me that he loved Hagia and always would, and her child by the foreigner was his own child, too, for when her belly was great he bit the scruff of her broad back and she said his name with such tenderness it cut him, and he loved that child because it was broken, because with every breath the child said: *John and Hagia should have let each other alone.*

I understood him without his needing to growl out his passion into the snow. I chose to be moved. I would go. What harm could it do me? Ah, poor Vyala. Even you can be fooled—love can always hurt you.

I settled on the amethyst floor of the al-Qasr. The sethym columns twisted with silver rising up like bones around me, and the smell of incense and bowls of banana flowers in my nostrils, and my claws clicked on the stone. They brought her to me, in a little palanquin of emerald and black silk—draped with a weight of coppery veils which served to hide her face. The child could not have been more than ten or twelve years of age. Neither Hagia nor John came with her, only servants, and at the time I thought this cruel. Later I understood that if they were to leave her with me they wanted to know how we two would behave toward each other in their absence; as with two cats who are strangers, often one must simply place them in a room and let them have at it, if ever peace is to be hoped for afterward.

"This is ridiculous," I growled. "Take off her veils. She is not a leper."

The servants, a pair of bull-headed boys, drew back the cloth and for the first time I regarded Sefalet, the daughter of Prester John and Hagia of the Blemmyae, princess of Pentexore.

I confess that when I heard of the results of the Abir that throned them, I wondered how their child would fare. A blemmye has no head and a chest full of her own face, and a man most certainly does have a head, and a blind, mute chest without so much as an eyebrow on it. That afternoon I had my answer: Sefalet had a head, but it was bald, and had no features upon it—no eyes, no mouth, hardly a nose at all, perhaps a ridge of bone beneath the flesh, but the rest smooth and blank as a page unwritten. It was certainly very unsettling. Her dress, all copper-colored like her veils, fell loosely enough that I could see no face upon her body. Poor lamb, to be deaf and dumb and faceless. But had we not all seen stranger? A tensevete has a body of ice—why should she be so singled out and veiled away?

The girl put her hands up over her face where her eyes ought to have been. On the backs of her hands opened a pair of calm and beautiful green eyes, though red and wet from some past crying. She watched me for some time out of these strange eyes before turning over her left hand and placing it where her mouth would have been, had she been born her father's daughter. On the palm opened a mouth, with dark lips and teeth gleaming.

Out of the left-hand mouth she screamed horribly, a scream from the very bottom of her being, where all had gone black. She let her left hand fall and put her right over her mouthless face, and out of a second mouth on her right-hand palm she cried out: *I'm sorry, I'm sorry, I'm sorry!*

In her distress, the princess crawled toward me from her palanquin, the mouths of her hands kissing the floor, her blank face nodding miserably, her fingernails breaking against the amethyst, and I could not help it, I growled at her, my muzzle drawing up, my teeth showing in the shadows. What could I ever do for this tiny maiden? The growl came without my meaning it to, as one growls when a tiger is near, a cat as great as oneself, as capable of rending, of ruining. I feel shame now, when I think that the first sound I gave that girl was a rumbling snarl.

Sefalet collapsed at the sound of my growling, flat onto the floor, as if by sinking into it she might escape forever. And as I watched her, she began to shake and quiver, a kind of fit taking over her body, and out of her hands and feet poured a kind of awful light, illuminating the corners of the hall, the palanquin, the bull-headed servants, and me, turning us all the color of the moon.

When she had done, and by the expression on the servants' faces I knew this was not the first time she had quaked or shone, I rose and padded over to where the child lay, her faceless face pressed into the floor, her arms and legs spread out like the spokes of a wheel.

"Well," I said to her, "you're alive. What will you do about it?"

I settled down on my haunches before the girl, waiting patiently. A cat is good at waiting; perhaps the best. I lashed my tail from side to side. The bull servants watched me, and I watched her. Finally Sefalet lifted her head and put one hand over her face so that her eye regarded me coolly.

"Tell me your griefs," I purred to her. "I know that your body is strange and that you suffer fits—you may skip those. Tell me what is wrong with you. Tell me and I will take it away."

"You can't take it away," said the left-hand mouth.

"I can, though. It will be a long journey, and at the end of it perhaps you will not be Sefalet anymore, but I can take grief and bury it under a stone."

"That would do no good, a sorrow-tree would only grow in its place, full of little unripe princesses weeping sap," said the right-hand mouth.

"How old are you, child?"

"I am nine years old."

"And tell me the truth, the lion's truth, which has teeth and delights in blood: do you know what afflicts you?"

She held out her palms to me: the left-hand mouth smiled, and the right-hand mouth frowned.

And at that moment I agreed to care for her.

Her mother left with John and Anglitora and the rest of that long chain of fools dancing along their sandy dunes with death at their head, laughing all the way to Jerusalem. That tale is none of mine and I do not want it told in my presence. It does not matter what happened out there in the desert. Let the historians have duels over who gets the writing of that mess. In my heart, where it is always snowing and a girl with no face is always weeping, it matters only what happened in the al-Qasr, between a gryphon, a lamia, and a white lion; it matters only what happened to a child-princess in her violet tower.

THE CONFESSIONS

I recalled the white lion from John's epistle concerning his journey to the tomb of St. Thomas, and how Hadulph discussed with him the slatternly nature of his mother and her corruption of the words of St. Paul—whose twisting inversion I confess haunted my heart: *Love is hungry and severe. Love is not unselfish or bashful or servile or gentle. Love demands everything. Love is not serene, and it keeps no records.* I did not like the white lion then and I liked her less when I heard her cold, pale voice echoing in my own mind, unmodulated by her kinder son. She was unfeminine; her maternal nature lacked some vital component. Something wild and untempered in her turned the gentleness of a mother's spirit into a thing cold and utterly other. She spoke of love in such a way that I questioned my translation of the word, whether I in any way understood what the animal signified by that handful of letters.

If I am honest, and I suppose if this is a confession in truth I must be honest—and a confession of my own now, for Hiob dreams on and on of some sacred dark and greening jungle of heaven and the heart. If I am honest, Vyala's imperious letters bring my own mother sharply to mind. My dim memories of her, of her black hair around me like the branches of a winter forest, protecting me or threatening I could not know then. I did not love her—I was afraid of her, I lay in abject adoration of her, as of God or an archangel, for so she seemed to my tiny soul, but the lion is at least correct in that love is a thing between those who can speak and barter for the terms of love. I remember only a terror that I would be abandoned by her, a terror of her beauty and her nearness; and abandoned I was. In my memory my mother moves like a lion, soundless on dead and blackened paws.

Into my reverie Brother Reinolt broke, his tremulous voice piercing and unwelcome.

"Brother Hiob is moving!" he cried, and pointed at the verdant bier, still knotted with vines and flowers, and now, I saw, the beginnings of a pink and furry fruit budding here and there among the glossy green leaves. "His hand!"

And I turned to see it, the motion of his deft fingers, not idle or twitching as an insensate man's limbs will sometimes do, but purposeful, sure, though his eyes remained shut, his breathing labored, the huge vine no less swollen and bright. I went to my brother and tried to hold his hand in mine, to comfort him in his evident distress—but his fingers shuddered and jumped and shook in my grasp and I let him go once more, watching as he seemed to work an invisible pen over a parchment of blue flowers veined in violet and gold.

Without being sure it was the correct thing to do, I drew some portion of my own parchment out, and a fresh quill, and the one I put into his hand and the other I put beneath the nib, to see if perhaps he wished to speak to me out of his dreaming, out of the landscapes clotted with pollen and spores and orange, tiger-colored dust that must have flitted beneath his eyes as such things grew over his body.

"Tell me what troubles you," I whispered to him, half in Latin and half in Aramaic, our old game of mixing tongues, hoping to rouse him, or at least inspire his hand to scrawl out some wry assurance in several dialects of the Turk.

But I received no reply in kind. Instead, I will write here what his elegant hand scribed out on that parchment, already moist with the glittering excretions of the petals beneath it.

Fortunatus brought Qaspiel before John, its delicate feet hardly leaving depressions in the thick black soil of Nural, which was not unlike the fine, moist sand of vanilla deep within the pod. It had shorn its hair, and strewn it with little beads of hematite for the occasion. Its dress gleamed nearly colorless, a cobweb that would flatten and spread out in flight—and its wings, taller than itself and a deep sort of cobalt that played tricks with the eye. I went to embrace my friend, but before I could hold out my arms, John fell to his knees between us. I stared at him as he wept, his jaw slack, his body shaking in a kind of rapture.

"An angel," he whispered.

"Qaspiel," the anthropteron laughed. Its wings fluttered briefly.

I found it profoundly strange to watch another so utterly laid bare. John put his face on the earth and cried. His body seemed to fall apart; he was racked. I cannot remember ever being so wretched myself. Perhaps when I first tasted the Fountain, in my mother's arms, her eyes against my cheek. Perhaps then I looked like that poor man, small and unable to speak at all, bowing before Qaspiel and whispering some strange prayer and making the winged creature terribly uncomfortable. He was keening, and I thought we might have to call Grisalba to concoct something to put him into some sleep. Without meaning to, I put out my hand to comfort him. His skin burned. I felt his bones beneath it. That was the first time I touched him, and the hand that smoothes this page remembers his shoulder, too, and the bones, and the heat of him, and the wind of that day under the portico, with Qaspiel's grey gaze and its wings like long shadows.

John raised his head. "What is this place, where I sit at the feet of an angel, with a demon touching my shoulder?"

I drew back my hand. It would not be the first time he stung me, and specially me, among all those he loved.

Qaspiel looked curiously at his earnest supplicant. "I do not know what an angel is," it said gently, "but I do not think I am one." Nevertheless it put its hand on John's head as though it *meant to bless him, and John began to shake as though sick, as if something in him had come loose and rattled all through his bones.*

"Take it away," rasped John. "The crane and the lamia and the gryphon's stew, all of it, everything alien I have taken into my body and everything I have entered with my body. Erase it, I know you can, I know you can smooth my soul until it is colorless and shining. Make me as I was. Make it all never have happened. Make me wake up in Constantinople with the sun on my back and my hands sticky with dates." But Qaspiel only shook his head, and not without some sadness, for such a sorrow is awful to witness.

"I cannot," it whispered. "Nor would I if I could, for all those things are blessings, and I am not so cruel."

John answered Qaspiel: "And Jacob was left alone; and there wrestled a man with him until the breaking of the day. And when he saw that he prevailed not against him, he touched the hollow of his thigh; and the hollow of Jacob's thigh was out of joint, as he wrestled with him. And he said, Let me go, for the day breaketh."

The Virtue of Things
Is in the Midst of Them

An Encyclopedia of Those Things Which Exist Beyond the Wall, Composed by a Certain Knight of St. Albans who was Also Called John, and who Also Came from the West Into the East, though this is merely a Coincidence and not a Commentary on the Lack of Imagination Shown by the World at Large.

When I first arrived in this country I tried to lie as often as possible. I did not lie because I was a bad man—or at least not primarily because I was a bad man—but because it is in my nature to tell fictions. These are nearly always more interesting than the sad truth, which most often concerns not having enough to eat and wandering around with little enough idea of where one means to end up. Who among us wants to listen to that all day? Certainly not I—so I endeavored to falsify everything that would bear falsification. I said that my name was George and I had killed seventeen dragons on my crossing of the icy northern sea, just to best the saint. I said that my name was Geoffrey and I had married a mermaid whose tail was split in two and clinging with ice that smelled of all the perfumes of Araby, and I loved her and had many children by her and only after she died and left me king of all the arctic oceans did I become bored with royal life and drift over the cap of the world to find myself here. I said that my name was John of Mandeville, and that I had come from England seeking delight and wealth, and along the way I had already breakfasted with both Popes and found their tables wanting, and that last was true, as far as true goes with me, which is only as far as it can pay its own way.

As to my character in other respects, well, I admit I traveled not out of wanderlust, which is a noble sort of thing, but because I happened to have killed a certain count in my own country and needed to absent myself until his relations got over the matter and started behaving reasonably toward my person. After all, the man was a rake and a pinch-penny and short to cap it all, and it isn't really my fault that he took such offense to a simple transaction involving sheep and a girl with red hair. A gentleman says no more. I talked my way into a ship by the pleasant name of *Proserpina*, mainly by claiming to be already her captain Marcus de Boin, and in quite a hurry to get after a crew in the next port. You'd like to think such simple lies wouldn't work, that they would be too feeble to carry their own weight, but a straight back and a level gaze will purchase more or less anything you might like to possess if you are comely enough of face and sufficiently quicksilver of tongue, which I am on both counts.

Proserpina was a fit little craft—hardly worth stealing if she were a trash heap that couldn't crest a tide! I had a fine time in several harbors before irritating the Sultan of Egypt in the matter of his daughter. She was a tortoiseshell of a woman, all her many colors polished by her handmaids and shining: black hair with flashes of blue, lips brown and rose, skin like brandywine and, most unusual of all in that part of the world, she bore eyes bright and blue and pale among all her other features, and on her person she wore jewels to match, lapis and sapphire and the occasional enormous emerald.

Of course I had her within half a fortnight—princesses are princesses wherever you go. They are tied down so tightly that the merest glimpse of a shear will send them into fits of passion. And I am a blade if ever there was one. I tasted her lips and they were honey; I tasted her pedigree and it was gold; I tasted her fortune and it was heaven on earth. A gentleman says no more. Since I'd spoilt her (all with her a willing and happy party to her own defloration) her father the Sultan demanded I marry the maid, and to this I was most amenable. Do not be surprised! I am not one of those cads who loves the flesh but hates the ring. I was happy to be her husband and Sultan thereafter—what man would be miserable in her arms and in her crown? But her father insisted on a knife's point that I abandon Christ and embrace the infidel faith. This I would not do, for I am the Lord's own child and I cannot even spell Mohammed. Thus I nobly took my leave of them in the night, leaving no trace save the wake of my ship.

Ah, but it's not true. You knew it even while I told the tale. Readers are always cleverer than the writer, that's the nature of literature, which, incidentally, *never* pays its own way. The Sultana would have none of me, and she had very little in the way of breasts or cheek—though the blue eyes were enough to pay for all that. Her younger sister, though—no pearl of Africa ever shone so bright as that maiden, though she might as well have been locked in a prison for all that any man was allowed near her. Eight eunuchs with collars of gold and onyx stood round her at all times, though surely in their ruined anatomy she must have excited some stirring, so astonishing was her purity and beauty. I made my seduction through the gaps in their muscular arms, glimpsing her hip, her hair, her flashing eyes through the wall of male flesh between us. *John,* she whispered, *slay them all with your sword and take me away on your ship. Until my sister is married I shall never be free of my guards, and she is so cruel with her tongue no man will have her.*

I shall wither to dust, surrounded by men who cannot touch me!
And between the thighs of two guardians she kissed me with
a sweetness like stolen gems, her pleading mouth small as a
bird's. The battle commenced and I handled myself well—a
gentleman says no more. But in the end princesses are tiresome
and know nothing about sailor's knots or weathering storms
at sea and I left her with a tribe of savages who knew the art
of harnessing ice floes to pull their chariots and hunting the
spotted seal.

Well, the truth is I have not had a woman for many years.
I am as good as a priest, or as bad as one. I have a notion
that Christ is but the face of God you can drink with, and
that suffices for my faith. I suppose I'd be just as happy with
Mohammed sharing my table if it came with a Sultanate and
a pearl of Carthage like a ring encompassing my thickest finger. Alas, as I have said, real life rarely offers such simple and
delightful choices, or else we would all be Mohammedans and
what would the Pope do for work?

It so happens, however, that after not experiencing much of
anything I have claimed to enjoy in Constantinople, Egypt,
Russia, or Persia, I turned my vessel northward and crossed
the hat of the world, where a black rock divides the waters into
the four oceans and pulls all compasses towards itself. There I
did not encounter a narwhal who had broken his horn on the
moon, nor did I meet with the Papess of the Pole, who did not
take me into her iron bedchamber nor compel my body into
hers by force of her magnetized flesh, nor did the archangel
Uriel (Michael is far overused, you know. You might as well
just announce yourself a liar and a fool if you drag Michael
into the business.) appear to me in my extremity and indicate
land, land not far, his outstretched arm dripping with manna
and diamonds and tiny blue fish.

You begin to understand me. How much better if life
were more like books, if life lied a little more, and gave up

its stubborn and boring adherence to the way things *can* be, and thought a little more imaginatively about the way things *might* be. I can hardly bear my own boredom in relating how it was somewhat cloudy when I passed the Pole, and the ice not too bad, and several large black birds devoured silver fish in my sight but none even had the decency to harry my mast or transform into a maiden with a coat of feathers and a need for the love of a mortal man.

Now, I suspect my passing was made mild by my new friends here. I suspect that whatever dwells in my nature that loves tales and falsehood and shining, pretty stories commended me to them and made me attractive, so that they drew my ship over the high blue sea and down into their country. A country, finally, strange enough that I do not have to lie in relating it to you (though I may if I am moved—I cannot be blamed, I am the man I am, and if my nature brought me here I shall follow it and not grovel to be forgiven. God made me, Christ drank my health, and the Devil took the rest).

Given how the rest of my writings have exaggerated and aggrandized as I saw fit I did think it would be amusing to set down the very truth of the underworld in which I beached my *Proserpina*, and from which I have slim hope of departing. I shall make a good work, and I believe this will be a good work, to shine in the dark when I cannot.

I shall organize my thoughts and set them down as an encyclopedia of the end of the world, after the fashion of the Spaniard Isidore who jotted down this and that about the nature of everything, and in future days perhaps you will call John Mandeville a liar, and my shade will laugh at you and say: *true, true, I was, but not always, not so. When the world was good enough in my sight, when it behaved as wildly and gorgeously as I always knew it could, I told the truth of it.*

HOW TO USE MY MOST EXCELLENT ENCYCLOPEDIA

I believe the following two scenes will illuminate how I would prefer this compendium to be used by whatever poor devil comes upon it after I have gone.

When I was a boy and avoiding my lessons for some superb reason or another, an erstwhile and much beleaguered tutor said to me: *John, what is it you hate so about books?*

I replied to him as quick as a bite: Books think they can boss me about. They think they have the upper hand, and can make me read them and pay attention to them and say nice things about them after I am done. They are snooty and think they are smarter than me. They insist on being read page one to page whathaveyou, and no stopping for good behavior. Well, I cannot be held still! I shall jump about and today read the machinations of the dark prince of Motteringdale and how he beheaded his herbalist, and tomorrow I shall read about how the herbalist wished his country to be free of taxation and red dragons, then next Thursday I shall read about how it was all an allegory concerning some early Popes I don't care about. That's how it is in real life, anyway! You hardly ever know anything important until the thing it was being important about is already over. Books think they can rule me, but I shall show them.

My tutor disapproved of this first attempt at philosophy.

And later, when I resided at the Sultan's court, I heard from a eunuch who had it from a concubine who had it from an alchemist-astrologer with a weakness for certain pleasures that the Sultan had a great book in his innermost chamber, and in the great book lived a demon. The demon and the book could not be separated; the demon was the book and the book was the demon. The demon lived in the spine of the book, had skin of iron and golden horns, and was called something irrelevant and unpronounceable. The Sultan was utterly in thrall to the demon, who each night took the form of a maiden with those selfsame golden horns and iron flesh, and when he made love to the succubus she whispered a chapter of the book of herself in his ear, and the writing meant to be in the pages of the tome scrawled itself instead across her breasts in fiery letters, and the Sultan loved the book to distraction. All of his concubines went unused and to be honest they were glad for it, having none of them been what a generous soul could call love matches. Every night when it came time for him to sire an heir with a woman of less metallic and sulfurous disposition the Sultan whispered: *only a little more. I shall just read a little more, then on to a proper bed.* When asked what enthralled him so in the book the monarch could only answer: *I have only just begun it, I cannot say, I cannot say.* Who can say what a book is about until one has nearly finished it? Even after five years of intent study and molten lovemaking and the searing read-ing of the flaming chapters upon the cold iron bosom of his beloved, the Sultan would insist he had hardly begun the tale, had scarcely turned the first page.

It went on in this way until the demon had by degrees suc-ceeded in drawing out all the life of her besotted reader and he was discovered one morning slumped over the book, which looked as innocent as you please, while an iron ball with golden sigils worked upon it rolled discreetly away from the palace, cheerful in the sun, gaining speed as it went.

What I mean to signify by all this scene-making is that books can harm you, and a careless John I would be if I were to let you open this volume and think you had a nice plump dog on a satin leash who would do your bidding and ask for no more than you liked to give. Books are not like that. They want to eat you up. They want you to spend yourself on their iron hearts and submit to their wills. An unsuspecting man who happens to find himself in this unfortunate world which is practically ruled by books has but two choices—give in and go under the page with the secret smile of the slattern on one's lips, or become the thing the book spends itself upon, become himself the iron princess with horns of gold, become fantastical and gorgeous beyond measure, nearly impossible to believe, but not so impossible that the spell is broken. Become the thing the tale tells of, something so strange that some book somewhere simply bursts into being to record your supereminence.

I have chosen this latter route in order to reign this book into the world. It is my hope that you will joust with its boisterous nature, struggle with its lack of alphabetization or order beyond my own sense of what thing should follow which; for I am a kind tyrant, and will not force such snooty, bossy schemes on you, my reader, my alchemist-astrologer, my eunuch, my most gentle concubine. You must always fight with a book, or else how do you know who has won when the last page is cut?

I am the demon of this book. I am the book itself, and I am the iron thing lying next to you in the morning.

1. On the Wall

They told me it was made of diamonds. Countless enormous gems, piled one atop the other a thousand years ago and more, diamonds so massive that two giants had to lift them into place, and in raising these prisms toward the sun thus blinded an entire generation of blue-bellied lizards. They tell me all blue-bellied lizards are now blind, as the elders told the youngsters that the world was white and featureless, and out of deference the little ones went right on behaving as though they could see nothing, and now no one can tell the difference. My friends in this country enjoy perverse stories with no moral or point. It appeals to their conglomerate nature, I think. In any event, the wall was raised and put in place and now it is so clotted with moss and tangled roots and stiff leaves and fern fronds like quill pens frozen in the act and huge orange blossoms that smell like bitter tea that I could not testify to the truth of the jewels—I suppose there could be diamonds under all that verdancy. I would like to believe it, or else what happened to the poor lizards?

According to my hosts, the Wall divides us from the fallen world on the other side; it keeps the fell knights of that world at bay and preserves our pleasant land of red stones and pomegranate orchards. On the other side of the Wall lie ugly, bloody, profane places called Nural and Nimat, called Babel and Shirshya, called Lost and Perdition and Decadence. *Be happy we dwell on this side, where the phoenix still sing at dusk,* they said at supper. *Praise the Wall and love it, for it is all that stands between us and ruin.* They touched my hands and whispered: *The day it closed we could breathe, and sing, and delight again. Should it ever open, well, it is too much to think on. Everyone knows it is our shield; everyone knows those on the other side possess a monstrousness best left unconsidered by virtuous souls.*

So they regaled me when I first arrived. Isn't it interesting, to know what everyone knows?

THE BOOK
OF THE RUBY

The cranes say the Sedge of Heaven was ruled over by thirteen clouds, each of them extremely complex and cold, but beautiful, frightening, heavy. In the long life of a crane one might encounter a single True cloud, drifting among the lesser and unintelligent wisps of moist or frozen air, moving stately and alien as a whale crusted over with diamonds. In her youth, before her Fall, Kukyk had come upon the Wooden Cloud, and she felt its presence like a blow against her body, as though something inside her was battered and squeezed with a hundred hands; yet the pain gave her also a ferocious pleasure, and she both forgot and remembered her name several times as the gold-tinged cloud passed by her, whispering its many canticles into her heart.

John the Priest said the Kingdom of Heaven was ruled over by a man on a throne, seated on a sea of glass. He is unencounterable, and unknowable. He is not fertile, having only managed one child since the beginning. He should not be blamed for this—mothers are rare on the sea of glass.

What do my stepdaughter and I have in common? The gates of both universes are closed to us. They are very pretty gates, but they cannot let us pass. We can neither of us fly, and will never find ourselves in the presence of a cloud, and—well. Our bodies are too shocking to be permitted entrance to the Kingdom of Heaven, even if we should build a ship of glass to sail it.

What do you do with a girl with only one wing?
Half the things you'd do to a girl with two.

The letter Anglitora had wrested from the mouth of her soldier's skull came among us like a True cloud, its complexities beyond us, its weight hideous but invisible, inciting a horror and an unseemly pleasure. I heard it read so many times before we launched the ships. I remember it perfectly, every word, as if it were written in oil and set blazing.

> *Emanuel, prince of Constantinople and the Eastern Empire, to John, priest by the almighty power of God and the might of our Lord Jesus Christ, we send you greetings in return, and all good wishes for your health, the peace of your nation, and all the divine gifts of this Earth.*
>
> *Our Majesty has received your letter and taken it to our bosom. With great interest did we read of the glory and power of your Kingdom in the East, and with delight did we read of its great Conversion to Christ. In brotherhood therefore we greet you, Prince to Prince, and Christian to Christian. We have sent some few objects that represent our affection, made of gold and emerald and costly perfumes beside, and look forward with joy to the day when we may meet and clasp hands in true friendship.*
>
> *However, our missive is not an idle one. Having subdued a country of infidels, we trust you will have some sympathy for our plight, as we are beset on all sides by the armies of the unfaithful, and moreover the unfaithful are uncommonly prosperous and numerous, and threaten to overcome our walls and claim both Constantinople and Jerusalem under their sway. We are strong in faith but admittedly weaker in arms, and we beseech our friend John*

to take up his great armies and come forth from the East to defend us, leaving behind only those souls who remain undedicated to Christ. If victory follows, which surely it must, Our Majesty will be pleased to divide the spoils of the Holy City with those we hold in blessed fraternity and grant whatsoever lands, titles, and honors such men may desire.

Surely the favor of God is with Us, whether or not Our Eastern Friend arrives to deliver Jerusalem into the bosom of the Church, however, the turning of the infidel tide would be much delayed if you do not immediately set out for our country with a great force at your command. We trust that you will accomplish this with swiftness and come to our aid no later than September, since you have at your call such flying creatures as you have described to us, which will be much use against the enemy. In utter faith we make this compact with you and take your assent as granted. We have set the table already in anticipation of your arrival, draped as you are in the blessings of the Lord.

Who stays and who goes? Who goes and who stays?

We lined up on the shore of the Rimal in our best finery. War was a game, after all. What happens when you go to war?

You kiss a pygmy boy, you dance a little, maybe you bite a corporal if it is a very serious battle.

Oh, of course we know better now. But then wars in which folk actually died were so far in the past as to be hilarious tales of fools and blowhards, and we were not like them. John was our king—of course we would rescue his people! Of course we would set our banners flying and march on Jerusalem! Why not? What a delightful sport! What a lovely idea! We would be back in a fortnight still covered in the flowers the humans showered upon us. We could already feel roses on our shoulders, red and white, white and red.

You all wanted to be chosen for the army, as if John were choosing guests for a dinner party. Even I, even I, for what did I know but that war meant mating and keening, the promise of a new drake between my legs and silver for my belt. How we must have seemed to my father; a nation of virgins, sure it would all go well enough once we were in the thick of it. Instinct would take over. What tales we would tell of our prowess.

In the end, a lottery seemed fairest. We are sometimes a people with little imagination. The bronze barrel of the Abir was draped in blue silk and filled with red and white stones. Red meant go, white meant stay. I held Sefalet in my arms, and she put her hands up so that she could whisper to me.

"Mama," she said out of her right-hand mouth, "everyone looks so pretty!"

"You're all going to die," growled her left-hand mouth. I winced. My daughter, my girl, whose mouths dropped such words into the well of my heart. Red stones and white, red stones and white, and I never knew which she would bring me. The way I loved her was like a bruise. It blossomed black and golden; it hurt me so. And when my stone came red, I was not sorry, and for this I am ashamed, even now.

And I, too, for I was the easier daughter to love. I had no second mouth to harm you, only my single, frank self. And with that self I fought at your back. If there was shame in our leaving we have all been punished for it.

One by one they came and drew their stone. Dressed as if for a play, in armor dug up from a cellar or hastily made from sheets of glittering sea glass or hardy ginger-flowers sewn together. One faun drew her stone hesitantly from the barrel, wearing a breastplate of antlers cast off that spring in the molting season, crisscrossed over her slender torso. When the pebble gleamed white in her hand she wept bitterly.

Fortunatus the gryphon drew a white stone; Hadulph drew red. Qaspiel my winged friend would put a sword on its hip, and Grisalba the lamia would stay behind. Hajji the panoti, her ears drawn close around her, kept her fist tight over her scarlet stone, peeking at it and shuddering. Our little court, divided along invisible lines. Most would stay, and I would like to think, oh, how I would like to believe that the war lottery was fair, that John did not seed his friends to come with him, his wife, his favorites. I choose to believe that. The rest lies easier if I believe it.

Sefalet struggled out of my arms and ran to the barrel, thrusting both her hands inside. I called out to her but she ignored me. She raised her fists high in the air and when she opened them we all saw that clamped between the teeth of her right palm she held a white stone, and in the teeth of her left a red one. She laughed out of both mouths, but tears dripped off of her wrists as her green eyes wept, turned away from us.

When Sefalet was only just learning to speak, we took her to the blue mussel shell. At first I could not do it. She was what she was, unique, alone, but not sick. Just ours, unavoidably and unutterably ours. John said to me: "She is broken. She is miserable. We will make her well."

If you ask what convinced me I will tell you that one day she looked up from her toys, a little golden cockatrice that whistled when you pulled its tail and a cedar ship with sails of silk. She put her right hand over her chin.

"When I am grown," she said with that mouth, "will I be queen like you?"

But then she let her right hand fall and raised up her left, and out of that mouth came a voice as deep as a man's, with a growl to it, a cruelness:

"Everything you love will pass from the earth," my daughter said with her second mouth, "and only one tree will remain, in a field of empty dirt. You can be queen of that, if it makes you happy."

And at those words she began to shake all over. Light poured out of her body, beading like sweat and trickling, then streaming, so much, so fast. Wherever the light touched me my flesh went cold and frosted over, and I screamed in fear of my own child. John came to her and put his hands on her forehead, but she would not be stilled. He trembled, too, and prayed, and who knows what his god said to him but we took her to the mussel, for that is what one does when a body is ill.

The two old men guarded it as they always had, their mustaches so long they trailed in the swampy, lily-clotted water of the pool, their wrinkles so heavy their eyes sank shut under their weight, and they said to my daughter: "Do you wish to be healed?"

My husband said to them: "Instead you should ask, 'do you accept Christ?' and if they answer correctly, heal them, and if not, turn them away."

The twin old men glared stonily at him, even beneath their wrinkles. In those days we treated John's missionary work as a charming quirk, as you will do with a friend who has become suddenly fascinated with astrology or some obscure historical period and cannot cease discussing it. Yes, he was king and some of us had been baptized—which seemed to consist of putting our heads underwater, which is more or less pleasant and thus no trouble to us—and it seemed to make him happy. He was king and that meant we were Christian, but this meant little more to any of us than when Xenophy the sciopod queen made us hop on one foot for a century or two so as not to make her nation feel self-conscious concerning their anatomy. Kings enjoy it when a nation imitates them. It makes them feel less alone. We hopped on one foot, we swore by Christ, but it meant nothing. John found few takers for his dreams of empire. We behaved towards him as water towards a staff—we flowed around, however hard he tried to direct us.

However, you cannot move the wind with a lyre, and the old men of the mussel were far too ancient and hoary to care who sat on any throne. They did not hop; they did not say the *Ave*.

"Do you wish to be healed?" they said to Sefalet, and she replied with her left-hand mouth:

"I am not sick. It is the rest of them you should pile into that shell."

And her right-hand mouth only trembled a little, saying nothing. That was that—if you do not ask for healing the shell can do nothing for you.

My father told me once that he believed he had not fathered the girl at all. That when he moved in you the Word of God, the Logos, stirred in him. Into the darkness between your bodies the light of the Word poured out, and it was that which made Sefalet, not his seed. I asked him: would that not make her a christ, and you the mother of god? He became angry and told me there was but one Christ and one Mother of God, and if the body is not perfect the soul must be marred. I felt his words on my cheeks, stinging like hands. I lifted my wing, my imperfect body, and he was sorry, but I think I only reminded him that he could not sire a whole child.

She was mine and his. That's all. Curse enough for any child.

John drew all who would stay behind together in the Lapis Pavilion while the stars pricked the night sky with wounds. He was flushed and happy, a health in his cheeks I had never seen. He was going home. What man would not rejoice? I looked into the violet evening and felt nothing but shadows on me, dread whispering in my daughter's left-hand mouth as she moved it against my shoulder. I suppose I ought to have denounced him. I suppose I ought to have said: *Wait, I remember from stories what it means to be dead.* But if all men in the nation of John were as small and weak as he there could be no possible trouble, and if he saw his home and greeted his friends with claps upon the shoulders and tales of old times, well, perhaps he would come home satisfied, ready to settle and take his last walk to the Fountain and be one of us in truth. Leave us be on the subject of God and live forever like everyone else. I did not believe, as many did, that war would be a delight. But I thought it would salve him.

Perhaps there is no salve for my father; perhaps the wound is part of his nature.

I do not even remember what he said to them, so deep was I sunk in my own thoughts, my desire to stay warring with my longing to see the places he dreamed of, Constantinople with her endless cisterns and golden domes, Yerushalayim where Imtithal's love had lost his brother. Autumn strewn with palm fronds and quince-wine, where my husband was a child.

I remember. He told them that they could not be idle while he fought his happy war. That the Devil sought idle hands for His own work. He told them to go to the ruins of the Tower of Babel, where you had taken him years past.

Where we first were lovers under the crescent moon, among the scarlet flowers.

He told them to go to that place and with the stones of it raise up a cathedral to rival any in Christendom. When he returned he expected it finished, and would dedicate it to Thomas and Mary, Mother and Child.

Yes. I recall it now. And I remember a man with huge hands and dark eyes, who stood tall and brown in the night, and he said to John: "Just because that letter says we have converted, and the letter you wrote lied and called us Christians, does not mean anything at all. Two letters have lied to each other—so what? This is not Christendom just because you call it so. Call me Gundoforus, it does not mean that is my name."

John colored darkly then and said to the young man: "I am

your King." And no one could argue. Being king is also a kind of game. The governed pretend that the king has power; the king pretends he is loved, and as long as no one breaks the mummer's dance, all is peaceful.

All I could think that night in the strange flat bed you gave me was: how long does he expect us to be gone?

I went to my daughter after all had wandered into sleep. I opened the veils of her bed and crawled in with her. I held her tight, and she put her arms around my neck. She smelled sweetly of child and tiredness, and as I always did when she was quiet I thought: how I love her. How mine she is. Usually she interrupted such thoughts with screaming and hissing about how the sciopods would have their feet severed and bleed out onto the hands of Christian men—but not this time. She nuzzled my shoulder with her blank face, and as she had when she was small, her hands sought my breasts, her mouth needing me, and I felt the old pull of my nursing self, and also of the grief Sefalet called up in me. I began to weep, tears seeping up from my flesh and into her mouth, which worked greedily, as though she starved for me. She drank my tears as she once drank my milk, and the sacrament of it was terrible, but still, what communion I could have I took, and my body shook, and so did hers. I suppose she did starve for me. I did not mean to be such a poor mother. Perhaps I should have severed my finger and buried it as my mother did, or kept a little book for her—but how many times could I hear my daughter predict my death by gruesome means before I began to fear her?

She will forgive you. I know it.

But she could not help but see that I chose the new daughter, the crane-girl with the lovely, normal face over her. When we come home, she will see that we fought together and love each other, that there is no fear between us. And it will cut her.

To be a child is a terrible thing. To be a mother worse.

For a moment, with her mouth on my breast like a helpless babe, I resolved to take her with us. After all, it was a holiday, really. No one would be hurt. John was so frail—his country-men would take one look at us and fall into a rictus of terror. And then, with a smacking sound, Sefalet pulled her left hand from me and said sweetly: "Everything and everyone you love is going to die, and you will see it all happen, and be spared nothing."

I cannot bear to think of how it must have been for her when she woke. I was gone. She was motherless, suddenly. I suppose, for her, it was the first Abir of her life.

The Left-Hand Mouth,
the Right-Hand Eye

This is how I began to understand Sefalet: she came upon me sleeping in the great gardens of the palace, between a peach tree and a mango, and the stars jangled overhead and the perfume of the many fountains trickled down the throat of the night. The child walked so silently that I did not wake until she leapt upon me like a tiny animal, and put her hands over my ears. She told me two tales that night, and the next day the capital as one body moved to Babel and everything happened as it happened and not otherwise. It was a moment between girl and lion and darkness, all three of us, before. The first I heard through my right ear, and the second through my left.

I wasn't always this way, Lion. I mean, yes, I was always this way—my eyes and my mouths were always arranged like this and I never had a face. But when I was little I had only one voice, and it was my right-hand voice, and no one thought I was awful and I didn't have fits. I don't remember how old I was but I remember the

I was always this way and will always be this way and I cannot escape anymore than anyone can escape who they were born to be. Where I was before I was born it was cold and the sky was always dark. I saw the same stars turning in a thin, tight wheel over the top of my head. I do not lilyfruit tree outside my window didn't come all the way up into my room the way it does now. I started to have dreams. In my dreams it was cold and dogs ran everywhere around me, sleek ones with narrow heads, and they had marvelous leashes, the most extraordinary leashes and collars, too, crusted with black gems but soft and coiling, so that when the dogs leapt into the air the leashes snapped and curled like ribbons. The dogs had a huge black bowl filled with the ocean, and I have never seen the ocean but I know what it is meant to look like, how the waves crest with little white hats made of foam, and how it is purple and blue and black all together. The dogs lapped at the bowlful of ocean and looked at me as if I were being terribly rude not to drink as well. The earth below the bowl crackled with ice and tiny pale snapping bits of lightning. On a shard of ice I saw a black collar and leash just my size. The dogs continued to stare as if they could not believe

remember how old I was (I am a rope attached to nothing, a black line on a black background, I have no beginning or end) when I began to have bad dreams (I am the eye that dreams of opening). I dreamed of a girl in a bed in a high room where a lilyfruit tree did not quite reach, and the girl had a body she was not using, and the girl had been a twin but I slowed her sister down until she melted away into the girl (time is like that, you can pull the leash from very far away) and now I can be her twin, I can be her sister, and you cannot blame me, she wasn't using that mouth for anything, and I needed it. I dreamed of a girl on both sides of a wall. I dreamed of twins. The universe is its own twin, and the two of them walk hand in hand down a golden road, into the impossible distance of space, and that is where I came from if I came from anywhere, the end of that golden road, and I tell the truth but no one listens to me, and that is more or less how it always my manners. I dreamed this dream over and over, night after night, until one night in the dream I put the collar around my own neck, and the leash of gems pulled taut, and I bent my head to drink the ocean from the bowl, and the ocean tasted bitter and heavy as iron. After that my left hand began speaking, and I couldn't stop it, or even understand it most of the time, but if I had not drunk the ocean it would never have happened, so I think I am as wicked as they say, after all.

has to go—if people listened, nothing would turn out as it should. If you ask my name I will tell you it is Sefalet and I will not be lying; if you ask why I am hurting the girl I will say I am not, I am her, and she is me, and we are twins but we are not mirrors, if she lifts her right hand I lift my right hand, if she lifts her left hand, I lift my left hand. When she kisses her first kiss I will kiss mine. Did you ever hear of a girl named Cassandra? She had it so easy.

The peach tree dropped a fruit; the mango tree moved its leaves in the night wind. I didn't understand most of what she said and she would not explain, only curled up between my paws and went to sleep, where I cannot imagine what she dreamed: of the dogs or the child dreaming of the dogs, dreamer and dreaming turning around each other like two huge wheels in one little body.

Love begins as it ends. The beginning is only a mirror held up to the end. Thus, you must pay good attention to how love first appears—what it is wearing, how it stands, with what colors and objects it decks itself, and in this way the rough prophecy of love may be practiced. It does not take an expert to predict that, in the end, I would understand little of anything that had happened, and no one would explain it to me. I accepted that, and hid the girl from the world beneath my chin.

In the morning Sefalet claimed no memory of her speech to me, and in fact seemed quite horrified at the idea that she could speak with both mouths at once. She asked very shyly to ride upon my back as the advance architectural parties went out to the Tower Waste to survey the ground and I took this as an excellent prognosis for our uneasy new world, populated only with lion and girl—the gryphon and the lamia and the inventor were still to come. We would have much time together to do the work of love, which is mainly the work of knot-making, tying breast to breast, binding and hauling tight. I could see how she struggled to speak only with her right-hand mouth: it was a dear and awful thing to see. I spoke to the princess as I would any soul who came to my crags and my caves seeking to understand as I did, and it seemed to delight her, to be treated as though she were not about to say something dreadful at any moment.

"When I was a cub I wanted to love something, but I did not have anything to love, my parents having gone their own way," I began.

"My parents have gone their way," whispered Sefalet's right-hand mouth. "But I'm not angry about it! Who can blame them?"

"Do you know, I think it is a parent's job to be unsatisfactory in some way? Then a child has something to hurt about early on, and such irritants usually produce heroes. Children who never hurt grow up to be many things, but rarely do they vanquish much, or start revolutions, or have extraordinary love affairs. If you have nothing to hurt you have nothing to heal with battling or politics or mating."

"How are you hurt, Vyala?"

"I will only tell you my first hurt today. I have four, but three will wait. The first was that my parents were solitary lions and treated me as a solitary lion, though they didn't mean anything cruel by it. As I have told many folk: love is a thing you can learn. But if you do not apply yourself to your lessons you will be as good at is as at mathematics you never took the time to squint at. The result of my solitariness was that the thing in me which could love (some call this a heart and I suppose that's well enough for poetry, but a heart's main use is to bleed, not to love) hung out of me like invisible ribbons, all loose and tangled. I was so young, I only felt the pain of them, and how they longed to be knotted together with others. These ropes hung out of my chest and streamed before me like braids, but I did not know what to do with them. I had to learn. Just as you do. Your mother and father love you but they are afraid of you—for every knot they tie, another slips loose. That's not your fault and it's not theirs. Fortunately I am not terribly invested in anything below the snowline, so you do not frighten me. My knots usually hold fast. I think we shall be able to get on quite well for however long this nonsense with the war lasts."

"It will never be over," hissed her left-hand mouth, and Sefalet clutched it with her right hand, her large green eyes filling with tears.

We rested in a town called Ecbatana Secunda, which a gryphon named Fortunatus said used to be called Shirshya, before John renamed everything. Gryphons are cousins to the lion; I smelled Hadulph around him like a red halo, and knew they must have been friends. We would have spoken and shared our dinner, which we cats prefer somewhat more raw than most, had Sefalet not bolted at the sound of the word *Shirshya*. We sprang after her, darting down little roads and into darkened orchards where the shadows made chessboards on the earth. Everything smelled of skin, and in the thin moonlight I saw trees full of parchment, some with tiny hoops already stretched with pelts ready to become pages, some heavy with ink-berries, some dropping pinecones full of shimmery silk that cracked open when they struck the ground. The gryphon and I rounded a tree heavily laden with scrolls shaped like thick papayas, their skins green and ripe and ready for the harvest.

And saw Sefalet sitting beside a gnarled trunk, under a canopy of branches spread wide and low. Everywhere on those boughs gentle hands grew, a woman's hands, and each missing their smallest finger. Those hands strained to cup Sefalet's faceless head, to stroke her skull where she might have had hair, to wipe the tears from the backs of her hands.

The Virtue of Things
Is in the Midst of Them

2. On the Hexakyk

My first act in this country was this: I lashed my boat at a tidy little dock clung with frozen barnacles and a kind of glistening seaweed covered in crystalline buds that sloshed with a turquoise liquid. I crushed a capsule between my thumb and forefinger and was pleased to find the viscous stuff sweet and clean to the taste. Indeed, only a few drops warmed me quite thoroughly with a winey intoxication. The whole place seemed quite civilized, if empty. Shards of ice floated here and there but on the whole the sea flowed kindly around bleached white boards and jetties. Whoever built these things, I thought to myself as I battened down the sundry aspects of my ship, has no reason whatever not to be hospitable to a traveler. Building a dock is an act of friendship. It says: *Come in, sell us things, make eyes at the locals; we will not eat you until after the feast if we eat you at all. We have never heard of your English count nor the Sultan of Egypt nor either of his daughters.*

The cold shore extended only a little inland, being replaced immediately by the most generous country, full of long grass and bright sunshine, flowers of blue and violet and gold, and well-kept orchards groaning with round, red fruit so deep a shade of scarlet that I thought the trees might be bleeding— later I would discover I was not far off. The difference between the shore and the meadows at which I found myself marveling was so marked that a line ran through the earth on the one side of which was snow and on the other was summer, as though some fell creature had dug his heel through the world and separated the fertile from the cruel.

Some distance ahead, in the mist that sometimes collects near the close of a warm and pleasant day, I saw two figures standing on the crest of a small hill. I could not make them out in the golden haze, but hailed them and moved further still inland to make their acquaintance and begin an understand-ing of their country—most importantly who ruled it, and how I could become friends with that fellow. Indeed, if I have any advice for travelers which is applicable in all nations and situations, it is to befriend immediately whatever king, caliph, or pope you can get your hands on most quickly, and if not them at least their brother, daughter, advisor, or dog. Wives are tricky—only for the advanced student.

I cannot say what occurred just then with any accuracy, but no sooner than I stepped toward the pair I stood quite close to them, on that same little crest of hill, and now I saw a large, spreading hedge upon that hill, and as I looked closer at that hedge, it seemed to be thatched of green bones, lushly leaved, but bones nonetheless, and the bone hedge dwindled off in either direction as far as I could see, down from the hill and off into the gentle fields that lay beyond under the deepening golden sunlight. (This was not the wall I spoke of earlier.) I was quite startled but of course showed nothing of the sort—it is not wise to appear too much the rube, wherever one finds oneself.

The pair I had sought looked mildly up at me, smiles on

their small faces, for they were but children, a boy and a girl, with large dark eyes and dark hair—the boy's cropped like a page's, the girl's very long indeed, falling nearly to her slender ankles. Their skin was a peculiar color, very nearly scarlet but not quite, tempered with a golden sheen. They wore clothes of deep green and silver, with pearls glinting at their belts. They appeared as the children of nobility usually appear—slightly vacant but ready to be bid by their betters if there is an iced cake or a duchy in it for them. However I have not mentioned their most striking feature, which was that both children, whom I took to be brother and sister, had six arms, three upon each side, arranged in a sort of wheel around their torsos so that the last set of arms rested at the waist. They held hands, by which I mean each hand of three of their arms, and their nails shone very pale against their damask skin.

"Are you lost?" they said together.

"A traveler cannot be lost if he has no destination," I demurred.

"I don't think that's true," said the girl.

"You can be lost any time. Sometimes you don't even know how lost you are," said the boy.

"I have come from the West seeking knowledge of the wide world, adventure if you can spare a cup, a good tale if you can't, and if you've nothing at all, a good rumor about the bad habits of your neighbors I can take home to amuse my friends. I am happy wherever I find such things."

"Is it very boring in the West?" The girl wrinkled her little nose.

"There do seem to be rather a lot of you all of the sudden," sighed her brother. "Anyway, our neighbors are truly wicked and terrible, but you don't want to hear about them—if you say their name it draws their eye."

"Where are your parents?" I asked the small ones.

"Oh, we don't have parents," the female laughed. "Where are *your* parents?"

"In England—dead as dogs, both of them." In fact my father lives quite well off his wool and mutton-selling, but I find an orphan, even a grown one, lends a certain amount of tragic dash a sheep-merchant's son just can't grasp at.

"Poor lamb," crooned the boy, his smile odd and crooked.

I had begun to tire of them if I am frank. I have many talents but only a few are of any interest to children, and the day would go better with me if I had something alcoholic and a bored queen in my sight.

"Who owns this country, children? Who rules it? How far to your lord's holdings, or better, to a city?"

The children looked at each other, the sun turning their black hair fiery as oil burning.

"We do," they said together.

"You must be quite a bit older than you look."

"Oh, ancient," giggled the girl. "But a lady never tells."

"And a gentleman says no more," the boy added, grinning again, and I did not like his grin nearly so much as hers.

"We're hexakyk, you see. We age very slowly. My brother has had nine wives already, and only five of them were me!"

They flared their six arms rather fetchingly.

"If you are a king and a queen, what are you doing out here in the countryside with no retinue and no servants, no pa-lanquin or canopy to keep out the rain, no jesters or cards to amuse you?"

"Why, we were waiting for you," the girl breathed.

And that was how I came to meet Ysra and Ymra, twin mon-archs of Pentexore. I must, however, point out that I never met any other hexakyk, and thus cannot say if they all bore the characteristics of Ysra and Ymra, only that the monarchs told me all hexakyk possess the following attributes: six arms, long life, great appetites, imperviousness to fire, a taste for poul-try, excellent skill at games of chance, pleasant singing voices, and an organ somewhat to the left of the liver for storing up grudges to be dealt with at a later and more convenient time. I certainly found all of those claims to be accurate.

I confess that nowhere in the world did I have it quite so good as I did in Pentexore. No sooner did I wish a thing than that I found it around a corner—no quicker than I became irritated with walking alongside my diminutive hosts when a proper king might have had at least a horse and preferably more than one but that Ymra, the long-haired queen, took my hand and squeezed it and a palace of extraordinary complexity and good features rose up before us.

3. On the Mount

The Mount rises out of a wide violet wood whose trees have a kind of fruit shaped terribly like hands covered in blue ink in swirls and patterns, held up in gestures of prayer or supplication, all of which aim for the palace. The castle itself, if I may call it a castle, seems not so much to have been built but grown, each wing or tower or buttress winding slowly out of the main body like blossoms. Indeed, the tips of the towers open very like camellia blooms, stone petals wide and graceful, with marble stamens arching up to fashion delicate courtyards on the topmost heights. Lanterns in every window give a tremendous glow, thousands of pricks of light, as though the Mount had called down all the stars of heaven and compelled them to burn only there, bright and pale and captive. Black stone, marble and granite and perhaps some gems, even, onyx and black sapphire, make up the entire edifice, which might frighten and domineer if not for the extreme loveliness of it all, how the palace seems to lean in to listen to the quiet prayers of the wood, and the moon positions herself just so as to be the crown of that dark stony maiden of the vale, as if she could not help but take her place in the grand design.

Once, in Spain, I had cause to walk among the singing fountains and pristine arches of the Alhambra, to converse with a woman who dressed as a man, who kept her hair shorn and her face unpainted, and this woman was a student of the heavens, not an astrologer but dedicated to recording the movements of the heavenly bodies for no other purpose than to understand them, not to predict weddings or imperial pratfalls. I loved her abjectly, though I and the rest of the court accepted with sadness that she was most likely a witch. What can you do in this degenerate age? Women are either nuns, mothers, or witches. If she's a nun you'll never have her, if she's a mother she died abed, and your best chance, lad, lies with the witch. A Christian man abhors such things, but I say it's good to have a trade.

She would not take me to bed, however, for I did not like to ply the woman's part and she knew only the man's. We merely kissed, for kissing is egalitarian. Had I spent another fortnight there I am sure I would have played the salamander's part if it might have won her. But between kisses she told me her favorite theory, for she had such favorites as other women have among their lapdogs, and she said to me that if a great house could be built so that its every arch and cornice and wall and gate lay on the earth as the orbit of the sphere of Saturn or Jupiter lay in the heavens, the house could take on the attributes of its celestial twin, such that the house of Saturn would be cold and imperious, and its lord would devour his children and beat his wife before bedding her, and the house of Jupiter would be decadent and worldly, its lord having many wives and lovers and children all trampling over the place, but merry as anything.

When first I saw the Mount I felt the memory of that Spaniard rise up in my chest, but I could not yet say what sphere might own that house.

THE CONFESSIONS

I cannot say if I find it a comfort that Hiob lives still in his dreaming, that some spark of his intellect has survived his trance. I want to know, of course, I want to know what he dreams, what he thinks, what he knows if he knows anything at all. I remember his going on about Seth and the grains of Paradise, that he ate the seeds of the great tree of Eden and a great tree grew in his mouth, from whence such marvelous wood was harvested. If I were to cull the woody fibers that lash Hiob to his bier, what could I build of them? Would anyone ask whence they came if I sent up a chapel of green vines and twisted half-lily monstrosities, if I honored God with the fruits of my brother's flesh?

Such strange thoughts invade me with the perfume of the Hiob-hedge. I tried to cut the leaves from his face, where two white blooms had opened in the place of his eyes, their centers shining red. They possessed a horrible verisimilitude to his own steady gaze. But the leaves swarmed back as thick as ever, as soon as the blade's shadow ceased to fall on them.

And yet, perhaps it cannot safely be said that what writes on that parchment is Hiob. It is an automatic thing, what he does, and perhaps the book Hiob devoured burned him quite away, scoured his flesh clean of anything that was the man, and left only itself, only its words and spores and fruiting seeds, only its memories of a land long dead. The book still wrote itself through him. Those blank spaces that so maddened my brother—well, he has them now.

And I note that all thought of this having been some strange fiction fled me sometime after I saw the tree with my own eyes, after a girl with one white wing spoke of war.

I could hardly concentrate on my translation, hardly give attention to that hideous child of John's—and how Hiob would have balked at *that*. Bad enough John had a wife, but two deformed half-breed children, neither of them sons, neither of them whole, both damned by their monstrous mothers. I imagined my brother shaking his head, flattening his hand on the page as if to make it not have happened by sheer force of his desire not to know it.

In our little house the evening shadows, rimmed with orange and shot with violet, had grown long. I bade Reinolt and Goswin to eat, and each of them dutifully supped on boiled eggs, some mashed red root I had discovered the woman in yellow paring and cooking under the embers of her fire, and quaffed down a yeasty beer I could not myself stomach. I changed the page beneath Hiob's withered hand, braceleted as a woman's in a lattice of vines studded with tiny yellow blossoms. I could spare little time to check his work—soon enough our own books would start to rot, and we would all ride the same ship across the same sea, towards perdition and flowers in the sockets of our eyes. But I am weak, after all—I could not help glimpsing the passage he scribbled, and I recalled it, that thousand-year past night when we raced the red mold together, and he brought me to his side to marvel at the colors, the colors moving as if with fell purpose, to defeat us and keep what is secret secret.

Qaspiel held out its long-fingered hand, and made its palm flat. Out of the flesh a single, stark red passion-flower sprang up, its petals ruffling slightly in the night breeze.

I confess I was at a loss to speak. Hagia laughed cruelly, and the passion-flower began to move, a sinuous writhing, and from it a kind of music came, though like little music I had ever heard. It was a plucked string, a lyre, but also a thing with breath, a flute or a trumpet or both together—but so soft, so quiet, and all of it came from Qaspiel's body, and all of it filled the night around us, slowly, water dripping into a goblet until it brims over.

"It is my voice," Qaspiel said gently. "My second voice, the voice of my self that was once part of a bird that was part of a woman. It is not less than my first voice, but only more fragile."

I took up my work once more. I had only one voice, and it owed allegiance to Hiob's work, to the finishing of it. Whatever singing blossom is Alaric's own voice, it is drowned in the bombast of Hagia, and Vyala, and that other John, the trickster-fool Mandeville—and that is the scribe's lot, the translator's fate. I do not envy Hagia in the least—it is a horrible and painful thing, to stand naked on a page before the world, without someone else's passions to protect you.

THE BOOK
OF THE RUBY

N ow tell them how we crossed the Rimal. Tell them about the sharks. It's very exciting; it'll set the right tone—they will feel what we felt, thrilled and interested in the world beyond, not thinking for a moment of death or darkness or a door beyond which we could not pass, a river we could not cross.

She would have me skip over the hedge. I had intended to tell that next. I think she does not wish to remember it—nor I, nor I.

John told me a story once, just after we were married. He was sunk in a black mood, as he had attempted to give the Eucharist to Fortunatus and a few other gryphons who had stumbled upon his lonely Mass—he had been delighted to have parishioners, but they only gobbled up his bread and drank his wine and snuffled for more beneath the altar cloth. This story happened long before his Christ, and perhaps John longed for that world, when he would not have been burdened with the terrible and thirsty work of conversion.

There was a great war, he told me while we cut pages for his improved Bible. Some say it was over a woman, some say over trade routes. I did not understand why anyone would fight a war over a woman. She chooses the mate she chooses. You cannot force her, I insisted, but John promised me you could. Anyway, a certain pleasant country was situated on the mouth of a great sea, and had grown rich because of it, so the whole business with a queen called Helen and how she had left her husband for a prince of that pleasant country was probably a pretty thin excuse to do what everyone wanted to in the first place. But when all the armies were assembled and all the warships painted with dread and glowing eyes upon their prows, and all the nations come to a place called Aulis, where they would launch their fleet, no wind would come. And some of the generals believed the wind had died because the gods thought the war unjust.

"Christ thought it unjust?" I asked.

"No, no," John said. "Christ had not yet been born. They believed in gods called Athena and Zeus and Ares. They were infidels, but it could not be helped—they were born, grew up, fought in twenty-year wars and died before Christ came to redeem man. They could not know the truth of the world."

"I have heard of Athene, and of the lightning-god Zeus. Alisaunder's gods—did Christ kill them?"

"You misunderstand, my love. They were lies; they never existed. People were afraid and lonely and they made up false stories to stand between them and the dark, until the truth came upon the face of the world."

"I don't think so—some of the centaurs worship Athene, and the astomii, too. And besides, how can you tell a false god from a real one? They all promise the same general sorts of things, and hold the same things sacred, and are generally in agreement on how we are to behave."

"Christ is the only true god," but his voice was less sure than it had once been on that subject, and he cast down his eyes from mine when he said it.

In any event it seems that the wind had turned against the ancient Christless armies, and no matter how they burned meat and bone and sang to their gods (who were never real) it refused to blow. Finally, a gaggle of priests had a revelation, that a certain maiden should be sacrificed to the moon-goddess, as it was certainly not the war that had offended heaven, but the fact that a pair of soldiers, bored and hungry, had killed a doe sacred to that same goddess, and she demanded blood for blood on this matter. Well, it so happened that the king's wife and daughter had come to bid him farewell, and the king had a cold heart. He chose his own daughter to sacrifice, which sent his wife mad and began a whole awful tale which would not end until twenty years later, and perhaps more than that. They tied the maiden onto a broad, flat stone, and unknotted her hair so it fell back loosely over the stone, raised a long knife, and plunged it into the girl's heart. She screamed, then she died. As though her last breath had the strength of a storm, the wind began to blow. Some people, John said, said later that they saw a fawn substituted at the last moment for the king's daughter, and that she was spirited away to a temple at the end of the world, but most likely they only wanted to make it all less miserable, and comfort the queen, whose fists clenched in the deafening wind.

I thought of that story when we came to the edge of the Rimal, which is the rim of the world I knew and loved, the world which had loved me and brought me up and given me golden fruit to eat and a mountain's blood to drink and promised me I would never have to grow old; I would never have to die. If I crossed the sandy sea, I wondered, would the spell break? Would I wither up into a crone, a husk of a crone, all my years collapsing upon my spine until it shattered? I did not exactly fear such fate, but I did not feel so confident that it did not occur to my heart, that I did not think of myself as that girl upon the slab.

I am the king's daughter. If there had been no wind, it would not have been you with your hair unloosed.

But it looked so like the scene John had painted for me of that other war—our little army standing with our ships, ships planted and grown in our dear soil, pieces of John's old *qarib*, the Tokos, torn apart and planted in the dark, giving earth, coaxed and wheedled into fast fruiting, so that on some of the ships you could still glimpse a raw, green shine to the black wood, and one or two spring blossoms still fell from their prows and sails the color of green wood.

The wind blew stiff and strong.

But of course we could not leave until the astronomers said that the road across the Rimal was nearing its apex, when it would lead to the Western world, that other place full of Johns, and not simply in circles, over and over again, concentric, leading back to the land of the cranes and Pentexore, which would perhaps have served us all better, in the end. The astronomer in question was a stout fellow, a minotaur called Sukut who wore silver caps on his horns to show his docility. When he moved they jangled slightly, so that he always announced his presence. A week, he said, two at the outmost. But if you asked his advice, we'd have all gone right home and had stew and wine and called it a very nice, long walk to the seaside.

"But we shall be able to wrestle with humans, and feast with them after!" laughed a satyr, his grape-leaf waistcoat starting to brown at the edges. "What could be more fun?"

Sukut shook his enormous bovine head. "The stars say: Sukut, your stew is getting cold."

"Do they always talk to you like that? Wouldn't you rather something more concrete, to impress the king with?" The satyr was already bored, however, and eyeing an amyctrya girl over the astronomer's shoulder, her huge jaw brimming with wine. The satyr made no attempt to conceal his rising interest.

"The stars speak how they speak, and they speak to me, and they say stew is better than war, for only one has nice carrots in it." Sukut looked up into the heavens and nodded glumly as if to say: *Might as well rest your argument, I've heard it before.*

You're talking around the ugly part. You're telling nice stories about the camp—but we spent the whole two weeks talking to the hedge, all the time, and only Sukut was talking to anything else at all.

Perhaps if she'd warned us. Perhaps if Anglitora had said: I should mention that in addition to a lonely helmet washing up with a letter in its mouth, a great number of bones and bits of armor have gotten wedged in the beach, and taken root there, and grown into a great hedge of knights leering at the horizon, trying to get home.

Perhaps if I had. But if I had made anything sound difficult or ugly, no one would have come.

Well, the hedge stood between us and the West. The hedge of knights, tangled with faces and muscled arms and sticks like bones, sword-blades tangled up with plumes, leaves of banner-colors and heraldic shades, fluttering in the sea air, and each of those faces helmed and wide-eyed, staring, able to speak and eager to, their arms twisting away from the blades in pain. Green ooze dropped from their skin. This morass of men stretched down the beach in either direction—so many dead, so many washed away to us, to the end of the world, as John kept calling us, though really, we were as much the beginning as the end.

Christ preserve us! Cried some. *Allahu akbar!* Cried others, though we could see no real difference between them. Perhaps their leaves shone greener and more silver than purple and gold. But they all looked like John and they all wished to talk endlessly like John, and we could not tell them apart.

Some of the younger blemmyae, noting as I had once done so long ago that their own appearance proved especially upsetting to John's folk, lit upon a game that soon became all the fashion in our little two-week nation. A female, so as to be most alarm-ing, since none of the knights seemed to be on speaking terms with naked flesh, would saunter up to one of the heads on the hedge and ask it to tell her the nature of God, or whether one ought to draw pictures of God, or how many fingers one ought to bless oneself with. They came up with endless variations.

One would howl: "The Trinity, the Father, the Son and the Spirit, all in one and one in all, the Father who made the world out of the void, the Son born of Mary who died for our sins, the Spirit who moves in all things!" Or some version of that. And at least this was succinct.

But another head would contort in fury and cry out: "Allah is the only God, and Mohammed is his prophet! Christ was a man only, and when Sarah could not bear children she gave her handmaid Hagar to Abraham and Hagar produced a son—" Rarely did the second head get that far before the first would attempt to leap out of the hedge and bite him, which he could certainly not do, being a plant and possessed of minimal locomotion. But the furor incited in that part of the hedge would spread up and down until the whole thing quavered and shook, and those heads on the far end had no notion of what the original argument had been, but they snarled and spat all the same. The blemmyae girls and their friends fell into fits of giggles, and soon the better part of the army spent their delight in tormenting the hedge. We could not even understand half of the words they said. The pleasure was in their fury, as when you watch two beasts fight from a safe distance.

Once, at night, when the moon was high and everyone slept, I went to a face and spoke to it. It had a handsome gaze, and I sensed he had been young, like me.

"Who are you?" I said to the face, and then: "Who were you, before you were a hedge?"

And he said: "I was called Yusuf, and I lived in Edessa, which is a city like on a hill, terraced and lovely, where my table forever groaned with olives and pomegranates and almonds, and I had two wives, Sarai and Fatima, who did not quarrel with one another, and out of them I had two daughters and two sons. I loved the daughters best, though I know that sons are the favor of Allah.

But my daughters saved honeycomb for me and made my shirts
with their deft little hands, and what did my sons ever do but wait
for me to die so they could inherit the olives and the pomegranates
and the almonds and the honeycomb and all my shirts? My eldest
daughter could play the psaltery, even the most difficult fingerings,
and she played it each day at sunset, every day without fail, so that
in my memory every note is gold and red."

"Why do you hate the other heads?"

"They are Christian heads."

"Our king is Christian."

"I am sorry for you, then. It is hard to live beneath such a king.
If I were still living we would probably be enemies."

"But Christians are harmless. Our king is annoying, and tries to
get us to play games with him involving crossing oneself a certain
number of times with a certain number of fingers, but that's no
worse than chess. It's nothing to do with us, really."

"Then he is a bad king," the head sighed. "If he lets you believe
it is only a game. He has counted your souls in his ledger already,
I promise. If you are truly going West, you will find this out soon
enough, and so will he, I wager."

"Did the other heads convert you?"

"The other heads came thundering into Edessa with horses beneath them and golden hair upon their heads, and they broke my
table and ate my olives and my pomegranates and my honeycomb,
and took my daughters to bed and made my eldest play her psaltery
for them, and wore my shirts and made my sons swear to a cross.
They turned out my home looking for gold, but I was rich only in
family. So they dragged my wives behind their horses for sport."

And then one of the other heads strained toward Yusuf and
hissed: "And did you do less when your cursed people took Edessa
from us? I had a fine house there, and everything had begun to
quiet down—Edessa accepted us, and I married a Saracen woman
who took Christ as her Lord, and she was as beautiful as any Gal-
lic girl, and we had a baby son, and our table, too, had enough

brown bread and yellow oil and black vinegar and green limes. We went to Mass, we rested on Sunday, Edessa was becoming a virtuous place before you trampled in with your filthy, shitting horses and your burning oil and you drove us into the wilderness and cut my head off in front of my wife!"

"That house was not yours, Baldwin! Not the house, nor the wife, nor the son, nor the brown bread nor the yellow oil nor the black vinegar nor the green limes! Not even the table! What kind of shitting craven wolf complains because what he stole was stolen back from him? You slaughtered us because your Pope was bored one Tuesday! You are demons, all of you, demons and pigs."

Their rage threatened to burst the skin of their cheeks. "Oh, stop," I whispered, "please stop. Why did you not just plant your own lime trees and bread trees and oil trees? Why could you not plant your wives' bodies and love them still? Why do you fight over food and gold? Surely nothing could be easier to come by."

And they stared at me as though I had suggested they fly to the moon. Oh, what was going on in that world, that even its dead cannot stop arguing over it?

In the end, I tried to make peace. "What is the difference between a Christian and a Muslim?"

Yusuf said: "A Christian takes what is not his and calls it God's will. A Muslim is a civilized man."

Baldwin said: "A Muslim takes what is not his and calls it God's will. A Christian is a civilized man."

And I wept for both of them, and for myself who understood nothing.

John never told me who won Helen's war. I suppose it was only important how the war began. Wars end how they begin. The beginning is only a mirror held up to the end.

The Left-Hand Mouth,
the Right-Hand Eye

The child is driven to the ground of her making, Fortunatus said. *Without her mother she is unanchored, and bolts to anything that reeks of maternity. Let her have comfort in those hands.*

Gryphons are sentimental. Sefalet would not be moved, even for food or water. When finally she fell asleep, we gathered her up and the winged cat carried her on his back. Behind us, the tree of hands made mute, miserable, grasping motions after the girl, the pale of its palms receding in shadow.

Some mornings later, the better part of the architectural expedition turned off the well-planted road in order to reach the Tower ruins—but Fortunatus and Sefalet and myself went on down into a silent town without a name, and the gryphon said this was in order to wake the architect.

John had left us no plans for this cathedral, no preferences for this or that many gargoyles, towers, flying buttresses, what style he envisioned for it, or how many folk he meant to be able to fit into the place. We were, in humble fact, somewhat unclear on the meaning of the words cathedral, gargoyle, and buttress. Therefore, Fortunatus had settled upon a plan to rouse a strange girl from a strange sleep, and as if sensing a kind of sister, Sefalet shrieked and wept until it was agreed that she could be the one to whisper in the sleeping architect's ear. She would wake and do our work for us, and all would be well. I would hold tight to her left hand so that the poor genius might not be terrified by some guttural song of death and horror blurting from the princess's palm.

The town shone at the bottom of a valley, a wash of blue. Every house had been painted some shade of deep, lovely inky blue, from cobalt and indigo to a pale sort of sky color, and each roof had been woven by a blue-mad thatching of lavender and vanilla leaves. Not a sound issued from the wide, single street, no market dinned in the center square, no man put out his washing; no woman tanned her kill in the runnels. When Fortunatus whispered, it echoed like a shout.

"It is on account of Gahmureen," he said, pawing the earth. "Her father was a great goldsmith, perhaps the greatest, until his daughter was born. She dismantled her cradle and built a mechanical knight to protect her mother from roving lizards when she went out to hunt. It could not speak very well, but still, such a wonderful thing! And that when she was but a child! However, the works of Gahmureen are so intricate and so great that she falls into a depthless sleep as soon as she completes them. After building the cradle-knight (who doddled after her mother all through the forests and did not let the lizards bite her) Gahmureen did not wake again for a whole summer. Her father thought her dead until she woke when the first autumn apple fell and asked for breakfast and if they did not need the roof mended. She has invented many astonishing things over the many years, and she never seems to be awake during the Abir. Of course her parents draw their chit from the barrel along with the rest and have gone off to be blacksmiths and pearl-divers and who knows what else. For a long while, a little machine woke her every century or so. But she has not come up out of dreaming in many years, for all built things wind down. Still, we have always known where she was, if we needed her. She sleeps deep and soundless at the bottom of her valley, in her blue village, Chandai, where folk left her in peace, dreaming of machines and waiting to be woken by her father or her mother or her clock, none of whom will ever come now. But we will come! And she has slept so long that surely she can build a cathedral—am I saying it right this time?—which will amaze John into shutting up and leaving us alone. This is my hope. I also hope she is kind, and does not snap at her assistants, and perhaps that she has green eyes like Hagia, whom I miss so."

For myself I hoped she would be good enough at her job that I could laze in the sun with Sefalet on my belly and have very little to do with it. Lions, lacking thumbs, are not greatly interested in architecture until it is finished and ready for us to nap in.

We crept through the village and toward a great cobalt house with a round black door and a number of flourishes at the windows, the chimney, and the corners of the roof—I could only call them flourishes, but they clearly had a purpose and just as clearly I could not understand what they might be. One flourish was a knot of pulleys and empty water-spouts folded together and rusted to unusability. One was a serpent with an apple in its mouth, all of sapphire. As we came to the door a flourish hidden in the hinges creakingly unfolded and rose up to regard us: a face of bluish ceramic, with silver eyes that opened and closed at intervals, and a mouth that opened through a series of weights and bellows, which also, I supposed, produced the voice that wheezed at us while blue dust spilled out of the mouth.

"Shhhh," the face said. "Gahmureen sleeps."

"We have come to wake her," Fortunatus said. Sefalet kept quite still, her hands clapped over her face so that her eyes could take it all in, large and round and roused. The face seemed to think.

"You are not Gahmuret, the father. Nor Gahmural, the mother."

I could tell that the gryphon meant to have a conversation with the face, to discuss with it why we should be allowed in, and keep up his manners all the while. It is a good way to be. But I had been living in the mountains so long, with only such company as sought me out, and perhaps now I feel I could have behaved differently, but then I simply nosed the face aside and pushed the door open with the flat of my head. Sefalet reached mutely for the face as though she meant to console it for its failure to keep the threshold fast, but I, crouching, pressed forward into the blue house towards a great blue bed. It took nearly the whole space of the central room. A stove puffed away near it, keeping the sleeping inventor warm in her rich bed, piled with turquoise pillows and purple coverlets, ashen silks and ink-colored blankets. Gahmureen slept unpeacefully, on her side with her knees brought up to her chest, one bare leg tangled in the cerulean linens, one arm thrown over her head, as though her dreams tormented her. Her temple shone damp with the night-sweats of countless years. Two straight horns, pearly and bright, the horn twisted around itself but straight as a staff, came up from her head, and each of them had impaled a pillow. Her black hair wound around the horns many times, tangled, drifting in the breeze through the door.

Sefalet climbed down from my back, keeping her left hand up so that her mouth was clamped shut but her eye stayed open, afraid of the lovely woman in the bed, her great horns, her very likely poor temper at having been woken. She reached out her right hand tentatively, as if to a wild dog, and placed the mouth of her palm next to Gahmureen's ear.

"Wake up, lady," she whispered. "Don't you want to build something beautiful?"

The inventor stirred in her sleep; she moaned lightly, as though her dream had torn at the edges.

"Wake up," Sefalet whispered again, more loudly. "Don't you want to see how high a tower can go?"

Gahmureen turned toward the voice but did not wake. Her arm fell limply to the coverlet, and her brow creased, as though her dream bled and pained her.

"Wake up," growled Sefalet's left-hand mouth, pressed against her face, but not so tightly that the words did not echo perfectly clear. "It's time to do the Devil's work."

And the horned woman sat up straight in her bed, her hair falling over her naked breasts, her eyes utterly clear and sharp.

"Did you say something, child?" she said, and her voice sounded hard and bright as first light.

I had to ask her. You would have asked too, if you'd been her lion, her great cat. I didn't even love her yet, but I had to know, because worry comes before love. Doesn't mean I wanted the answer.

I let her eat first, I'm not cruel. I can afford to wait—so can we all, forever if it takes so long. I said: *One more grape, girl. You have to keep your color up.* I said: *If you don't eat your meat you'll have bad dreams.* I said: *Sit back in my tent, royal child, there are pillows here for you, and a bowl of water to wash your hair in.*

And around our dinner a city rose up, bustling, makeshift, the thousand tents of the cathedral town to come, ready to work when Gahmureen could hold the whole thing in her head, when she could see it building itself under her long hands with their black nails. Torches lit, blue tents and green and gold along the wide plain, and the red moths gathered around the flames in their own concentric cities, and adzes were cleaned and axes were sharpened and the grinding of blades floated around our little space where grapes and meat and clean hair met.

I asked. I had to ask. "You used a word, before. Devil. Do you know what it means?" Because of course I knew. When John says *devil*, he means *us*.

"Yes, Father told me," said Sefalet shyly, her right hand clamped over her face. I was always making her talk, and she could never be sure which of her would answer. It made her nervous and it made her stutter. But a child must speak, or how will the world know how to behave in its presence?

"What did your father tell you?"

"The Devil lives in the other place. He tempts us into sin."

"Where is the other place?"

"I don't know. Father didn't say. Maybe it's beyond the wall," Sefalet said sullenly, and balled her left hand into a fist.

"What does the Devil look like?"

Beneath the girl's hand, a dark circle of tears grew. "Like Qaspiel, he said. Only black and red all over and with wings like a terrible bat, and horns, too. But Vyala, Qaspiel is beautiful, and I've seen Utior, its friend, and *its* wings are black like a bat's, and it has horns that are just so awfully red! And Utior is beautiful, too, and gave me a ride on his shoulders, and didn't even flinch when my left hand told it that it would mourn forever and still be weeping at the end of days. Everyone has horns and wings and a tail and everyone lives in another place and everyone sins—"

"What's sinning, little one?"

Sefalet wailed: "When you do something that Father's book says you oughtn't! But everyone does, and so maybe this is hell and the other place and me and mama are the Devil too! I don't want to be the Devil!"

"Hush, love, hush, my cublet. What did you mean, then, when you called the cathedral the Devil's work?"

And finally her left hand won out, and seized her right with vicious claws, throwing it aside to clutch her jaw like a hideous starfish and tell me:

"The Devil's work is entropy. Don't know what that word means? It's beyond a lion's ken. The Devil's work is time and death. The Devil's work is not the building of a tower to heaven but the throwing down of it—his work is the cracking of the world, and we will build but the guardhouse over the chasm. But don't let Father convince you there's a morality to it. The Devil just is. Entropy occurs. Extropy, too, and you can call that God if you're lonely. Want another answer? The other place is Constantinople, and the Devil sits on a purple throne."

The child turned her blank head upward, abject in her shame and her unhappiness. I padded to her and let her fall into my chest—it is a big chest, and deep, and sometimes a body needs a place to fall. I tucked my chin over her poor, bald head.

"I wanted to be good for you," she whispered. "You had never met me, and if I could only be the right-hand Sefalet all the time, you would love me, and never be afraid of me or angry with me, and my life would be clean, with no awful things in it."

"Oh, child," I purred. "No one's life is like that."

Grisalba the lamia came for us in the morning, a flaming orange chiton concealing her coppery tail and revealing her more human beauty, and though I don't believe Grisalba knows anything but stern expressions, she gave her softest one to the sleeping princess.

"Bring the girl," she said. "This won't be pretty, but better it's now than if she finds it on her own."

I roused her, nipping the scruff of her dress and bidding her sink her hands in cold water and eat the last of the fat green grapes, grown warm and soft overnight. The three of us went peaceably through the work camp, and I marveled that Pentexore could remember how to build things when growing them was so much easier. John had a lecture about the greater virtue of sweat and labor that he kept for such occasions. Anyway I was not even sure one could grow something so large as a cathedral. The al-Qasr had always been there, since before we came. Certainly half the purpose of this church of Thomas and

Mary was to outstrip our native palace, a thing greater than the land could gift.

Breakfast fires crackled, and the smell of sizzling fruit and fatty lamb made the air rich. The huge black stones of the Tower ruins lay strewn about, slabs of darkness in the dry, sweet grass. Some had grown pelts of rope and hooks already, ready to be moved on Gahmureen's command—only she had not yet presented herself or made known her desire.

Grisalba said nothing. She did not like me, I suspect, the newcomer in their little family, stranger, who had not seen the great man come. She stopped finally and gestured at a tree that sprang up in the center of the ruins like the root of the Tower itself.

In the trunk of the tree, Hagia's wide green eyes and her frank, laughing mouth opened in the expanse of golden-brown bark. In the leaves, the stout, short, twisted branches, among the last of the stark blue spring blossoms, golden crosses hung, tinkling in the warm wind, and in each of them was a mouth, as strange and separated from a body as Sefalet's, and from each mouth came John's voice, calling his daughter in a chorus of delight.

THE VIRTUE OF THINGS
IS IN THE MIDST OF THEM

4. On the Creation of the World

One cannot listen to origin stories on an empty stomach. Fortunately, my hosts understood that instinctively, and fed me in a most extraordinary fashion. I would be remiss if I did not record that first feast, for it reveals much of the nature of the country in which I found myself. I was not compelled to present myself at a long table for a stingy meal made up for with golden goblets and diamond plates, nor to stroke the dozen wretched hunting dogs of a lesser lord and comment on their obvious qualities before I could eat. Ymra, the feminine hexakyk, showed me a room appointed in a manner I can only call familiar—on the wall hung tapestries depicting a countryside that could only be my own England, green and fair, with the standard dragons and unicorns going about their allegorical business, spotted spaniels leaping that might have been my own boisterous dogs, and even an exquisite scene depicting a young woman with almond eyes peeking out through a fence of eight strong men. The bed stood sturdy and large, its posts carved from good Breton oak, its linens stitched impeccably, gold and violet upon red, my own family's colors. I had to myself a wash basin of black marble and milled soap smoother than any I had ever seen, the color of a new and perfect rose. I should be cleaner than ever I have been, with such items at my disposal.

In the midst of my wondering the meal arrived, brought to my room by the king and queen themselves, though I found this quite beyond the pale. When I inquired if there were not servants to do this work, Ysra assured me they would make themselves known presently, but intimacy, rather than convenience, was what was wanted tonight. They set out my food and sat upon the floor like the children they still appeared to be in my eyes, and watched me eat.

The food itself could not have been more alien. For each eerie and homelike tapestry on the wall, foodstuffs past my understanding glittered on ivory trays. The meat remained crusted with the skin of the beast who had given it up, broiled and roasted emerald-colored scales, as though a supper from St. George's own quarry. Fruit there was, but each of them encased in crystal I was obliged to pry open like a glittering clam's shell. A thorny fish course stared up at me, a piscine marvel with long, twisted horns and scales of sapphire and gold, whose meat, too, glistened like precious metal (oh, but it tasted softer and sweeter than melon or pears) accompanied by wine which might well have been blood. I found it impossible to tell the difference—either I quaffed an unusually thick, rich, and salty vintage, or with equal relish a cup of somewhat thin, sour blood. (I have nothing against blood—it can be quite a boon on a long voyage, as the nomads of Araby will happily tell you. In fact, I once, in dire need, drank the blood of a crocodile when a duel had left me so wracked and wounded that I feared death had finally noticed poor John. The crocodile did not seem to mind the cut I made in her flank, and I woke quite utterly healed and refreshed. One must not be squeamish about foreign foods.)

"Are you sated?" asked Ymra, and I allowed that I was.

"Are you rested?" asked Ysra, and to that I also confessed.

At which point, they began to tell me the following tale, with a great urgency, as though it was of paramount importance that

I not only hear all they had to say, but believe it wholly, as surely as they believed it, and not doubt their smallest word. I am a clever John if I am a John at all, and I know that when folk are that keen to have you swallow their tale, they are most certainly lying about some or all of it, more often all of it, but a tale follows a meal like Sunday morning follows Saturday night, and I was content to hear anything. I heard the following:

Once, long ago, there was a war and everyone involved behaved very badly. The war is not important—war is never important. It is the same, a sort of mummery that everyone knows how to perform but agrees to pretend they can still be surprised by it. War is only ever a joint or a hinge, where the world becomes something else, swings open or swings closed. What is important comes after the war. What came after this war was twenty years of coming home. What came after *this* war was a man, a very clever man, so full of cleverness and schemes he could hardly open his mouth before the boldest and most beautiful lies flitted out of him like fiery green butterflies. He got lost in stormy seas, and after he lost all his companions and all hope of getting home, he ran aground on a little island, so small it had only one house and one inhabitant. The house glittered with blue-green sea glass and bits of metal and wood that looked to the clever man as if they might have come from ships like his. But he didn't think about that. He thought only about the woman who lived on the island, who had so much black hair that it ringed the island twice and wore a net of emeralds over her naked body.

Her name was Calypso.

The clever man stayed with her for nine years, and told her all his secrets, how he had been weaned early to make room for a sister, how his father thought him too skinny, how he'd married a grey-eyed girl who was good at weaving, a girl he hardly knew and she'd gotten pregnant faster than he'd gotten over his wedding hangover. How he could still hear the pocking of arrows, even though the war was done. And Calypso loved him. She gave him her body, her emeralds, her house, her hair. She wept for his sorrows and cheered for his clevernesses. She did not tell him that she was a goddess, and if you ask us what a goddess is we will say: A goddess is a kind of trick the world plays. It is a good trick. The world only has good tricks.

Why did she love a skinny, lying mortal man, this woman with a heart like a sun? That is what men like him are made for, to pick the locks inside of a woman far bigger than he.

Finally nine years were over and Calypso asked her clever boy to make a choice. She took him in her arms and wrapped him in her black, black hair and said: You have suffered so much. Let me erase your suffering. Let me make you live forever, and never age, never hunger, never thirst, never become bored or listless. Let me make you like me, and you can stay on this island for all time—or else range over the whole world and all its oceans, one foot on each wave like a racer of the tide. Let me be generous with you; let me give you plenty of all the secret things I know.

And the clever man said no. He said: If I go home my father will have to be proud of me. I went to war; I am a man. He will have to see that. If I go home that grey-eyed girl will have grown up and I'll find out who she is. I'll meet my son. I'll be an old king like my father and have a chance to disapprove of everyone. If I stay here, if I stay here and live forever, no one will ever know my name. You can't be famous without dying—death is what puts the final seal on a man's life.

But a goddess is a trick the world plays, and Calypso means *to conceal* and *to hide*. What Calypso hid was that the choice she gave her clever man had a vicious echo, and he chose for all men, and all women, and their children, too. So the world is full of those who die, and some become famous but most do not, and they certainly become bored and listless and old.

Calypso called him a fool and wrapped her hair three times around her island, dragging it out of the sea and to the edges of the world where no one would refuse her, would refuse anyone, would refuse anything. A place where the only answer to any question was yes. And that place became Pentexore, when it grew up.

The opposite of Calypso is apocalypse. And it is coming, when a trick with eyes that carry the whole sea in them will offer a choice again, and we will all drown in it. We are looking forward to it. We are setting our clocks. We are very curious to see how it all turns out.

I drank a bit more of my wine-that-might-have-been-blood and tapped my fingernail against the goblet.

"Now, is that true?" I said with a twinkle in my eye—I have a most effective twinkle that I can deploy at will.

Ymra gave me back my twinkle trebled. "Not really," she said with a smile. "But the grey-eyed girl *was* very good at weaving."

"To begin to tell the history of a thing is to begin to tell a lie about it," said Ysra. "Tell us again about your adventures in Egypt?"

5. On Literature in Pentexore

I have written a great number of excellent books. In addition to the books detailing my travels I have also written charming fiction involving a circle of Italian nobles telling tales in the countryside, and a most exciting poem concerning a certain English monster and his mother. I spent two years as a bard in the court of a Carthaginian heir, compelled to tell and retell the story of Rome's conquest of Carthage so that Hannibal and Hasdrubal won through, and marched the Scipio down the broad, palm-lined Phoenician boulevards in chains. To tell them how Aeneas did not humiliate Dido to suicide. No, when he left her after marrying her in that long-lost cave while the lightning crashed and Hera howled, Dido hunted him down through all the isles of Italy, and cut his throat in front of his new wife Lavinia, whereupon Rome was founded by Dido the queen and all of those red-cloaked bastards were Carthaginian to begin with. It was good work, and well paid, but it did not fulfill me, to constantly sing of victories that did not happen to an heir who would never sit on the throne, but longed for a world that never came to pass. It was, if I may be frank, and I think I may, depressing.

So you see that I am quite accomplished, and one morning over the royal breakfast, in which every dish was soaked in yellow cream and rich with eggs, I announced my intentions to Ysra and Ymra.

"When I get home I wish to write an expansive account of Pentexore. No one in Christendom would not like to read of such wonders, and I do not deny wonders when I can give them, with both hands. I have already begun my preliminary notes. But I wonder if perhaps many books are written *in* Pentexore. Perhaps the salamanders too might like to read my thoughts on their doings."

Ysra and Ymra smiled identical, tight, small smiles. "What would you say about us?"

"Oh, I would not criticize, if that's your fear! I only want my countrymen to know what an extraordinary country you rule, what marvelous inventions and natural resources you command, how charming your daily works!"

Ymra swirled a flat black biscuit in her creamy cup. "If we allowed this, would your people want to travel here, do you think?"

"Most certainly!"

Ysra looked hungrily at me. "We want that. We have heard that men visit Pentexore-Beyond-the-Wall, but you are our first foreigner. We want your country and our country to meet and court and kiss. We want to merge, to see what is extraordinary in England, what marvelous inventions and natural resources Byzantium commands, to observe the daily works of Flemish knights. We want to sniff at them, and see what they are made of, and what we could make of their world. If you think a book could accomplish this we welcome you to write it. Write it beautifully, write it so beautifully they have to come, and pay tribute to us, and build roads from Spain to Simurgh. Build ships to cross from Sweden to Summikto. We find these words so bright and alien: Sweden, England, Flanders. They sound rich enough to eat."

I confess I was taken aback by their enthusiasm. I had not thought much on trade between our nations. My heart unfolded like a map: a picture of a town I knew in Scotland, in which a seam of silver was discovered, rich and deep. Several dukes and princes swarmed their vassals over that town, digging out the silver and taking the women to wife and carousing until nothing remained of the village except a hollow mountain and a few burnt houses. That is how it often goes in Scotland. That is how it often goes everywhere, I suppose.

"As for Pentexoran books," Ymra said sweetly. "We have heard that on the other side of the Wall they are enamored of such things, but here, we find they…inflict a distressing order on the world. Surely you have noticed that once you write a thing down, it is as good as real. People aren't strong enough to resist the spell of authority ink casts. It *is* a kind of magic, and we don't generally approve. You must be so careful with that sort of thing, or else all sorts of things you never intended start becoming real, and soon you've no control at all anymore. I suppose, if we could enforce that folk only wrote about what was real, and virtuous, and only told good tales about their monarchs and their compatriots, it might be all right."

"I believe Plato would agree with you."

"Is she a relation of yours?"

I laughed. "No, but *he* proposed just such safeguards."

"Perhaps then, when you write your book, Plato will come and visit us and advise us on the dangerous questions of literature." Ymra said in a way that made me quite aware the issue had closed.

"But you must understand," I insisted, though I could see it annoyed them both to continue the discussion past the polite placing of the queen's napkin on the table, "there are weak books and strong books. Yes, certainly, sometimes a man writes things not strictly true and folk have no way of knowing otherwise, or perhaps the things he wrote seemed so much bigger and brighter than anything they knew that they wanted it to be real, or perhaps a king wrote it, and could pass a law requiring people to behave as though it was true—you know, that sort of thing happened with the Bible and Constantine, though I would be struck down for saying so at home. But I told tales of Carthage Triumphant for years, and it did not unmake old Rome, it did not rewrite the history of the world, it did not do anything but sink a black-haired prince of a dead kingdom further in despair and bitterness."

Ysra considered. "But in that prince's court, did everyone behave as though the tales were true? As though the kingdom were not dead and the prince puissant, Rome a meager, trollopy sort of place?"

I answered slowly. "The prince held a ball once, where he compelled half his courtiers to dress as Romans, and the other half as old Carthaginian nobles. After the dancing and rich eating, the Carthaginians threw goblets of wine at the Romans, and beat them, at first with mock strength and much laughter, but soon with vigor and anger, and at the end of it the Romans were made to stand naked before the 'conquerors' and parceled out as slaves. The next day they were emancipated, but that night was pleasant for no one."

"There you have it," said Ymra smugly, folding her six hands over one another. "The world is too fragile to bear the weight of books."

6. On the Phoenix

I had much freedom in Simurgh, the city of the phoenix, over which the Mount looms like a great black mother bird. The phoenix do not hold Simurgh alone, but rather it is a haven for all fiery creatures, and a large population of salamanders call it home as well. It is a most pleasant city, full of green domes half-blackened with smoke and beautiful birds strutting through the streets with their tails heavy and golden behind them, for it is considered gauche to fly unless one is coming of age (and soon to conflagrate), of a rank lower than margrave, or an appointed sheriff. The salamanders, who range in size from that of a hunting dog to that of a long and undulate pony, and in color from deep beryl-green to iridescent coppery verdigris, carry crystal globes of living fire around their necks on thick chains, and when they are exhausted, they sip from the sloshing fire, and are refreshed.

In Simurgh, two activities consumed most of her inhabitants' energies: The making of young, and preparations for the Bonfire, a great ball held in honor of all Simurgh's most premier folk, as well as Ymra and Ysra, who are certainly monarchs as they claimed to be, for I had yet to see any other soul move in the Mount, and whenever I mentioned their name to an incandescent bird or portly salamander, I was treated to much in the way of imprecations for their health and favor. The phoenix asked me if I have been to the Wall yet. They say: *The land on the other side of the Wall is rich and beautiful, and they have a hole which is full of everlasting life, and we have none of those things, and they will not share. They are decadent and weak. In all the world there is only the land on one side of the Wall and the land on the other side, and we are in one place, and they are in the other place, and we cannot get there, and they cannot get here.*

They sang with such bitterness of the Wall. They sang for Ysra and Ymra to give them what that other land has.

The rearing and breeding of young, however, comprised most of the economy of Simurgh. Both phoenix and salamander required a great deal of fire to effect their peculiar processes. The lizards possessed great silver urns of flame in which their worms, very like silkworms, writhed and grew until they were ready spin their cocoons. The cocoons shimmered blue, gold, amber, and deft handmaidens appeared as if out of nowhere, the only other humans I had seen, their eyes hollow and their limbs thin. They plunged their hands into the molten creche and spun out a wondrous thread from the cocoons. Their fingers were in no way scorched, so I may have to reconsider whether they are human. They certainly kept their own counsel and company, for I could not get a word from them. (Though I found in my rooms a most extraordinary suit of clothes the day after I observed this rite, with hose of fiery red and the rest golden, amber, brassy and bold.)

The phoenix, of course, give birth to themselves every five hundred years or so. However, this is not quite sufficient for population growth, and I gathered that at some point in their past they suffered a great reduction in their numbers. Their eggs, when they lay them (a rather difficult proposition, I gather, as the hen must ingest a monstrous amount of cinnamon in order to achieve fertility—the woods surrounding Simurgh crowded thick with cassia) must be roasted for one hundred days on a bed of embers. One might imagine such a blaze would cook the egg, but I am assured the chick cannot survive without it.

I was treated as a minor celebrity and given a goodly number of ales and cakes. The streets of Simurgh glowed with red leaves shed from stately trees which never seemed to grow new green shoots nor run out of their scarlet foliage. Anything red is beloved. To date I have not seen a conflagration of phoenix, but I gather it is quite the to-do, and the main purpose of the Bonfire, to celebrate the old phoenix and the new, and to glimpse the sacred dance of the salamanders on their round and gleaming feet.

When will this great event occur? I asked every phoenix and green salamander I met.

Soon, they all said. *If not tomorrow, surely the day after.*

I have been here for some time now. The answer is always tomorrow. Surely the next day. No longer than the day after that.

THE BOOK
OF THE RUBY

You don't have to say how they sent us off. It's embarrassing to think about now. Even my mother came—Kukyk, waving her wings in the air. How they cheered. How they blew kisses. How the wind sounded on the golden waves. How they cut the hedge apart to let us through, with axes and beaks. You can skip that part. The part where we were so happy to be going to save John's world we pretended not to hear the heads crunching and crying under blade after blade. The part where we thought our own king would love us if only we killed a whole heap of people we had no quarrel with.

But the sharks? I should still make that scene?

Yes, the sharks.

We learned from John that whichever ship bore the king was most important, the flagship. I rode upon that ship, too, along with Anglitora and Qaspiel and Hadulph and Sukut the bull-headed astronomer and many others. I could not say why then but I felt it important that we stay together. The whole business had been timed so that the road through the sand would form when we had nearly completed the crossing, so that we could sail as long as possible, so we could make good time. John seemed to have little enough idea how far it would be from the opposite shore of the Rimal to Jerusalem.

"I am not a cartographer, no matter how much I might wish

94

it. Hopefully I shall be able to orient myself when we arrive. I will do my best, wife, that is all I can do."

He seemed so kind, now that we were at war. At peace, even joyful.

That is how humans are built, I think.

The sharks came in the evening of the fourth day at sea. We had encountered a calm patch in the wind, and lashed the ships together so that folk could move from one to the other, clap their comrades' shoulders, share some wine, practice with their new weapons.

You have forgotten to say how we brought barrels full of black, soft earth and how we had planted in them swords and bows and arrows and axes and polearms, hoping for the best. This is how Pentexore plans for war—they become farmers. The bushes had begun to bud just as we set out, so the smallest of us, pygmies, cannibals, panotii, plucked green swords, still hard and unripe, bows with a pinkish cherry-cast to them, polearms barely as long as your leg and smelling strongly of green apples. Only enough to train with—the rest to be given their due time to bloom.

It was as you say. I was only hurrying to get to the sharks more quickly.

We had a lovely supper of fish and brandy and all had enough to eat (how I relish the thought of that now). The panotii were showing off their bows when Sukut spied them—glassy strange shapes moving in the sand. I did not and do not know if you could rightly call them sharks but the effect was the same. Nearly transparent in the dusk, they seemed truly to be made of glass: Teeth, gills, fins and all. The setting sun exploded through their bodies, and they surrounded us, terrible crystal fire-fish.

But no fear came over us—had we not come to prick flesh and draw blood? The hardy green polearms flew from a dozen hands—anything that could reasonably be called a harpoon shot out from our city of lashed ships and into the diamond bodies of the sharks. The poor wretches took bolts and arrows and blades in their flanks, and they cried out—

Like bells ringing—

—Like goblets pinging against one another when a toast is called. Everyone shouted and hallooed—well, not I, who could not credit how fast Pentexorans could become something else entirely, and fling weapons at beasts they did not know. Not Anglitora, who did not fight what she could not mate with. And not John, whose face went white before he pressed his brow into my shoulder and whispered:

"I had forgotten, when I crossed, how terrible is the life of the sea."

The blemmye boys whose arms bulged to the task hauled the corpses on board. They sliced into them with triumphant yells, hacking and cutting at the stubborn stuff, only to find the creatures quite hollow save for a translucent swim-bladder and some vestigial digestive flotsam with little more to it than a scrap of silk twisted into a rope. These tossed aside, the skins proved hard and not at all as prone to shattering as glass, and big enough to make an impressive number of breastplates and cuirasses.

A great success, the first victory of the war. Never mind how we heard those ponging, bell-like wails of despair following us across the sea, never ceasing till we made landfall, an endless, impotent weeping.

A young phoenix made berth on the flagship with us. Her name was Niobe, and unusual among phoenix, her plumage shone pale blue with flecks of gold, much as some terribly hot flames glow. She clutched a pot in her talons, and sat upon it most of the time, protecting it jealously. Though I could see how seasick she often felt, being unused to ships when she might well have just flown and saved herself the trouble, she never let the little jar go.

Do you suppose there is a road through the sky over the Rimal, too? If some crane flew west, would she find herself back in Pentexore unless she flew at some special time of year, when a path through the clouds might open and lead her to Jerusalem? I suppose I shall never know, flightless maid that I am.

"What is in your pot, Niobe?" I asked her one hot afternoon, when the glare off the sand slashed like blades at my eyes. The pot gleamed, several metals winding around each other, silver and gold and copper and tin, with veins of malachite and carnelian and other gems.

"It is myself, queen Hagia," she answered, and I begged her not to call me so.

The blue bird went on, her golden gaze cast low. "Only four of us remain, now. Rastno is gone, the wall stands firm, and the phoenix have no hope of finding Heliopolis more. By this I mean the city of the sun, where we must inter our old ashes, stand watch at our own funeral. We met in the dark, we four, under wide and fragrant trees, and I had the least to stay for. I have had no chicks, nor did I wish for any. I have devoted myself to diving for gems into the crevasses of the earth—it is good work and the Abir chose it for me, but others will take up my slack. And—well. I was Rastno's mate, years and nights and ages ago. We burned a cloud to death in our passion and when I mourned for him I screamed so loudly a lake boiled away. I should seek out his birthright if anyone should. You know he was our king? We say Bazil. He should have held the secret of Heliopolis in trust for us. Instead we died and died and died. It is our secret shame. Alone among you the phoenix are short-lived. The Fountain has nothing for us. But if I can find Heliopolis we will all be saved. We can go on. We can have children. Lakes may live. I made my nest of pearls and cinnamon and roses and sugar cane, and burned myself—I had held back for centuries, as long as I could, for without the rites in Heliopolis even the resurrected phoenix must waste and die.

In this pot are my ashes. I have hope that the city of the sun lies in the West, and I might find it among the wreckage of the king's country. It is a small hope but small can be good and I am cheerful—the air is very sweet at sea."

I remember her. It always shocked me how big the phoenix grow—I had never seen one; I had always wanted to. Among birds they are considered the best and most beautiful. And Niobe did shine. Nearly as tall as John—and that tail! I wish I had a tail so bright.

The crossing was full of people telling stories. Telling their lives to anyone who would listen. To strangers they hoped would be friends, to friends who might have forgotten. That was how I discovered that Ummo the sciopod had won all the foot races in his village as a child, only to suffer a knee injury while truffle-hunting—but thankfully the next Abir had made him a herald, at which he felt he had aptitude, being louder than any of his siblings. It was how I heard the tale of Aya the astomi, who took the veil in her third century, tattooing her nose with extraordinary patterns like starry ferns and buds. She showed us the markings that indicated her as an adept, a huntress of the first order, sworn and bound. Even those I knew well could not resist the fish-pot and the circle of tales— I had not heard that John had occupied much of his childhood running errands for the bustling, big-armed fishermen of the harbor, on a sea called the Bosphorus, bringing chopped or rotten or otherwise undesirable fish for bait, gutting mackerel, selling baskets of blue tails to wives of little means. Some told of their journeys to the Fountain, and how they had choked on the water, and how they had got some bauble of a tigress or anthropteron along the way. Some told of their last Abir, and how the barrel had spun, and how they had held their breath—oh, the anticipation of it!—and how they had kissed their mates and learned to make cloth or laws or soup, as their glittering stones commanded. Some of the stories were dear, some plain, some boring and poorly told. But the telling of them passed the time, and when we ran out of true tales, we made up new ones, and they were also dear and exciting and plain and boring and poorly told, but how we laughed at every one.

We bet with them. When we played Knuckle with Niobe's glass beads. If you lost, you gave up a secret. Aya never cashed in, she saved up the secrets they owed her. You never know when I'll need them, *she said, and her eyes shone. I think by the time we made land she had a fortune in secrets.*

There was a serious young man named Houd with enormous hands, his body like a dancer's, and he told two tales—the one he spoke, in which he worked as a glassblower and loved it, because his breath permeated everything he made, his own, private breath that moved like a secret in the glass that gathered dust in homes and huts and palaces, and how he had once known a phoenix who saw his work and called him a good boy. And another, one we all knew but which he did not tell so much as allow to sit beside him while he talked of glass. Of a nursery, and two sisters, and a governess. None of us could call out that second tale. The Abir forbids mention of other lives, other selves once we have passed the barrel and into the new century. But we all knew him, even though we did not say, and I saw Hajji weeping by the stew-pot. Later, in the dark below decks, I saw her wrap her ears around him, and him close his great hands around her tiny body.

And then there was Sukut, who adjusted the silver ring in his nose and the golden one in his furry ear as he spoke in his slow gravelly way, how would I have come to know and love him if he had not ladled out his portion of stew one night and lowed:

"My mother was a maze-maker. It's a traditional line of work for my kind. Even my cradle, the size of a little boat, full of twists and turns I had to solve before I found her at the end, her breasts heavy with milk for me, her expression proud and mild. As a calf I was always looking for her, seeking her, and everything in the world was a maze. At the center of every maze, warm arms and a furry cheek and praise and sugar-reeds to suck. My bull-father would hide in the corners and leap out, snarling and roaring until he could stand it no more and collapsed into laughing and ruffling my hair. I was fully grown before I realized some roads just run straight, with no turns at all. Some houses don't have traps and puzzles to solve to get to the kitchen and supper in a clay bowl. To tell you the truth I miss it. I'm always looking for the false wall and the invisible lever. Nothing seems quite real unless you had to seek it out, peek under rocks for the key to it. I thought I'd be a mazer as well—I was brought up to the business, I had an aptitude. But the Abir said: *No, instead, an astronomer and a seer, and no calves, either.* I went down to the al-Qasr to find the last astronomer, a salamander called Lyx, and I asked her to train me, so that I could be good at seeing, and be happy in my life. Lyx wanted her belly rubbed, for this is a sign of fraternity among salamanders, and I was honored to do it—her skin felt like baking bread, hard and soft and hot all together. *Cow,* she said while I scratched her, and I didn't mind it, I am a cow, at least half of one. *Cow,* she said, *you have to make the fire yourself. And don't be stingy; if it's not hot enough, the portents will freeze to death.* I asked if astronomy didn't mainly have to do with the stars. Lyx laughed, which sounds like crackling, sparking branches when a salamander does it. *Listen, cow. The Abir's just a bunch of rocks in a box. If you want to be happy, you have to interpret the text a little broadly. Stare at the stars if you like. I am what I am and what that is is a fiery lizard, and I say astronomy is mainly to do with fire. What else are stars made of? And you know, when I did use the broken old looking glasses and spying lenses to see the sky, I found that the heavens are a maze, the most beautiful and perfect and difficult one you can imagine. And astronomy, I say, is mainly to do with mazes, and the solving of* them, and the finding, in the center, warm arms and a furry cheek and breasts heavy with milk, and praise—and also trapdoors and invisible levers and roaring and snarling. It all depends on which way you turn."

Oh, Sukut. You smelled like new grass.

It was that night, after he told us about the sky and the salamander. That was the night the cloud came.

I should have known it for an omen.

The moon rose up so high, like a hole in the sky we might slip through. Nearly all slept; I had the night watch, and you boiled grasses to keep me waking. It came down like a curtain, as golden as the sand, a mist so thick I could hardly breathe in it. But in the mist I saw lights, like distant lanterns, pale and green or bright and glittering amber, floating lazily in the fog. And my stepdaughter's face, I remember her face so clearly—

It was not a cloud. It was a Cloud. Descending to the sandy sea to close me up in its arms, me, who could not fly to meet it, most unworthy child of the Sedge of Heaven, it surrounded me and made an agony of my skin but also a hideous pleasure, an ecstasy like death and like birth and like the breaking of the egg. The Cloud spoke and did not speak, it loved and loathed and longed for unnameable things, and this is what God is like, what John thinks he understands but does not, that clouds and gods land like luck or bloody mishap. All you can do is survive them—

I looked up into the lights and felt the weight of them, heard voices and heard nothing, and when I turned Niobe filled my vision, her wings outspread so huge and so wide, her body illuminated, burning and not burning, her head thrown back and her beak aglow, and rapture was everywhere but I could not touch it—

You do not have wings, it was not for you, though you had a part in it—

—And then it was gone and the light vanished out of the world, I could breathe and I could weep, which I did, all of us did who saw it, but when I think on it now I remember a private thing, with no other soul to witness but two birds and a poor blemmye.

I have had some space to think on this now. Some distance. And I cannot decide what it meant. Why the Cloud would come to me then, and not after, when I had such great wounds. When it would have mattered so much more, when I would have felt the touch of the mist like forgiveness.

John was always wrong about God. God is not a man who looks like men, God is not even a blemmye who looks like blemmyae. God is a random event, a nexus of pain and pleasure and making and breaking. It has no sense of timing. It does not obey nice narratives like: a child is born, he grows, he performs miracles and draws companions, then sacrifices himself to redeem a previous event in an old book. That is not how anything works. God is a sphere, and only rarely does it intersect with us—and when it does, it crashes, it cracks the surface of everything. It does not part the sea at just the right time. God is too big for such precision.

Maybe it was only a cloud. Maybe the cranes don't really know anything. My mother was not educated as the scribes in the al-Qasr are. Perhaps they all just love the sky, and sing their songs of praise to the thing they love. Maybe Hajji is right and there is nothing, only brothers and sisters and lovers and ships on the sea and mistakes on your hands like a branch of orange.

I would prefer that. It would make a better story.

THE LEFT-HAND MOUTH,
THE RIGHT-HAND EYE

You must be careful of the earth in Pentexore. It is hungry. It is fertile, but like a pregnant woman, it will devour anything it can in order to feed its young. Sefalet sat at the base of the tree and would not be moved. She clapped her hands up, no mouth, all eyes, and the tree could not put arms around her, but all its mouths smiled down, and she bathed in its shadow like a turtle soaked in the sea.

"Do you suppose it's king now, since they're gone? Or queen? I'm unclear on the politics here." Grisalba chewed on the end of her tail, coiled in the long grass. "It hasn't said anything yet. We did that when Abibas died. Just planted him and let him rule from his pot."

Fortunatus, fretting, pawed the earth. The sun played on his fur. "I suspect I know what's happened," he said gently. "Hagia and John mated here. It was their first time. We all pretended not to hear. They were not...careful. Even his own book says not to spill seed upon the earth! I am in wonderment that he took that not at all seriously."

Sefalet spoke without turning. "Is it my sister, then, like the girl with one wing?"

How were we to interpret it for her? A snake, a lion, and a gryphon, to explain such signs to a child. I began to offer my best notion—the tree was like an aunt. It came of love, but of the king and queen before they were king and queen, it would not know her nor have anything useful to say, but it was pretty and friendly and from time to time we would leave her with it when we cannot think of anything better.

But the tree spoke first. Hagia, her face rosy on the golden trunk, sighed.

"My baby," she said. "My own girl."

"You're so big," sang the crosses jangling in the branches. "Grown up, and we missed it!"

Sefalet wept from her hands, and inched closer to the tree. I believe she would have traded anything to hear herself called baby and girl and grown and big forever. Grisalba started in on me immediately, to cover her discomfort with the great naked tree, to give the child a screen of words that might grant her a sort of rough privacy.

"You know, I could have looked after her," the lamia snorted. "They didn't need to bring *you* here. What is it you do, teach people to love? That's not a job."

"It's difficult," I began to say.

"No it isn't! I love nine people before teatime, most days. Now, making potions in your gizzard, that's difficult. That's a trade."

I grinned, my muzzle drawing back. It looks alarming, but it is never meant to be. I liked the lamia—lamia are like lions. They have appetites, and are not afraid of their own teeth. I watched Sefalet, whose world consisted now of herself and the tree and nothing else.

"How do you make a potion, Grisalba? Let's say a drug, a hallucinogen or something similar. Something spectacular and complicated."

Grisalba flushed green with pleasure—she loved to discuss her methods. "Well, you know, making a body hallucinate is nothing, really. Bodies are made up of fluids—don't we have a lovely illustration of *that* principle before us today! Adding a new fluid is as easy as kissing. Putting someone to sleep, waking them, arousing their flesh, making them see the unseen, it's all simple, beginner's sorts of secreting. What's difficult, what's really interesting is permanent change. Convincing a body to change over from producing its native fluids and humors to producing what I want it to. Making ants speak. Mushrooms, that sort of thing. Making a girl who's devoted herself to her studies into a libertine and back again at my pleasure. Making luck that can stick to a soul. Yes, yes, I know what you meant; the higher levels are too complex for our little morning chat. Fine. If I wanted to make a body dream—hallucinating is just dreaming with your eyes open—I would eat. Radishes, for bitterness, some mangoes, for remembering, coconut or possibly butterflies if I could catch them, for depth and resonance. While I digested them I would tell my gizzard to make a liquor with a pearly sheen, using phlegmatic humors and a little of the sanguine. I would try to kiss my victim, or at least lick him, for sweat contains much I can use. Sweat is memory the body secretes. Then, when the gizzard was full I would pass the fluid into my heart, where I could let it ferment, and when the time was right I'd bring it up through my mouth, and my kiss would taste of radishes and dreams. My body condenses and distills and sorts out everything that is not the potion, that is not dreaming or waking or arousing. I am a machine for making fluids and so are you, but my machine takes instruction."

I kneaded the ground with my paws. "Love is like that, you know. It's easy to arouse a person or make them dream. That's nothing. Permanence is fiendishly hard. Bodies are made up of fluids, as you say. They sizzle and they ache. Loving is aching with your eyes open. You take in all the bitterness and sweetness and remembering and depth of the thing you love and your body crushes it, distills it into a kind of lightning that keeps you living. It passes through your heart and up through your mouth and the machine of you churns along. And that's fine, as far as it goes. When your lover opens his body to you so sweetly, or your child sleeps in your arms, or your comrades tell you their secrets, or your work comes easily. Love is easy when love is easy. What is difficult is when the machine slips, or when other machines refuse to make the fluids you wish them to, or when your lover runs off with a minotaur, or when your child has two mouths and one of them hates you. You can practice love for all your days and still, it will be hard when it is hard. Love is an unhappy beast who only smiles when it is full of meat, of hearts. You could have raised the girl true. But they hoped I would teach her left-hand mouth to love. Her left-hand heart."

"Do you love the princess?"

"No," answered I. "Not yet. I am only obsessed with her. There is a difference."

"I don't think you really know what you're talking about," frowned Grisalba, and shook her iridescent hair like a horse.

"Probably not," I agreed. "It's only that when people come to you for a thousand years asking you what love means, eventually, you've got to come up with an answer for them."

Sefalet would not leave the treebed. She called it mother and father. She slept there, curled up beneath Hagia's woody mouth, which had a burl beneath it like a mole. When Gahmureen determined that the center of the cathedral should be precisely where the tree marked, according to whatever arcane geomancy she practiced, Sefalet shrieked and wept and her left-hand mouth snapped and bit at anyone who came near. She clung to the trunk, her arms stretched in a wide half-circle around its girth, digging in with her fingernails. Her palms kissed the wood.

Gahmureen retired to her tent, a tall, narrow affair of yellow and orange silks with the ceramic face who guarded her house mounted at its apex. If its eyes opened, she was within, if they closed, she had left for the building site. She napped.

When she emerged she announced that they would build the cathedral around the tree, preserving it, and the sun would enter through a maze of glass holes, finding its way eventually down to a soft silver pool wherein the tree would grow forever.

Sefalet looked at her feet, and then at her tree, somewhat mollified, though still eager to bite anyone who came near her. I sat a short distance away, and we made a tableaux, the three of us: the child, the leafy parent, and the lion, half-drowsy in the hot sun.

Gahmureen and the cathedral loved each other. The horned woman, so tall and lithe, her hands always still, but with the impression that they moved so fast they only appeared still to us. She was full of her cathedral, the panes of its windows were her eyes, the heights of its spires her spiral horns. It loomed so great inside her that she could hardly speak to anyone about it, or she would weep with the beauty of it that only she could see. It took her a week to explain that the foundations should be laid out in the shape of a star. Another to direct the clutch of six-armed hexakyk in the sculpting of the gates, which should depict a tree bursting with fruit—every people of Pentexore should hang happy and serene from a branch, all of us together on the black sethym wood. I found her presence peaceful. She owned purpose, even her blood owned it, and love is purpose. She loved that church even if she did not care that it was a church or had to have a certain number of crosses in it. I knew she didn't care because she called the crosses compasses, as if they merely showed the directions, and Fortunatus had to tell her many times not to tilt them all so that they pointed north together.

Once, at night, when the moon fell on everyone sleeping and the glistening stones of the foundations, she said to me: "When I slept, I dreamed of my mother Gahmural, and every time she laughed, a cathedral came out of her mouth, and I wore them all around my neck like jewels. I will never make anything else so huge and perfect as this, but no one will know it, for it will belong to a god who has never come to court me."

After we had been hauling rocks for a fortnight, out of the tangled briar-wood a little creature came toddling, creaking and squeaking as he went. Finally it accomplished the long plain and clasped Gahmureen's pale bluish hand in his. The architect looked down, surprised, and beheld a little knight made of pieces of cradle: rocking runners and good red wood and a carved canopy and bits of swaddling to keep his joints together, looking up at her with adoring yellow wood eyes. The cradle-knight she had made to protect her long-gone mother had returned, and it remembered her. She smiled and squeezed its hand. I thought the tiny warrior might shake himself apart with joy.

The tree spoke often. The Hagia trunk said things like:

You are so beautiful and clever. I think you will grow up to be like a gourd, hard on the outside, for hungry elephants are always about, but on the inside soft and orange and sweet. I love you, my gourd-girl. It was so thoughtful of you to visit me.

Do you have brothers and sisters?

I am not a monster. Now I am divine, like the Ophanim, and God is a kiss.

Did the Hagia who is not a tree teach you this song? All the blemmyae sing it. It is about the hero Guro, who had shoulders so big they gave her the Axle of Heaven to hold up so it could steal a kiss from the sun.

The crosses with their mouths that spoke in John's voice, clinking against each other in the wind, said things like:

You are so beautiful! Why, you look just like me, with all your mouths! Who could doubt you are my daughter?

My sweetest, the Logos is the Word and God is a Word, and the Logos is light, and when Christ was a boy he suffered fits, too, because his body was not big enough to hold the light. There is no shame in it. Perhaps you will grow up to be a saint. What an addition to the family crest that would make.

This is Eden, Sefalet. This is the navel of the world. Somewhere, somewhere here, I promise you, there is a gate of gold, and a sword thrust through it, blackened and burnt, its flames long since gone out. Somewhere there is an apple no one was ever meant to eat.

I love you, my child. I will never leave you.

No wonder Sefalet could not part herself from it. This is what every child dreams of—a parent who cannot leave them, who loves only them, who knows songs and rhymes and tells them they are wonderful over and over. The tree was not John nor Hagia—it was their love, it grew out of love, it was only their loving portions, only the parts of them that made a child. What they gave her was not mammal love but tree love—permanent, unchanging, growing but slowly, asking for nothing but a bit of water in return. But it sounds like mammal love, and it binds like love, and by the time you notice it is bitter, it's the only kind of love you can hear or see.

I wanted to get the girl free of it. But what could I offer against her parents, come home to her, kinder and simpler than they ever were?

Her left mouth had said nothing for days. She was happy. But she did not eat, she did not call for water, she did not even speak back to the tree. She only listened, and wept, and ate all the love they could drop from their boughs, asking for more all the while.

The Virtue of Things
Is in the Midst of Them

7. Some Questions I Was Asked in Pentexore
by Phoenix, Salamanders, and Hexakyk

Are you a Christian man?

Do you understand Christ to be more like an ox (excuse us, three oxen) or more like a door?

Do you find our country pleasant?

Do you think the world, having had a beginning, must have an end?

Do you need help to build your nest?

Do you believe in the holy apostolic Church?

Are you the male or female of your kind?

How long will you stay?

Do you have any dark secrets or crimes in your past? They are our favorite, tell us immediately.

What is an England?

Are you immune to any common poisons or weak against fire or perhaps lightning?

Do you have any peculiar talents?

What can your body do?

Do you think it is as moral to destroy things as to create them?

Are you lonely here?

Do you know how to fertilize an egg? It's easy; it can be taught.

How long will you stay?

Will you sing us a bawdy song of your country?

Is everyone in your country named John?

Is everyone in your country a liar?

What will you tell your people about us?

Will you remember how green and pretty my skin was?

Will you tell them we are good or that we are wicked?

Have you ever come back from the dead?

What did your father do?

How long will you stay?

Do you think the earth goes around the sun or do you think the sun goes around the earth?

Are any of your countrymen blood-drinkers or eaters of offal?

Have you ever fallen asleep and woken up a hundred years later?

Have you ever had three daughters, two of whom were wicked, one of whom was fair and good?

How did you punish the fair one?

Have you been to see the Wall?

Do you think your soul is sufficient to approach it?

How long will you stay?

How long will you stay?

How long will you stay?

8. Some Answers I Gave

Inasmuch as a man from England is an Englishman and the son of a thatcher is also a thatcher, I am a Christian man. By which I mean I was born so and not consulted on the matter, and therefore not as hardworking or dedicated a thatcher as I might have been if I had my choice of a dozen or so professions.

An ox plows the earth uncomplainingly, so that others may eat and grow. He applies his individual strength to the benefit of the group. But really I have found scripture to be rather full of complaining and the group plowing the earth for the benefit of the individual, so if those are my only choices I will say: a door, for he leads into the world after this one.

Most pleasant, and extraordinary, for I have discovered a tree in the courtyard which bears as fruit nothing but the most extraordinary shoes, in motley silks and with bells or ribbons upon them. I cannot see a good purpose to this, but a certain lady's slipper tasted marvelously of orange blossom cake.

Certainly, though may the saints grant that we do not live long enough to witness what is certain to be a disturbing event.

It will be some years before I have need to conflagrate, but you are most thoughtful.

One answers that in the positive when within earshot of the Church, but when out of sight and mind, well, one cares rather less.

That certainly depends upon whether you are the goose or the gander of your kind.

As long as I am fed and amused.

Oh, many. Once, in Turkey, I came upon a man called Odoric. He was uncommonly handsome, with a large and prominent nose, blazing eyes, and skin like good tea. I made his acquaintance easily, for he loved to speak of his many travels, to the north and south of the world, across the four seas and the seven deserts, how he had been feted at the courts of no less than nine emperors including the Japanese, the Holy Roman, and the Matanitu, been sacrificed bodily to a sun god with green palms and found himself wholly restored upon the morning, and possessed of no less than twelve wives, one for each Apostle, each ample of hip and excellent cooks, and each of them named so: Matthew, Mark, Simon, Judas, Peter and so forth. At this time I was but a callow and inexperienced youth, and Odoric asked if I should like to see some of the world, and if I would travel with him to Cappadocia, where he had heard that Death was hearing cases on a pale bench, and Odoric planned to plead for at least another fifty years, having used his previous time on earth so well. Death, he said, was in fact a young girl, very plain of face and quite short, but a fierce one at the joust, despite her appearance. Well of course I went with him as squire, and endeavored to learn all I could about Odoric's favorite arts, which were jousting, marrying, juggling, and lying. When we reached Cappadocia, to my great surprise we did come upon a court in the midst of a lilac field, where a high marble bench stood, brushed with pollen, as if it had galloped ahead and forgotten its courthouse behind it. Men and women gathered all around it with their hands outstretched to a girl with hair of no particular color, and she had on a black curling wig over that colorless, and a black cravat.

Odoric and I waited our turn at the docket, and shared a lunch of cheese and bread with some of the other plaintiffs, who had on rags and shoes which were little more than sackcloth bound to their feet with rope. When his name was called by the bailiff,

Odoric plead his case eloquently, telling all his best tales: how he had fought pirates side by side with his wife Peter; how he had rescued an Italian girl from the depredations of a duke who was also a black magician, and not even taken her virginity in exchange; how he had circled the globe in a Greek ship rowed by Gnostics who escaped the purge, and when they passed through the Sirens' country, he sang the harmony's part and danced upon the crow's nest. I felt myself near tears in admiration. All he asked of Death was another fifty years, a hundred at the outmost, having shown his ability to spend time as daringly and gorgeously as any man.

"My sentence is as follows," said Death, who had a crone's voice in her girl's mouth, "you may take your fifty years, but the coin I take will be equal to the coin I give. The coin is fifty years. Your fifty years well spent I shall take, and give unto this boy at your side, and you shall have his plain and uninteresting life, for only beginning from nothing may a man make a true fortune. Fair warning, however, he has a count's vengeance on his head."

From then on Odoric recalled nothing of his former life, not his adventures nor his wives, but I knew it all in its smallest detail, such that when I happened to find myself in Thrace, I came home to James the Lesser, Odoric's sixth wife, and she guessed nothing amiss.

An island where counts have elephants' memories, ruled over by dragons and barristers.

I am immune to shame, boredom, and cholera, but I confess fire and lightning will do me quite in.

I daresay my talents are common to all men, it is only that I use them, while most stuff them in a cupboard to lure mice.

Anything you ask of it, my dear.

It seems to me that the world creates things all the time: children, castles, hereditary monarchies, apple trees, stockings. With such a great quantity of things being made every day, surely some things must be destroyed simply to make room. What morality can be attached to such balance?

I shall be your most humble servant, my fiery friend.

As long as the twins are content to have me.

All the men of my country are virtuous and know nothing of bawd—I, alone among them a man of appetite, have cut a swath. I shall sing to you of the bread of my wife Matthew, and how round and firm it was, and also of the pink fruits hid within.

Everyone of any importance. My wife John dwells yet in Spain, where she weaves a tapestry showing the Acts of my wives, and when it is complete I shall return to here, and all my wives shall live in one house together, and all our children, too, under one roof, made of gold, for there shall be a new roof and a new tapestry, and all my wives will ride upon beasts with ten heads, who are quite docile and enjoy the spearmint and heather of the fields.

All men are liars.

I will tell them it is a rich and gentle land, though much obsessed with fire.

Forever and always, and how blue your eyes as well.

I will say that on the whole you assayed against the wicked when you could see it, and against the good when you could not.

It so happens that I journeyed awhile in France, where is hid the capstone of the underworld. Some winemakers discovered it when digging for their cellars, and told no one, but kept their best reds near to the stone disc. Of course someone must have blabbed, for I had heard even in Sicily: *If you want to wrestle the three-headed dog and pledge a troth to the great red queen, high ye to a certain French valley, and quote ye Virgil to a black rock.*

When I grew bored of both Macedonia and my wife Judas Iscariot, who betrayed my eggs to my bread, my wine to my water, my horse to my cow, and my intellect to my other regions, I journeyed with a circus of some reputation through the countryside to France, where we performed the Passion (complete with peacocks, a sword dance, and four somersaulting fools) for wide-eyed, smudge-nosed children whose parents gave us two chickens on the bargain. After boiling the birds and sucking their bones I took a constitutional walk, whereupon I discovered a cave, in which I discovered a number of wine caskets which, when tapped, issued forth a black vintage which to my tongue tasted of licorice and quicksilver and time. Deeper into the cave I ventured, for it was well-lit by torches, until I came upon a huge black stone upon the ground, wholly flat and chiseled, and writ upon with many pictures and couplets. I remembered my Sicilian friends and summoned up a line or two of Virgil—my Latin has always been so-so—and the stone cracked down the middle, showing me a staircase straight into the earth.

Well, call John not a coward! Many long hours did I walk down that dark stair, which grew so wide I could not see either end of each step. I passed other souls along my way, but they did not look up at me nor pause in their walking, which was much slower than mine. Eventually I came upon a kind of landing in the stair, and a cameleopard greeted me, though its flesh was black and it possessed three heads. It trumpeted: Wilt thou wrestle me, John? And so I did, though its three monstrous necks twined around me and tried to strangle me, though its breath stank of the dead and ancient sorrows, though its hooves were iron and its teeth were ice, I strove with that odd Cerberus until I locked two of its heads with my arms and a third with my thigh, well muscled from battling my wife Simon in every damned thing, and the creature cried mercy.

I had a pleasant holiday in the underworld, where I soon discovered that everyone has three heads—one for the Father, one for the Son, one for the Spirit—one for Past, one for Present, one for Future—one for Child, one for Grown, one for Withered—one for Good, one for Evil, and one for Threading the Needle. I made the acquaintance of Persephone, who has three heads, one black, one scarlet, and one silver, which rotate in the morning, evening, and midnight. I preferred her silver visage, for in that guise she plied me with kisses and riddles and promises. *I must be true!* I cried. *I must be true to my wives! What would Mark say if she could see me in your silvery arms! Let me plight my shield to you instead, and write ballads in your name, and slay a dragon or a navy for thee!* But then I only kissed her the more, and more fervently.

Hades took me hunting on his estate, with his dogs, tiny things, like a noblewoman's lapdogs, silky and high-voiced, but with tongues of fire, running along behind as we rode black stags through the wood, seeking his chosen quarry: the souls of aristocrats. *What you give to my wife you must give half to me*, said the King of the Dead, and fair is fair, so I kissed my lord with half my mouth.

Finally, I longed to see the sun the more. I packed what I had brought with me—my honor, my name, my troth, my kisses, and made to pass three-necked Cerberus once more.

But, came the voice of the Cold Queen. *You have eaten of the pomegranate.*

Rather a lot of pomegranate, said the Fiery King. *And some grapes as well. And venison.*

What is the punishment? said I.

To stay as many months of the year as you have eaten, Persephone laughed, and was glad, to trick as she had been tricked. Every girl deserves her day.

Ah, but I have bargained with Death, and she has vouchsafed me fifty years in the land of the living, I countered. *I will return when I have done with Death's sentence, and serve out my time with my Lord and my Lady.*

They called it good, and so did I, and we spat in our hands on the bargain. I walked up the long stair once more and into the French wood, where I found my fellow mummers but waking from their night's sleep and ready to press on to the next town after a few sausages and pears had been enjoyed over a morning's fire.

My father, like his son, bed, wed, and bred; some of these better than others, some worse.

As many days as seeds I eat.

I am quite sure the sun and the earth have worked it out between the two of them, and like a good babe I do not meddle in the quarrels of my parents.

Of a certainty. I knew a vampire once in Kiev, who would only drink the blood of Boyars. He ate their beards, too, leaving them quite enervated and foolish-looking. They would present themselves to their Tsar only to find their laws unwritten, their advice unheard, and their taxes due. My vampire friend, who was called Robertus, passed unnoticed through their ranks, drinking blood and influence until he was quite fat and unpresentable in society. But by then the Mongols had come with their short beards and horses and disinterest in writing laws. Robertus had drunk so much influence that all simply presumed him to be the Tsar of Rus, even the Tsar Ivan and his wife Yelena, who bowed to him and hoped he might marry one of their daughters. Unfortunately, this meant the Khan had Robertus beheaded with a quickness. When they took off his head, however, they discovered his body was empty save the hair of a century's worth of long, pointed beards, which spilled out over the floor, and all the Boyars seized them once more. The beards affixed themselves gratefully to the lords' chins, and all was as it had been except that they were all Mongols now and no longer Rus.

Poor bastard—but let us have it as a lesson to move with the times!

I am a light sleeper, madam, and every time sleep tries to take a century from me the turning of January startles me awake.

I have seventeen daughters—ten wicked, five fair, and two bishops.

I believe Simon had at them with a spoon until they agreed to be courtesans like their father wanted.

I have heard of the Wall, but am assured that I could never stand near it, for I would be burnt quite up.

The state of my soul is my private affair. But look, come near, I will open my mouth as children do for the village doctor, and you may glimpse a bit of my soul sticking out, and judge for yourself if it possesses sufficiency.

As long as my wives do not miss me.

As many months as caskets of wine resting in the dark.

Fifty years, of which I have forty remaining. Possibly thirty.

Oh, how the time goes on ahead of a man, such horses dragging his cart through the mud and the rain and the sun and the snow.

Jupiter, Hot and Moist

*When we go to war, we have fourteen golden and be-
jeweled crosses borne before us instead of banners. Each
of these crosses is followed by ten thousand horsemen
and one hundred thousand foot soldiers, fully armed,
without reckoning those in charge of the luggage and
provision.*

*When we ride abroad plainly we have a wooden,
unadorned cross without gold or gems about it, borne
before us in order that we meditate on the sufferings of
our Lord Jesus Christ; also a golden bowl filled with
earth to remind us of that whence we sprung and that
to which we must return; but besides these there is
borne a silver bowl full of gold as a token to all that we
are the Lord of Lords.*

—The Letter of Prester John
1165

The Confessions

A rhythm formed; I felt mechanized. My eyes flitted, back and forth, from the blue book and its pale violet pages swimming with perfume, swimming with bluebell and plum and a deep, unsettling musk. My gaze was steady, fluid—the blue pages to mine, over and over, my attention a little silver spoon dipping into the war, into the winged girl and the bull-astronomer and emptying itself onto my own solid, assured page, in my own solid, assured hand, a page the color pages are meant to be, the ink smelling a little of iron, a little of wax, and that's all.

The danger of rhythm is its lull. I found myself soon drifting to sleep, as the moon came down, drifting to dreams and the long, lightless river that flows along the bottom of unconsciousness. In and out, the spoon moving, the man still, and all scribes know that distant feeling, as though he hovers over his text in a silk balloon—he knows what he is writing, can feel the text moving through his brain, but it is just so separate from him. His hand cribbing along looks like the hand of another man; his breath comes so slowly, and he can almost guess what the next line of the original will be before he glances over to capture it. Mechanized, perfect, oh, we will waste no ink this time! No scratching out, no imperfectly declined nouns, why, you could almost do it sleeping.

I was only a man. I am only a man. It was only that I was

so tired. So much to do, so little time, and my body drifted away from my purpose. I dreamt.

Hiob stands beside me, and he stands in a river, a river of impossible colors, so many and flowing so quickly I cannot even name them before they're gone.

"Not as easy as it looked, is it?" he says ruefully and I am just so grateful to see him again, without vines and blossoms like worms devouring his flesh. He holds out his hands. "It's the Year of Our Lord 1699 and the end of the world."

"It's not the end of the world," I say.

"It's always the end of the world. Why do you think they keep predicting it? Christ said some that heard him speak would see the end of days. Paul thought he would stand at the throne of the new city. And everyone since just can't wait for it all to come down. No one wants to be impolitely early to the ball, and fashionably late just won't do this time." Brother Hiob looks so happy, as though he has slept for a fortnight and awakened to a breakfast fit for a bear.

"The world isn't ending," I say again. My dream-mind moves slowly, syrupy, a blue sludge.

"Every day a world ends. Just not yours. Well, every week at least. Bimonthly at the outside. Circles close, trajectories complete. A new world is coming, and we are reading its conception. Really, it's rather prurient stuff. This is why one doesn't draw pictures of bodies tangling and merging—the beginnings of things should always be secrets."

"I don't remember anything about that."

"Oh, well, that's all right, Alaric. I already know how it ends. Privileges of seniority and all."

And it is not Hiob in the river, but it is my mother, wearing Hiob's habit, and her hair hangs so long and thick and bright I almost cannot look at it; it is like seeing her naked.

"To begin to tell the history of a thing is to begin to tell a lie about it," she says, and her voice is everything I remember.

"Is none of it true then?"

"Everything is true, and everything is permitted." She smiles and holds out her arms, and I remember saying that very thing to Hiob, uttering that strange and sacred dream of an impossibly generous and permissive world. "God is a cloud," she says. "He comes without warning, and His Mind is not a human mind, it is as different as your intellect from a tiny snail creeping across the floor of the sea. The snail thinks the sea is all the world. And in the mind of God there is softness, and there is lightning."

I weep and move to embrace her in the water, moving so fast around her, dazzling multicolored foam catching in her habit, a roar of water rising around her, and suddenly her head vanishes, and the habit falls away and within it is a blemmye, her wide eyes flashing in heavy breasts, and around her waist is a long yellow dress, and in her mouth is a mirror, and in the mirror is a child, fat and grinning, and he rips page after page from a book, stuffing them into his mouth and giggling as the rainbow waters rise—

I woke.

My brothers had sunk so deep in their own work they did not see my head droop and fall. My face stuck to the blue book and when I pulled it away the tiniest wisps of fragrant spore appeared where my cheek, my chin, my eyelash had been.

THE BOOK
OF THE RUBY

A man stands on the prow of a ship. Not old, not young, poised between like a jester with a good trick in his bag: watch him change faces in the blink of an eye—any eye, your eye, his eye. The sun makes his face look healthy, bright—he is clean-shaven, his eyes piercing, his hair neatly lashed with leather. You would not call the man a demon. You would say: there stands a just man, because no one living can escape the fallacy of the outside and the inside and a man with a piercing steady gaze and neat hair and a straight spine must be just, must know his worth and the worth of his world.

A man stands at the prow of his ship.

You have not wanted to talk about him. You have moved all around him, orbiting, and hardly touched him.

A man stands at the prow of his ship. He is not a man, not really. Not my husband, not a king, not a priest. At the prow of that ship, at the rim of that sea, where in my memory he stands forever, and nothing has yet happened on the other side of the sea, he has not yet even touched the hand of another human soul, at the prow of that ship stands not a man but a touchstone. Strike us all against it and see if we are true gold.

I was so young. Can you believe how young I was? I thought he was so wise. Is that what everyone thinks of their fathers? If he would only look at me, really look at me, he would see that I was wise, too. I wasn't, of course, but neither was he, so we both come out even.

A man stands at the prow of a ship forever. And he stands at a mirror and watches a city burn. He watches, watches, watches, and the world moves around him because he says: *God, please, move the world for me.* I said to him when he first saw his home through that mirror:

"Don't ask us. Don't say we must go. Because we will go, all of us, we won't think twice—novelty is the richest coin possible when you live forever. It won't be so bad that you asked us, but we will want to go. We will say to each other that our king has devised such a game for us. And I don't know what will happen—probably nothing, probably no harm will fall on the smallest of our heads, but we will have learned that your world is *fun*, and you will have taught your world that we are here. And no one will know how badly it's all gone until the gates of Jerusalem are ringed with empty pikes—one for every blemmye whose head they could not take."

"But Hagia," he whispered, already standing on the prow of his ship, "it's my home. It's my home and everyone is dying. What would you do, if you had come, starving, bleeding, to the beaches of Constantinople, and I had taken you in, washed you and fed you fish and grapes and taught you to read Greek and to haggle for butter—if I made you queen, if I made you Empress, and maybe not everyone felt sure of that, the Jews and the Greeks especially, but you were mild and soon pregnant and everyone forgave you for being foreign? And then, finally, one day, through magic or with a wonderful machine, it doesn't matter, but one day you could see—not just hear from a messenger but really *see*—Pentexore in flames, and Hadulph on fire, burning to death, and Fortunatus cut open on a wheel, and Qaspiel with its wings shorn off and weeping for mercy? If all that occurred, could I say anything at all that would keep you from going to them? More, rousing the whole Byzantine army with blades and pitch and shields and hell on horseback to ride behind you and obliterate whoever laid their smallest finger upon your home?"

What answer could I have made to that which would have altered our course? A king, if he is a good king, tells the truth when he wants something badly enough. He only lies to win advantage—and to win the game entire he flays his own heart and lays it before the tribunal. And the tribunal was me, and I said yes, and so it is all my fault, really. Everything that happened. If my crane-girl had never come with your helmet and your letter, still he would have stood at that prow. Nothing could move him from it.

Oh, Hagia.

And in our little tent, past the end of the war, where I am writing and she is reading over my shoulder, the candles gutter and the silks all look black, so black I have forgotten what color they ever were, and my stepdaughter is crying, and I want to sleep forever and wake up at home, never having done anything but stretch parchment on a wide hoop in the sun.

Cranes have a secret, Hagia. Inside them—near the heart, but not too near, in the mess of viscera somewhere, we have a little stone. When cranes die, their mates take the stone and add it to the nest's long line. We pray with them, looping the line of stones around our throats like a necklace, and we remember everyone, everyone we loved, everyone who has gone to the Clouds and the Sedge of Heaven. We don't care for their other use. They are touchstones, that we keep in our hearts, that are our hearts. For every time you have struck my heart, Hagia, I have called you gold. All of us, golden, a long line of stones, wrapping around and around.

In my heart John always stands on that ship. And in my heart the rest of us pull the ships across the hardpack road of the Rimal, ropes knotted over our shoulders that were so strong, strong enough to any task, dragging as one body the great galleons from one world to another. We are there forever, with the sun at our backs, and the drum-beat keeps the time of our hauling.

The Physon flows through the upper cliffs of Nural, grinding the pink rock there year by year. A river, yes, but we have many rivers. The Physon flows through all the world, and I think John's world, too. Catacalon, when he was a philosopher, said that the Physon dwells underground in most lands, moving through the earth, the breath of the earth, rumbling and coughing and rasping. But in Nural, and a few other places, it breaks the surface like a whale, and we see this breath in motion, rocks tumbling over one another, basalt and schist and granite and slate, crashing, rolling, roaring. Time smoothes the stones and grinds down the cliffs, but always we can see new, rough rock surfacing. A river of stones, its current never slowing, stopping, or breaking into tributaries or marshes. The Physon is constant.

Sometimes I think the road through the Rimal is only the Physon, finally slowing somewhere, pausing for a moment before rushing on through the flesh of the earth. A held breath. Since the Physon rolls through the body of the world, it could leave us anywhere, anywhere it flows beneath the sunlit land, in the dark, where we cannot hear or see. I should be grateful it spared us a long walk through the desert, which would certainly have been amusing, the first time we tried to plant our dried yak and peach-bread in order to have supplies for the trip home. Instead, the Physon, or the Rimal road, whichever pleases the geographer in you, brought us to another river, wide and blue, with eddies of golden silt shivering down its banks. A new river, and a bright day, and river-birds crying and calling overhead, so white and small. On the opposite shore, some ways south, we could see the dim, tiny shapes of a white city, white as the seabirds, shimmering and prickling with minarets and crosses perched atop the buildings. The wharf sang with movement, but the river yawned between us.

How fine we must have looked. With our ships behind us, and our armor in the sun, our flags—do you remember how the amyctryae sewed the flags, their huge mouths full of pins, arguing over our standard and what it should depict until John insisted on the cross. But they would not be placated, and on every blazing green flag was not only a silver cross, so many stars, crescent moons, ears, mouths, horses, hands, and other symbols of the people of Pentexore that the cross was rendered all but invisible in the riot. We flew those flags so proudly, glittering with their tangles of silver thread, and the centaurs put brass covers on their hooves, and the swordtrees had borne good fruit, and we must have looked so beautiful, like we were dressed for a holiday—for Christ-mass, that festival John was always trying to get us to perform in the winter, with gifts and songs about darkness. I cannot believe anyone could have looked on us and not fallen to their knees in joy.

And yet, the river. A blue ribbon bordering their country. I still do not understand. We meant to put our ships onto the current and sail into the white city, glorious, stately, and John would stand at the prow (forever at the prow) coming home with emeralds in his coat, and his wife and his people, a crown on his head. We all agreed he deserved that, that any of us, coming home, would want our folk to see us that way, it was a thing of the heart we were happy to give him. Rivers were never a trouble to us. In addition to the Physon the Indus belongs also to Pentexore, and its waters flow deep and green. Little rivers, some so little they have no names, and lakes, too. The ships would glide as smoothly on the river as on the Rimal, surely. They were built for water, after all. Sand was only ever a temporary dalliance.

My father shivered, so excited, practically radiant—he would rescue them all, and they would see how lovely he was now. I understood so well. Had not I wanted John to see me that way, when I came home?

"Anglitora," he said to me, and my heart lurched toward him, so surprised to hear him think of me, to call my name. "Stand on my left side, when the ships sail in? Hagia will stand on my right, and I would have a daughter with me."

I thought I might die of his approval.

We dug a trench to get the ships afloat. All stood ready. The sun, so low when we reached the end of the road, seemed to have flipped around in the sky so that it was merely early morning, and the light would show our wild army gorgeously as we descended like salvation, like a cadre of angels. And yet, when the trench gaped in the sand and the river moistened it, when we were so ready, everyone kept their place. We stood and stared at the river like we had never seen one before. We *meant* to move, to haul the ships in one by one to lash the ropes on and heave ho, but no one stepped forward.

"Forward!" cried John, and forward we went—except we didn't. We told our limbs to do it, but it would not be done. My body felt as though it had become a statue, built for that one spot, made for it, to watch over the river for centuries, a stone sentinel. Nothing could move me. I could not quite even feel my feet.

The winged soldiers felt the breeze beneath their feathers and it would not lift us. The wind said: stay, stay.

"Forward!" I cried, trying to rally us, in case our spirits had suddenly lost the taste of war.

Had they only!

The flags flapped in the air. A cannibal coughed nervously. I strained, willing my body to leap into the water. The blood beat in me, loudly, madly. Sweat prickled every inch of skin.

"Backward," John whispered.

And without the smallest effort, we all took a firm, easy step back.

Forward. Back. We could come to the edge of the water but not beyond it. Downstream, I saw the flicker of small boats, long white barks. Forward. Back.

John dropped to his knees at the water's edge. He wept so bitterly, as though his whole heart had vanished from his body and left nothing but grief in him. He clenched his fists in the wet earth. He screamed—it was awful, a voice torn in half.

I stood on his left.

I stood on his right. And he could not cross the river any more than we. His screaming turned to laughing and that was worse, that was ugly and we did not want to witness it.

"Demons cannot cross water," he laughed, and went on laughing, while the white barks drew nearer and nearer, and our green flags snapped in the blue, searing air.

The Left-Hand Mouth,
the Right-Hand Eye

In the end, Gahmureen saved her, where I could not.

She rose out of her tent one morning and crouched next to the cradle-knight, who was named Elif, with her chisel. I have never and I suspect will never understand what made that little imp move and speak and think. Gahmureen's invention passes my understanding as mine passes that of a very dense tensevete. I asked her once—she said that when she was a child she invented as a child does, without knowledge of what can and cannot be done. Elif was her first invention. He had all the ambition and none of the *well, perhaps we oughtn't*. She cannot remember how she did it, anymore than I can remember my dreams. Elif was a mystery, as much as the Tower, as much as the Fountain.

I asked: "Do you know magic? Is it a charm or a spell that moves him?"

The inventor wrapped her long fingers around one of her horns. "What is magic?" she replied. "Magic is what you call it when you cannot remember how you did something, or cannot imagine how you will do it. When you dreamed it, and then it happened. Nothing is magic. Everything performs its design." She paused for a moment, her gaze faraway. "I think there might have been a wind-wheel involved. Spinning around in his heart. I hear it creaking, when he is thinking hard."

And I learned no more of Elif's workings.

Gahmureen slapped the cradle-knight on the back and the little automaton strode jerkily over to Sefalet and her tree. I watched with interest, padded after him. His helmet, a bit of cradle-canopy carved from red wood, gleamed from a fresh polishing.

"Stop," Elif said to the child.

"No," Sefalet hissed through her right-hand mouth. Both of them were truculent now, angry and turned inward. "They're my parents. Leave me alone."

"Stop acting like a baby," Elif said. His voice was soft and whispery, like the wind in leaves. "Only babies have trees for toys."

"I'm not a baby!" The right-hand mouth.

"Gahmureen says you're like a baby sucking your thumb. If you don't stop, you'll hurt yourself."

"I don't care what Gahmureen says! You're not even alive."

"Neither is the tree."

"That's not true! They talk!" The right-hand mouth, again.

"I talk."

"They have names!"

"I have a name."

"They love me," Sefalet pleaded.

"I could do that."

The tree did not argue its own case, and perhaps in the end that damned it. If it had said: *Sefalet, you are our girl and we will never let you go*, she would never have budged from that spot, until the sun went out like a snuffed lantern. But trees are funny things. They are alive, Elif had it wrong there. They grow, they eat light and drink rain. But no matter how much they remember or seem to, they are not quite who they were before. They are at least half earth, and the Earth is a very strange creature, who often speaks nonsense and even more often says nothing. They do not have preferences anymore. The tree was deeply, wholly happy to have Sefalet. It was deeply, wholly happy to be alone. This is why Abibas was a better king after he was planted—he could not be swayed by passions or angers, by revenges or the desire to curry favor. He was deeply, wholly happy, and governed from a place of utter contentment, without grasping, without striving.

An extravagant wind bellowed down the plain; I watched it slip through the joins of Elif's elbows and ribs and knees; I watched it fill him up and make him creak.

"If all you require is someone to say: Sefalet is good and beautiful and I love her, I can do that," said the little knight. "I could be so good at it."

Sefalet blushed deeply, her blank head coloring from crown to chin. "No, that's not all." Her left-hand mouth growled; it made her fingers twitch. "The only love we need is the kind shaped like a knife. You are shaped like a fool."

"I would be better at it than a tree. I was built to watch over, forever. I am missing a thing to watch over. Gahmureen built me to protect her mother from tigers and other striped things. She built me out of her cradle. But she did not know what my cradle was built out of. Gahmural told me when we hunted together, and I rode on her back because she could run faster than me. I would ride on your back if you would like it. Gahmural was pregnant with Gahmureen—did you know that's how people make more people? It took me quite a long time to work that out. I hadn't any scratch paper. Gahmural was pregnant with Gahmureen and she walked a long way east, almost to the sea, where she knew a forest—but not a forest of trees. A forest of poles sticking out of the ground and on the top of every one lived a wise creature standing on one leg, whose job it was to think about things until their thinking was bigger than the original thing."

"Stylites," I said helpfully. "The Forest of Stylites."

"They are called that?" mused Elif.

"Yes. I lived there for a long time." I had, and felt a spreading pleasure at hearing my old home spoken of. I had learned at the foot of a thousand poles, until I found one who knew about love. Her name was Adab, and her fingernails had grown so long that they pierced the earth below her pole. I sat below her and listened for a hundred years, eating an unfortunate blackbird every month when the moon grew dim, but no more. *Vyala*, she called down, *I love you because you starve for me.*

"Gahmural asked each stylite to slice off a piece of their pole," the cradle-knight was saying, "and whisper their sutras into it, and give them over to her to make her daughter's bed. I am made of very interesting sayings, very hard-won knowings. I need a hunter to watch over or else I feel useless and despondent. It is a flaw in my making."

"I have a flaw in my making," whispered Sefalet.

The wind died; the golden grasses and red flowers stilled, and Elif slumped a little, out of breath, having spoken so much, much more than he had yet done. Sefalet crawled over to him, hesitantly, her mouths kissing the earth. She lifted her right hand and blew gently on the little man, and he swelled up a little.

"Sefalet," he wheezed, "you are beautiful and good. I will keep you safe from tigers."

From then on the three of us rarely parted company. Occasionally, Elif would look up at me, quite concerned, as though I might be classifiable as a tiger. Fortunately, I have no stripes, and that seemed to be a deciding factor in the categorization of threats according to Elif. Occasionally I looked down at him, and wondered what part of his body had belonged to Adab's pole.

As we built it, the cathedral slowly closed around John and Hagia's tree. In similar fashion, Sefalet held Elif tight, and I wrapped my tail close round her.

In the circuit of her arms Elif whispered: "Qutuz the stylite said: every creature is an infinite tower—her head knows not where her feet trod, and her dark cellars know nothing of the moon on her spires."

Fortunatus came to me in the nights. "I had a wife," he said. "I had a daughter. Then I had a friend called John and I loved him so much I made him king, just so he could be happy. I gave him a wife who gave him a daughter—those are the best things I know. Now everyone is gone, and it's either Grisalba's green fluids to make me dream or you. I only ever wanted to lie in the al-Qasr with all my dear ones, showing our bellies in the paths of sunbeams, and now the palace is empty. Even I left it. Hadulph said you were wise. That you bite broken cats by the scruff of the neck and drag the pieces of them back together. I was a good gryphon, I said yes whenever anyone asked me a thing, and somehow my whole heart got onto a ship and sailed away over the sand."

I purred and bit him gently. Tears flowed over his bronze beak. I offered him my scruff; he took it. It is not the only salve I know, but it is quick.

The clerestory started talking first.

Work proceeded well, Gahmureen's motifs were spirals, circles, and leaves, coils of leaves, tendrils of stone moving around and up and opening into more and higher belltowers, turrets, whole floors with their own green altars and naves, suspended between the spires of the previous level. It looked like it could all come down if you breathed upon it. It never swayed, even in fierce wind.

You could hardly hear it at first. A whistling, a whispering, but only if you stood quite near the stones on the scaffolding, or flew up to them like my gryphon, who told us of the voices, and flapped his great golden wings impatiently while I and my charge and her knight scrabbled up the scaffolds to press our ears to the cobalt stone.

Elif offered: "Usha the stylite said: only by saying a thing does it become real. However, realness spreads out in a disc, and changes everything that hears it becoming."

"Shhh, Elif," Sefalet hissed, "I'm trying to listen." And the little man was abashed.

We pressed our ears to the clerestory stones as if to shells to hear the ocean. Even so, it was so dim and quiet we had to strain to hear the gentle voices, as if they had come a long way.

Do you remember living on the ground, Kalavya? came a male voice, and it sounded as though he spoke underwater. *I have already forgotten what we meant when we said* grass *or* beach.

I think those were your cousins, Drona, answered a woman. *The twins, with moles on their cheeks in just the same place?*

Of course, how could I have forgotten?

Next week a new level will be finished, my love. We will all be going up the malachite stair. I hear the leopards have stowed away dried mangoes and quince and even lamb fat to celebrate, and we will sing as we climb, one of the old songs from level five, about the moon falling in love with Jupiter. I will put on my yellow dress, that I got when Bhaga fell off. Kalavya's voice drifted in and out, louder and softer.

I only hope the clouds stay off this time, Drona sighed. *Remember the last time we walked the stair, up to the floor where we made those rose mosaics? The clouds gathered so thick I could hardly get my foot up onto the next step. Almost like they hated the Tower, but no one hates the Tower, that's just ridiculous. Do you remember what* tide *meant?*

Isn't that a sort of sunshade you hold over your head?

You've got a memory big enough for the both of us, Drona laughed, and then it all started over again: *Do you remember living on the ground, Kalavya?*

We drew away wonderingly.

Sefalet's left hand flew to her face in a moment of inattention. "It'll all come down, just like before," it snarled. "Let me kiss that wall and watch it swoon."

The Virtue of Things
Is in the Midst of Them

9. On the Origins of Hatred
Between the Two Pentexores

A salamander by the name of Agneya made my friendship. I have only encountered female salamanders, though they assure me they have males, but apparently maleness is a thing easily misplaced, or spoiled, or forgotten. They only think about it when new eggs need making, at which point males seem to spring up just everywhere, getting underfoot. When the eggs are viable and the roasting time begins, along with the season for salamander racing, a favored sport, the males seem to wander off somewhere, but it doesn't worry anyone unduly.

I asked Agneya while I helped her turn her eggs in their fire why the land on the other side of the Wall hated us so much as to keep the Fountain of Youth from their brothers and sisters here. My friend confessed she did not know. However, she had heard the following tale from a sciopod:

The world has a twin. It burst at the same time as our world. It has similar features; it had hopes and dreams and ambitions not unlike the hopes and dreams and ambitions of the world. It has a body consisting of spheres and stars and moons and orbits; it has a gender. (The genders of world are complex, and the possibilities number twelve or none at all. Our world is female, obviously; its twin can best be called third neuter.) The world did not mean to be a twin. It was an accident with no morality attached to it. The pair grew up together, side by side, developing temperaments, vocations, loves and hates. They expanded together into the infinite wasteland of the previous world, which had perished after a long and mostly uneventful life. They chased each other into the grey corridors of the spherical void, they laughed the laughter of worlds, and their stars winked in and out of being.

But the twins also possessed a tragedy, for they could not touch or embrace as siblings long to do. They could not merge or know what the other experienced in its infancy or adolescence. They could not feast together as family. They tried it several times, and found that when the world's twin touched its sister, holes rimmed in pink fire opened up in the surface of her, holes which later filled up with brackish, strange water, or sand like a sea, or a river full of stones. Wherever the twin tried to reach out, things in our world became confused, and if the twin happened to touch a thinking creature by accident, that creature's limbs broke into pieces or rearranged themselves in odd ways. But the world's twin moved very slowly, and managed for a little while to hold our world tightly in what passes for its arms. When the membrane between them finally broke, shards of the world's twin splintered from its arms and fell down like rain. The shards ran off in many directions at once, and wherever they walked, our world erupted in pink fire and seas boiled and air clotted. The shards did not mean to do harm; worlds break, nothing to be done. Later folk in the other Pentexore called the shards demons and trapped them behind a terrible wall all of diamonds, but we have had no trouble from them, and in many years no one has even heard their names.

"That sounds very fanciful to me," I said.

Agneya snorted. "Well, yes, sciopods have some notions that fly right over my head. I heard one say we were all just specks of I don't know what spinning around bits of I don't know who, and the spinning gets so fast it looks like sitting still, and that's why I can say: what a fine calf my John has, and you can say: my, Agneya, you're looking green today. They can have it. I know about fire and fire knows about me. But they do say we used to have demons here. Lousy with them, we were meant to be. But do you see demons loping about, I ask you? No, just wholesome salamanders roasting their eggs, and some very flamboyant birds."

10. On the Unicorn

I have, in the course of my travels, taken part in many a unicorn hunt. Usually, they end quite merrily, with the horses and dogs exhausted, the men lying about in a forest clearing with a goodly number of wineskins open and a few kerchiefs of strawberries and walnuts and brown bread spread out on the orange leaves. The virgin, if we'd got a good one, sang a song or, if we'd got a *very* good one, danced in her white dress, spinning until the leaves flew around her like a little flame-colored storm. Unicorn hunts always struck me as civilized sorts of things, so long as no actual unicorns show up and spoil the fun. I've seen it happen—the beast all pale as bone, with a collar fastened round its throat from its last captivity. It fell on the maiden and upset the strawberries, spilling the wine and sending the poor dogs quite mad. I shouldn't like to think what the creature meant to do to that wretched girl, but I fired my arrow true and had both the horn of the beast for a trophy and, before the night was out, the trophy of the maid. Still, it's a nasty business when the quarry insists on being involved in the hunting.

Unicorns in this part of the world are discomfiting and I do not like them in the least. Ysra and Ymra asked me to a hunt on the equinox, when the cinnamon forest had gone entirely fragrant and scarlet. They put on green hunting jackets and long knives, which ought to have been my first clue, as everyone knows arrows are the preferred weapon, if not a pole-ax. I packed up my kerchiefs and my wineskins and felt quite ensured of a pleasant afternoon.

I learned the following points of interest with regards to the unicorn while on the forest path with the king and queen, who rode no horses nor even salamanders but walked hand in hand. I never saw them use any other means of transport.

First, there are exactly five genuine unicorns in the world, in my world or Pentexore, which fact I've no notion of how they could know. What I think of as a unicorn is a mutant, they said, no more desirable or attractive than a mule. They really would not like to speculate on how the narwhal managed it.

Second, the idea of the virgin was a result of bad translation. For catching a unicorn, what you want is a scholar. You can see why the clerks changed those nouns around—self-preservation has been the end of many a winsome couplet.

Third, it was important that, should we own our luck, I be the one to make the kill. It was just bad manners for monarchs to kill their own creatures, even the poor, stupid unicorn. Besides, they said. A unicorn dies a big death. Not like a rabbit or a fox. We wouldn't deprive you of it.

We reached a clearing in the cinnamon wood where the blue sky shone through and the spiced wind kicked at the brush. Everything smelled crisp, as though the day could be snapped in half. I saw the scholar readily enough—though should she have been chained to a stake in the earth? Surely she volunteered. Surely she would grace us with a song later.

"Scholars have temperaments little better than boars," sighed Ysra. "You wouldn't send a boar a formal invitation."

The scholar was quite naked; her silvery hair fell long enough to provide her some modesty, but her eyes darted quickly, here and there in terror, the whites showing, her wrists manacled and crossed over one another. I looked for her species but she seemed in all manner to me quite human, if small and delicate, and a shadow passed over my heart.

"The beast will come, if we wait," Ymra said, rubbing the cold from her knuckles in several complicated gestures of her six hands.

Wait we did, in the slight chill of the day, while the scholar whimpered and I suppressed my growing urge to help her, to put my hunting coat around her shoulders and give her hot wine—my hosts would hardly allow my eyes to drift to her, as if they caught the drift of my thoughts.

At last I heard a rumbling in the wood and I understood for the first time that the unicorn really meant to come for the girl, and I would be expected to kill the mute beast. A disquiet entered my soul and set the stakes of its tent there. The unicorn burst through the trees—and it was not a horse at all, or even a beast, but a young man with terribly white skin, covered in a soft down, glowing with a silvery countenance. His long hair brushed his shoulder blades and his eyes shone huge and dark, round and liquid as an animal's. He wore a collar, too, from some past hunt or captivity or sovereign lord who kept the young man in his gardens with a strong fence to keep him still. His muscles seemed carved rather than grown, so stark and leonine were his limbs—and if I should dare to offend the sensibilities of refined folk who may read my words—the unicorn's member stood rigid and enormous, a horn in truth, and a cruel one.

The unicorn spied the scholar and rushed to her, standing terribly near, and they looked at each other, afraid and aroused and alert, and he put his hands on her face, and she looked into his eyes and wept suddenly, as completely as I have ever seen a soul weep for another.

"Do it now," said Ysra mildly, without urgency, nearly bored. "In a moment you'll lose your chance."

"But sire, that's only a young man. I don't feel right at all about it. Why don't we let them alone and have our picnic?"

"Don't be simple," Ymra snapped, her gaze instantly terrible. "It's a unicorn. Kill it. You said you'd killed one before."

"And you said it was no unicorn but some kind of whale!" I protested.

"It will ravish the girl and leave her pregnant with its colts," insisted the king Ysra.

"She doesn't seem as though she'd mind," said I, and in truth the scholar caressed the cheek of the unicorn with tenderness. Her gaze said she knew everything one could know about unicorns, and accepted this one anyway.

"You are our guest and our chattel!" hissed the queen Ymra. "Kill the unicorn or call yourself a treason and look to your cell!"

The thing about lying is that it's best to do it only for fun, for delight and a prettier kind of world. Lies told to cover your own skin pervert the purity of the art. I want to lie to you—oh, how I would like it. To say I defied the king and the queen, I let the unicorn and the scholar make love in the autumn wood and drank my wine and went home to dry my socks by the great hearth. Instead I can at least say I made it quick. I cut his throat, and his blood flowed as clear as seawater, and the wood filled with howling: the scholar in grief, the unicorn in death, the monarchs in triumph, and myself, your John, in horror and shame.

11. On the Practical Results of Killing a Unicorn

I did not know until much later. I could not know. But it would appear that a unicorn's horn is little, if anything, like the horn of a man. It pierces the air; it is the mate of the wind; it is an anchor. And with the anchor gone, strange ships may begin to drift out to sea.

I did not like it so much in Pentexore after that. I wished for home.

The Book
of the Ruby

We made a city where we stood, on our side of the river. The barrels of our sword-trees, heavy with sticky hilts, made a barricade, our cannon-flowers, too, our buckler-vines. Our own knight-hedge, grateful for the water of the river, happy for the oily yellow sun of this new world, and the old world's black earth still deep and moist to suckle in. The tents went up, green and silver and rose and black, pits dug for pots to boil over, animals—when we found animals—to roast over, and all our little things we'd hoped to trade. We laid down our beds on the lean summer earth, we lay down and looked up into the stars, our stars after all, and each of us asked the other: *What is wrong with us? What is so wrong that the river has such grudges against us? Were we false to our own river, so that it told its cousin not to set her table for us, when we came?*

I asked John to kiss me and he would not. He turned his head so I would not see his tears—but I am stronger than his secret griefs. I have always had to be. I took his face in my hands and moved his mouth to mine, his head in the curve of my waist, and between kisses I whispered: "Nothing has changed. Nothing has changed."

He answered, "God has barred me from my home."

"I am your home."

But John would not take my comfort. "I am two men," he

said. "And one of them drank from that Fountain and felt its vigor though he knew how dearly he might buy it, and one of them never left home, never knew there was another land but the one that bore him. And I do not know which man is me, and which is dead and gone, as dead as any bone on the bank of this river."

I went to the water's edge, the water's edge in the moonlight, and stood with only the tips of my toes wet in the current. The sounds of the camp murmured and rolled behind me. A man joined me, lean and lovely and dark, and he had hands like a giant's.

"Is it Yerushalayim?" he said to me. "The white city, with the starlight on it?"

"I cannot know, Houd," said I, for I remembered him from the ship, and liked him well enough to call him by name. His presence felt rigid and thin next to me. "I think it might be. The hedge spoke of that place, where their god was born and died, and they said ugly things, about thorns and crowns and governors."

"I…have heard tales of it. Of autumn-time in Yerushalayim, and wonderful foods on wonderful tables, and wonderful men telling tales of a golden world."

If my girl had been brought up by us, she would have heard tales of Houd.

For his sake I called that city Yerushalayim, and dreamed of a hundred gods walking its streets, each with bull horns and wings like mine, each garlanded with orange boughs fiery with fruit. In his sleep Houd stirred beside me, and I pulled his hands over us both.

I could not bear him any longer. I have a limited capacity for despair. It takes so much strength to be sad. My muscles ached with it. I sought out, as I ever sought when my husbands were miserable and drawn up into themselves like night-snails, when Astolfo, my first mate, scowled and frowned, when John wanted to talk about God and I wanted his body in mine, or to eat sweet things, or to dance in the pavilion, anything but contemplate the wounds of a man I never knew, and their cosmological significance, I sought out Hadulph, my red lion. He eschewed a tent, finding the air warm, and lay on the side of the river, peering into the running water, the strong, strong current. I lay down beside him; I put my hands into his fur. With John there could be kissing, but the mouths of blemmye and lion do not fit together. Instead there are hands and paws and tails, manes and tongues and claws. He growled at me, and I knew—it had been so long since I had come to him, my marriage took so much work, I hardly had the time.

John had known long before we married, and, well, I think he learned a lesson in his world, and that lesson was that a king cannot dishonor. We draw little difference between a king and a queen, and this was enough to addle his ideas about adultery a little. I had no particular ideas about adultery; I did not consider adultery. Love is love. There is time enough in the world for everything. Hadulph, I knew, loved also a tensevete out on the icy wastes, and I did not begrudge either of them. Why should I? And since I loved Hadulph before John, he was the interloper, in truth. All this meant was that he chose not to think on it, and I chose not to discuss it. Only once did he tell me I endangered my immortal soul. I said: *A lion is worth a soul. And besides, I thought I didn't have one?*

Hadulph growled and rolled me as lions do, wrestling gently, biting softly. I lost myself in it, in scratching him, in the roughness of his fur, in the drawing back of his muzzle, in the light of the moon on his whiskers. I felt each tooth like all the teeth he had ever sunk in me, I heard his purring as all the purring he had ever made in my presence, all the occasions of our mating, in pepper fields and parchment fields, in palaces. I had known him almost all my life, and when he took me it was all the times he had ever taken me, that I had ever taken him, happening together, the young lion pouncing on me and knocking me to the ground, discovering the bigness of our bodies, the strength we could inflict on the other, comparing bruises and laughing so low and so long. All the wordlessness we had shared, for where John insisted on theological debates, Hadulph and I had enjoyed silence, or growling, and that seemed to contain all we needed to know. We were rooted in each other, wherever our branches grew.

Finally, we quieted. We looked into the water together. We leaned forward, pressing against whatever kept us back, the invisible wall which made us not even want to cross the river. Hadulph put out his great paw against it, flexing his claws.

"Why do you think we cannot cross?" I said. "It cannot really be that we are demons. If demons are as he says, I don't think water would pose much trouble."

Hadulph yawned. His vast pink tongue lolled out. "I think that they have all been praying on the banks of this river for so long that the weight of their wanting made it so. They wanted to believe the river kept them safe from anyone *not them*. That's all demon means. It means *not us*. It's obvious there's no such thing as God, and that's all right. I never felt the lack. There is so much in the world, insisting on a kindly god is greedy. But if there were I would say that God is wanting, the power of it, the incarnation of it. They all wanted to keep out the not-us. And they have." Hadulph scratched the soil. "Of course, that means John is not-them now. You and I…we never were."

The sun rose and fell and rose and fell as John brooded on our situation, reluctant to walk downstream and attempt to signal across the river. What if they should see us all, in our finery, in our scales and furs, and send their numbers against us at once?

I believe John simply forgot. He forgot what we looked like to him when he first arrived. How he cried out, terrified of the gryphon and the amyctryae, how he thought Grisalba a demoness, how he would not even look at me because he could not bear to look upon a woman's naked breast. He had come to love us, and forgot that his countrymen would see us as did he, at first, not as he saw now. He had forgotten the company of those who looked like him, and we seemed in his sight as beautiful as angels. John had imagined himself riding home with an army of angels at his back. Instead, he had only us. And the river saw no difference between himself and his countrymen.

"I cannot see why I should not be able to cross," he said weakly.

He sent Qaspiel to find a way around the river. He bade it fly north and west, to fly high so that he would not be seen, and return to us, tell us if we could walk the distance, if a path through the blue net of rivers that caught up the land John knew could be found.

"I do not wish to leave you, John. Nor Hagia—Hagia tell him, tell him I can be of use here, send a gryphon or one of the little dragons." I could only hold it, my closed eyes against its familiar chest that still smelled faintly of vanilla, as though his years in the fields had never ended.

John looked down uncomfortably. The fullness of it was coming to him. "If you are caught," he said, "they will not hurt you. They will think as I thought once, that you are…an angel. A gryphon alone, without me to explain, to teach them how to see her…she would be slaughtered."

And so it understood, and so it went. And the trouble of what we were to do unraveled itself almost as soon as Qaspiel became a speck in the sky.

A man came walking over the hill.

In green and silver, with a sword and a helm under his elbow. And handsome, black curls and a long nose, a clear narrow face, a shining black beard, and he looked at us and blinked.

He was not afraid, or disgusted by us. He did not run, or laugh, or swoon. He seemed surprised. We, too, watched him, waiting for his fear, looking for our own, wondering if we would find it, if this was the enemy we had come to fight, if we would be expected to fall upon him. If he would speak kindly. If we would understand him when he spoke. Without much concern the man walked down to the river, knelt, and drank with cupped hands. He looked up at the sun, and back towards us, most especially myself, and raised his hand a little, in greeting.

"Sir," said Houd, standing somewhat behind Anglitora, his huge hands shaking, his eyes wet and eager, "is that Yerushalayim? The city on the hill?"

The man in green looked toward the distant domes of the city and smiled. He answered us in Greek, for which we were grateful.

"No, my lad, that is Mosul," he answered, chuckling. "Where you stand now was once Nineveh, a thousand years ago, and five hundred more. I think you might be stepping on the Shamash Gate. Jerusalem is, oh, far to the south. But perhaps not so far. I expect only a few years away now. And in a decade, well, the distance between Mosul and Jerusalem may be small indeed."

We looked at John, whose face had fallen. He studied the earth, his shoulders soft and defeated.

"I am John of Constantinople," he said finally. "I came to defend Jerusalem from the Saracen, from the fire."

"Well," laughed the man in green, broadly now. "You're early! I haven't taken it yet. I am Salah ad-Din Yusuf ibn Ayyubi, and at the moment I am besieging Mosul. When that is done, I promise, I will devote all of my love and attention to the Holy City."

"Where is your army?" Anglitora demanded. "Where are your knights? How came you to be wandering around on the other side of the river from the thing you claim to be sieging?"

Salah ad-Din filled a flask from the river. "Have you ever commanded a siege, madam? It is a long and boring business.

Mostly, you stand outside a very large wall and try to keep your own army from killing each other for lack of anything more amusing to do. Occasionally I come to the ancient city you are all roasting birds over to meditate and pray. I get bored, too. Now, since I know your aim and you know mine, tell me, does your diadem indicate you are a king? Where have you come from? How did you come across such extraordinary beasts?"

Do not call us beasts. Did I say that? I would like to have said that.

Let us say she said it. Who is to know? Perhaps I put aside the insult, offered him a sword from our saplings, and quoted him a poem of the lamia Gnoskil, which went: *Listening to the constellation of the ox-cart, my heart is full of trinkets: a pair of scissors, an oil-jar, a jeweled comb. All of them are me, and the ox-cart, too.* And perhaps he took the sword, and gave me in return a blossom from the gardens of Mosul, which was white, and said: *O friend, seest thou the lightning—there, and then gone, as though two hands raised up together over a pillar of cloud.* And Anglitora smiled, because of the cloud he spoke of, and because once two souls have exchanged poetry they must love one another forever, as all know. So we gave him our tea as well, and shared a lunch of olives and oranges. Sukut offered to read the stars on his behalf. It happened something like that, after all. Until he said to John:

"Why do you not pray for God to open the river to you?"

And John the Priest was ashamed, for he had not thought of it. He could eat no more. He scowled into his chest. What sort of priest was he now, that he had not even attempted to call Christ to his side?

"We are all very curious," I said, to turn the tide of our talking, "to know what an infidel is. John called us that a great deal in the old days, and there was a good deal of private debate—some said it meant a person who has four legs. Some said it meant a person who interrupts John when he is speaking. Some insisted it obviously referred to a camel. But you are an infidel, and neither four-legged, nor impolite, nor a camel. Nor very much like us."

"He is a Muslim," John said bluntly. "I am a Christian."

Sukut tossed his cream-colored horns. "Easy then. Different systems of magic."

Both Salah ad-Din and John spluttered and began to talk very quickly, over one another.

"It is by no means magic!" cried John. "I spent years instructing all of you to accept Christ and honor Him and that is what you took from it? That He is some sort of wizard?"

The green knight insisted: "There is but one God and He is not a magician, but the Creator of All and Father of Prophets!"

"Ah, but prophecy, that's magic," lowed Sukut with his gentle, firm voice. "And did you not just ask our king to pray for the river's good graces? Well, I'll tell you what he's going to do just as soon as we're finished here. He's going to go into his tent and light candles and quiet his mind and say words in Latin, special words that he has taught us all, and he will chant them over and over again until he feels strong, and then he will whisper what he wants into the darkness, and say some more Latin things—he likes Latin a great deal—and then expect, *fully and utterly expect* to see his wishes made manifest. If that is not magic I am a fish, sir."

Salah ad-Din grinned impishly. "Well, perhaps when a Christian man does it, it is magic."

Sukut scratched at his brown hand. "Why do you not call your own wizards and ask them to break the spell of the river? It is not our river. We do not know it; we did not grow up with it or confess secrets near it; we have not washed clothes in it or carried it in buckets to boil. It is a stranger to us—we do not even know its name. Best to let family look after family."

"Yes," laughed John. "Call your wizards." He held up his hands. "Oh, please, do try to explain it to them. We'll be here for ninety years, and at the end of it they'll be quite certain you've told them that Mohammed is a turtle with an excellent singing voice. May you have better luck than I!"

Salah ad-Din pursed his lips. "When a horse pulls a plow through the furrow, you do not call it magic—it is only what the horse was made to do. He is fulfilling his purpose on earth. When a man prays, it is the same."

"Horses were not meant to pull plows," argued Sukut. "They are meant to be horses. That's all. The plow is useful to the owner of the horse, but not to the horse himself. Also, the farmer does not insist that the horse call himself bad and sinful and wicked all the while he pulls the plow, and in between abusing himself and laboring for the comfort of his owner, praise the farmer as beneficent and all-powerful."

Salah ad-Din slapped his knee. "I have always said that what marks out the civilized from the uncivilized is a love of arguing! What a wonderful country you must have, where horses need not labor if they do not wish to, and men eat well all the same."

Sukut blinked. "Well, yes," he said.

Much explanation was needed then, and showing of the trees in their barrels, how their mace-apples gleamed with spikes and bronzeflowers with five arrowhead petals each. Salah ad-Din became very quiet. I put my hand upon his wrist and asked the matter, for I liked him, how soft-spoken he was, even when laughing, and how he seemed to handle things very carefully in his heart before he said them.

"I was only possessed by an image, blemmye. That if Nineveh had died and been buried under her grassy hill in your country, then we might walk now through a forest of stone lions whose leaves were the beards of dead kings. An almond grove might shade my head while I recited poems to the sun, and their branches might form the fifteen gates of Nineveh, and nothing would ever be forgotten, no, in the long life of the world."

And the green knight seemed so moved by this thought that had he been alone, he might have wept.

Did you wish he had come to Pentexore in John's place?

Forgive me, daughter, but that day I did.

The Left-Hand Mouth,
the Right-Hand Eye

I met Adab on the Fountain road, on my final walk. Oh, yes, I forgot. They're pilgrimages now, aren't they? I did not love her till much later, when she looked familiar, and I had to spend a fortnight working out where I had known her before. Deep in my memory I finally recalled that we were young women together on that long path. Adab was a sciopod, which is an excellent species for a stylite, when you think about it. The traditional pose—up on one foot, balanced, poised—posed no trouble for them. Posed no trouble for her. On that long trail of lanterns, swinging back and forth in the warm, rind-scented night, I saw her hopping ahead, her hair in a hundred complex looping braids, her gait so eager.

"If I recall," I said to her, by way of introduction, "it tastes foul and looks like a lamia's sick. In such a hurry to taste it?"

And she turned to me with black eyes shining and said: "When I have swallowed it I shall climb a pillar and never come down, not until I am so wise the wind could go through me and come out the other side an adept in three disciplines."

In all the time Sefalet had spoken with her parents' tree, she had not had her fits nor extruded that awful light from her limbs. I was grateful. We all were. But once Elif and I had her fully to ourselves once more, it began again. She slept against my flank and her left hand cried in her dreams (*The ropes, the ropes! Ah, it's all coming down!*) and her tremors woke me, and then the light poured out over all of us.

"She is broken," said Elif softly.

I could not answer him. In her misery and her fervor, Sefalet arched her back, wrenching her body—and flung herself upon me. Her arms locked around my neck and her light tumbled over me like a snow drift. Her weight was much more than her size, as though someone had opened her mouth and poured silver into her, and now it was all coming out.

"I broke once," Elif said, touching the hem of the princess's dress. "Gahmuret, Gahmureen's father, took me with him to the market and a child pulled my arm too hard. She didn't mean it; she didn't know I'm alive. Sometimes I don't even know it. How could she? But my arm snapped off and the girl started crying. I wanted her to stop and I wanted to be fixed, and so these seemed like the same thing to me. When Gahmuret got me tooled and oiled and well again, I waited until the family got boisterous and busy with their projects and crept out of the house. I went all the way back to the market to find the little girl, whose mother owned the strained cheese stall. I showed her my new arm and told her to stop crying now, but it was not very satisfying because she had stopped days ago and did not know what I meant." Elif touched his arm slightly, and I thought he might be considering whether breaking it himself might work some sort of sympathetic, retrograde magic and stop Sefalet's pain.

"No," I said firmly. And the girl went still.

"Kalavya fell off the malachite stair," the left-hand mouth whispered. "She dashed her brains out on the ground."

"Ride upon me, Adab," I said, and she obliged me. "Tell what wisdom looks like to you."

"Wisdom is a pane of red glass," she said. "It colors every-thing—and you must be careful, because you can forget that the world is not colored red, if you only look through the glass all the time. I hope, in years to come, I shall hold my heart up and it will be a pane of clear glass, through which I see all, but nothing is distorted."

This seemed like very pretty nonsense to me. But I did not yet understand. When I look through my glass now I see everything colored by knowing about love, by having studied it with rigor.

"Why must you do it on a pole?" I asked. I was very young.

"I suppose I could do it on a lion," she said, and then blushed at her own boldness.

The stones continued to speak. Distant, always, and hard to hear, but laughter and weeping and dreaming of what life at the top of the Tower might be came wafting out of the blue bricks of our cathedral.

Do you think it's true what the giants say? That the moon is a girl, a duchess of their old kingdom, and when we build the Tower high enough we will discover her court, full of huge thrones and chandeliers and hunting trophies, the black and starry heads of the beasts who roam the heavens?

That's ridiculous. The Spheres will open up and show us a new earth within them, more beautiful than you can imagine, with a thousand crystal cities ready for us.

I like our earth. I liked having my feet on it, my toes in it. I want to go home.

And among all the voices, and Kalavya and Drona, too, Kalavya who was always putting on her yellow dress, always ready for the next day when they would go up the stair with her gold skirts blowing wild in the wind, among all of them sometimes the Hagia-and-John tree would call up. Sometimes they called for Sefalet. Sometimes for Qaspiel or Fortunatus. Sometimes for someone named Kostas. The cathedral sang with dreams and ghosts and all Gahmureen would say was that living leaves a mark.

I held Adab while she drank from the Fountain; the stylite held me.

"What I want," she said as we walked back down the mountain, "Is to have a little space where no one else can touch me. I'll own the space at the top of the pillar. The space will get to know me and I'll get to know it. The air of it will live inside me. I'll be so alone, but I'll be thinking all the time, and the space will be becoming more and more me until I—Adab—expand out like a star. And that's what the forest is, all those stars, radiating. And one of the stars is a physician and one is an alchemist and one is a historian and one is a poet. But we are all philosophers, and on one foot we will think so loudly it will be like music."

"What I want is you," I said.

Elif came to me one day. Fortunatus nuzzled my whiskers and the sun came filtering in through the silk tent.

"Sefalet says the unicorn died," Elif said.

Fortunatus yawned, his pink tongue showing. "Don't be silly. There are no unicorns anymore. Not since the Wall."

"She says it died, and Gahmureen says Fortunatus has to muster at the nave just like everyone else, because all winged workers were supposed to be there at dawn."

The princess slipped through the curtain of our little house. She held her left hand behind her back. When Hadulph was a cub he used to roll on his back while he thought about things, as though he needed to shake the solution free. Sefalet squeezed her hands to keep her thoughts in.

I loved her when she clasped her arms around me in her agony. I know that now. The flash and sharpness of that instant is always impossible to see until they're gone. But that was the moment.

"Don't be afraid," I purred. "I know everything about you,

Sefalet. Your body cannot hurt or horrify me. I will hold you when you shake and listen when you say cruel things—I will not believe them, no matter what. I will let your left-hand words wash over me with no more weight or importance than seafoam."

Slowly, grinding the teeth in her palms, Sefalet drew out her hands.

"There's a hole in the sky," said the left mouth. "She's here." And it began to laugh.

"I'll love you when you can join me in the forest," said Adab. "When you have earned a pillar."

I was barely grown. I wanted her now. I wanted to roll her in the snow. I didn't want to stand on a pillar and take up a discipline.

"If you don't become adept at something, you'll go mad," she said, and her dark eyes were so serious. "We live so long. You have to pick something that will take forever to get really good at it. It's the only salvation—study and love something terribly difficult. That or the Abir, but...for me that would be taking the easy path. The path of no resistance. I want to know this world so well it does what I say just to make me happy."

"What I want is you," I repeated. It was not a very good courtship. But it was my first. I did finally grasp the way to do it.

I sat on my haunches below her pillow, a wide, winnowed, wind-broken lash of stone. "All right," I roared up to her, my chest so full of her beauty up there, with the sun shining through her as if it wanted to climb inside her skin. "Teach me what you know."

The woman had collapsed on the north end of the building site, where the curls of stone the masons had chiseled and hammered off piled up in mountains of blue shards. Already the cathedral cast a long shadow—I remember John saying these took generations to build, that a little boy might be born, he might grow up strong with golden hair and grey eyes, might learn a trade, blacksmithing or glassworking, might go to war in the Levant and lose his blessing fingers in a battle with pirates, might marry a woman with a limp because she knew how to read and he did not, might have four children, one a son, and that son have a daughter who married a minor lord, elevating the whole family, and her daughter might marry an earl and own a strand of pearls that cost more than her grandfather had earned in his life, and in all that time still a cathedral would only be begun. Yet we were meant to have it done and dusted by the time the human king got home.

Already Gahmureen had begun to plan a long, winding stair to wrap the whole building, spiraling up and up, made of malachite with its endless green swirls. I suppose the gryphons helped it along, and the stones wanted to be together, after all, as they had once been. As soon as you brought two together the day seemed a little brighter. We'd done so much. Those mounds of stone chips towered, cast their own shadows.

And in one of them we found her. Very lovely, in a ragged dress that showed most of one breast and no shoes, her long dark hair tangled and matted, her skin ruddy and dark, but not healthy. Windburned and chapped, her poor legs had been slashed with tiny strokes, as though a thousand needles had scored her.

The cametenna lay as though dead, her huge hands thrown up over her face as if to hide herself from heaven.

THE VIRTUE OF THINGS
IS IN THE MIDST OF THEM

12. On Emeralds

Several enormous emeralds rolled along the hallways of the Mount. They were approximately the size of a healthy man, his limbs extended to make a wheel, should you run ribbon from his head to his hands to his feet. I was sometimes able to tell them apart by their inclusions, but often they simply dazzled me, or the late afternoon sun would stream through them, showering the chambers with green prisms. I counted at least seven that I knew by sight—there might have been more, indeed this seems very likely.

The unicorn was bad enough, I hear you say, and some of our visiting female cousins had to turn their eyes from the page when you mentioned his horn. And now you would have us believe in locomotive gemstones?

I have told you before, good readers, that when the world presents itself, properly dressed in its strangeness, I need embroider nothing with fancy.

As all men know, emeralds have great healing powers, but demons love them. A terrible trade for a mystic, but I have never been muchly concerned with demons. I met one while snowbound in Ecbatana and he seemed a nice enough fellow. Very long fingers, as I recall. A whiff of myrrh about his person. Other than that he kept to himself, wrote several very good poems, shot game, and with a great deal of sadness took a lord's youngest daughter to wed in remuneration for having cured the man's tumors. I remember the demon sighing: *I did not look to get married so young. I might have liked to have seen Pandemonium first, or finish my book. Nothing ever goes to plan, in the end,*

The emeralds do not have a language as such. However, they are more than capable of communication—in fact, their method commands much more attention than merely shouting down the hall. The gems glow with a great green fire, and their feelings flow forth within the flames—when the light touches the flesh, you feel what the emerald feels and have little choice in the matter. There they go, the grinding, glittering wheels, flashing here and there, sending a beam of well-being here, of anger and bitterness there, of love unrequited and unlooked for—whatever private operas play out among the jewels.

This was how I discovered that, after the unicorn hunt, I was no longer permitted to move about the Mount as I pleased. I attempted to leave my room and a queen emerald, one I thought of as Cabochon, for that was her cut (I assume she was a she—I suppose she could be a he as easily, or a nothing at all since emeralds are hardly sticklers on social points, but I prefer women's company so I shall call my Cab what I like), rolled across the door, shining with a strong sense of *not a chance, my friend*. I implored, but Cab's light did not change.

Cabochon seemed to be a sort of pack leader—an alpha gem, along with the one I thought of as Trillion, again, for the cut of him, a broad bull emerald. But Cab could spin down the halls at such speeds, and Trillion, with his points, had a slower, more plodding, more meditative pace through the world. She would roll around him with such merriment, throwing out rainbows of teasing delight, like a puppy nipping at a litter mate, and he would simply glow.

Having little else to do with a gigantic jewel wedged in my

door, sparkling with regret and chagrin, I asked her several questions I had been considering, but too interested in my friend Agneya's eggs (one had gone totally black—this is apparently considered an omen of great good luck) and the ever-distant Bonfire and the disturbing events of the hunt to interview the rolling gems.

"Do emeralds alone grow to such great size, or are there rubies and sapphires, too, roaming the hills in packs, jasper prides digging trails through the brush, carnelian wheels spinning along the seashore?"

Cabochon glowed pride: *only us, we alone.*

"Do you have a mother, a father?"

My sweet Cab flickered—*too complex.*

"Are you born?"

Green warmth: *yes.*

"From another jewel, a parent gem?"

Cabochon grew cool and dim: *no.*

"The mountain then. The mountain is your mother?"

A blaze of grassy color—*Indeed!* A dark piney flash: *more I cannot say.*

"Are you servants here? Like dogs set to guard a treasure? Or are you citizens of Simurgh, being fiery, after a fashion?"

Cab rolled back and forth, distressed. Her light took on a bluish cast. *The Masters will hear.*

"I do not mean to discomfit you! Let us move on to easier topics. Do you have art among you? Music, theater, epic and historical poetry?"

A bashful flood of dappled color: *yes, secret rites, secret dances.*

"Have you been to see the Wall?"

Several quick, angry peacock shades glared in succession: *the Wall hurts us.*

"Are you a Christian ornament?"

A spray of prisms: Cab's laughter.

"Pagan then? Perhaps a Jewish gem?"

And a kind of light came from my friend which I can only call sharp—clear and freezing cold and perfect, almost blinding, but as if all of those qualities of light were in fact emotions that could be felt by the heart, and this I understood as the approximation of religious feeling among emeralds.

God is a stone.

13. On Imprisonment

I knew a man named Boethius once. I find myself thinking of him quite often these days. He found himself in prison for one of the several reasons good men find themselves in prison—he offended a magistrate, refused to convert, intersected with someone's daughter in one fashion or another. I don't really recall—the reasons men stumble into jail are less interesting than what they do once they hear those doors clang shut. I, for example, have been writing this very long and interesting catalogue of my adventures in Pentexore. Boethius was a man of higher virtue than myself (not difficult) and wrote philosophy.

The pious old bastard cheated, though, when you think about it. See, the goddess of Philosophy has very little to do these days. Most of our best thinkers have gone over entirely to Theology, who, as a paramour, dresses less excitingly and will contort herself into fewer positions, but has a certain respectability—you can take her home to meet your mother and no one will be accused of wasting their time laying about uselessly on couches drinking wine. Thus, Miss Philosophy found herself bored and started visiting Boethius in his cell. I can tell you, I would have thought of something better to do with a girl of good figure who could slip in and out of cages unnoticed. But not Boethius—he just sat on his miserable chair and talked with her about justice or something, writing it all down, until even she'd had enough of him.

If Madame History or Madame Literature showed up to

keep me company, this would certainly be a more interesting book. Or perhaps the both of them, lascivious and rigorous all at once, their bodies draped in chitons of pages, the ink leaving snaking violet trails on their skin. Then folk years hence would say: *I knew a man named John Mandeville once*, and that would be enough to ensure their listeners that the speaker was a man of authority and wisdom as well as good connections.

The truth is, confinement wears on the bones and the brain. Men write in prison because they've nothing else to do. I do not even quite understand why I have been closed away with only my gentle Cab for company. I killed the unicorn when asked. They cannot demand that I also feel no remorse for it. They cannot demand I relish the memory.

"Cabochon," I called, and my green friend rolled into view, nervously peeking round the door.

"Was the unicorn important somehow?"

A sad springtime glow: *very.*

I suppose they always are. I suppose if you take all the pretty story away, they were always innocent young boys laying their horns in maidens' laps. I suppose it was always about virginity. The blood and the collar and the girl in the wood. The horn and the wildness of the hunt. The piercing. And I suppose we all knew what the allegory meant, or it wouldn't be much of an allegory. And an allegory is just a civilized way of lying.

If you take away the lie, the truth remains at the bottom of it, and the truth is shaped like a dead boy.

The sun comes up and the sun goes down. My tapestries change, though I cannot catch them in the act. No longer do I see my spaniels or my tidy English hills. Now I see my twelve wives, all of them in blue, their faces holy and upturned, as though they were in truth the Apostles whose names they bear. I see Death in a judge's wig taking the years off of a robust man like thread coming off a spool. I see Boethius, wretched, ragged, starving—but at least he had a visitor.

I do not have twelve wives. I have never stood at Death's bench, nor even owned a spaniel. The tapestries show nothing true, only what I have told them. To be totally honest I am not wholly sure I was ever English. I might have been born in Bourgogne. I have lied about myself more than anything else, for more than any other thing in this world, I have failed to be as fantastical as I might have been. I remember that unicorn and his terrified expression and he seems so like me. Everyone said he was a magical beast, but in the end he was but a boy whose desire showed in every aspect of his body—my desire shows in my mind, that is the difference if there is any at all. Take away the lie of the horse and all you have is the horn, throbbing and painful and yearning toward it knows not what.

Outside my window, it is a long way down. The phoenix and salamanders are piling up dry wood and leaves. They are breaking their tripods for kindling. The Bonfire is coming.

The Confessions

She came for me. I did not want to go. I had work, I had so much more to do. The mold had begun to creep back—slowly, but we were taking too long, we had to go faster, faster! I had no time for girls' games in the dark. Woman, leave me be. Woman, tend to thine own.

But the woman in yellow said: "I am owed. Leave your men to work. Give me my night."

What could I have said? If there is a currency in such places, one must pay the tariffs. Knowledge has an ugly tax. She drew me out and sat beneath the branches of books for all the world like the heathen Buddha beneath his Bo tree, shadows on her hands and in her lap.

"You came to convert us to Christ, yet you say nothing of your God, and only devour our books, only say: give us food and everything you know, let us gorge ourselves, fill us up, fill us up! Are you such empty men? Tell me about the wonders of Jesus Christ Your Lord. Tell me the good news. Tell me he has risen and I am saved. Do you think we have never met your like before? Every several years some troupe of you, yearning after sainthood or martyrhood, comes babbling about doves."

I was ashamed. When asked to minister, it all went to ash in me. I wanted only to return to the books, to know everything they had in them, and failing that I wanted, improbably, for the woman in yellow to look kindly on me and sit close to me, to take me into her confidence. The starlight played on the pale, thin down of her skin.

"You know we came for Prester John," I said. "Why humiliate me this way?"

"Do you think it is not humiliating to be valued only for what passed in one's country, long ago?"

"Who are you? Why are you called Theotokos? What god is your child? You must know that only Mary bears that title—and if you are not Christian, whence comes this Christian name?" I longed to put out my hands to her—I would still have said then that I did not want her in a sinful way—such thoughts had long ago seeped from my collection of recognizable states.

"No, Alaric. Who are *you*? Tell me the secrets of the country of Alaric. Pluck the books of his heart for me. Read them while they rot."

The only way back to my books—yes, I called them mine in my heart—was through. If I flayed myself for her I could be excused from her presence. I did not speak to be shriven, and yet, what would you call it, when a man sits in shade and tells his history?

I told her of my mother. It seemed the thing most likely to please her. I told her that when I learned my Greek letters I thought Aristotle would save me from the maternal influence, because he felt contempt for women, and wrote that they were not fully human—and that is how I felt toward my mother. That she was made of some stuff other than what made me, that she was an animal or a spirit, something wild and untouchable which came and went like a cloud, which one could not predict. I followed Aristotle into the company of men, where the memory of her could not come.

"I do not care about your mother," said the woman in yellow. "Blame women for your loneliness and misery—that is your business. Tell me a thing that is true, that is at the heart of you. Something as true as the things you copy."

"Why? Is everything in those books true? Am I to believe John Mandeville really wrote that black book? A separate and secret one that he left in this place? Well, some of it may be true but there is a lot of allegory in there, and the faux Mandeville lies as though it will save his soul."

"Perhaps it did."

"Do you know what is written there? Have you read the books yourself? Don't you want to know the history of your own country?"

She looked amused for a moment, staring me down. "Why do you assume I am ignorant of it? As you assume I am no god's mother, as you assume I am an animal, as you assume all we have is yours to take."

"You are angry."

"No, I am human, and I am beset by animals."

I could say nothing to answer that. I took a deep breath. The air tasted like apples and wood and the pages of books, blowing down from the tree.

"When I had just taken my orders," I said slowly, "I heard the older monks talking in the refectory. They drank the autumn's first beer and ate the summer's dried mushrooms and I wanted so to be older, to be one of them, to be learned. And they said the same name over and over: *Prester John. Prester John.* I think it was a game, really, by then. After all, the story is five hundred years old now. It has lost a little of its sheen. But everyone still played the game: What fantastical thing can you make everyone believe is really there, in that impossible kingdom? And they would weave wilder and wilder stories until someone asked for textual authority on the point of jaguars having souls, and they would dissolve into laughter. I watched them from the door the way a child watches his parents in their marriage bed—furtively, curiously, with shame and a kind of foreknowledge growing in one's breast. I felt towards the game of Prester John very like I felt toward the sexual act, in fact. I hated it because it was silly and old-fashioned and so earnest; it had no intellect, only base desire. Yet I longed for it terribly, to be part of its rites, to be welcomed, and I felt if I could seize one or the other or both I would finally understand something about the world. But somehow, somehow I missed it. Like a gear slipping, failing to catch. I could never make up a new beast for Prester John's pantheon, I could not make puns about gryphons. I could not be like the other boys. I could not even sneak out of the abbey as they did and into the village—my attempts ended with me red-faced and ashamed, on the outside, telling myself everything they said was a lie designed to cause pain to anyone not in on the joke. I could be neither in Prester John's kingdom nor in our own. The cameleopards and unicorns were not for me. They occupied another country, the same country my mother occupied, one where everyone spoke the language but me, where I could never belong. It got tangled up inside me, the body and Prester John and my mother. And when Hiob and the rest were chosen for this mission, I seethed, furious, hating them as they dug out all the old tales and drank the old beer and chewed the old mushrooms and it was all weeping crocodiles and phoenix again, fountains of youth and amethyst palaces."

"Then why did you come?"

"Because they chose me. The country of unicorns and mothers turned its head and looked at me at last. Hiob said: 'You are my friend and my best linguist. You are strong in faith. Come with me, take the chance that more in the world is truth than lies.' And for a moment I believed that I could belong to that place, that place where everything is true."

The woman in yellow kept her silence. Did I imagine it, that her expression softened, just a little?

"But it is Hiob's country, still. It is all through him, that country of lies and mothers and beasts and village girls. Eating him from the inside, making him into a grotesquerie. I do his work, but I am still on the outside."

Finally, she said: "The world is not made of countries and outsiders. We are all just humans, and most of us fools, and all of us longing for more than we have, to know more than we know—and yet even that is not enough, for if we knew everything we would only be disappointed that there was not one more secret to uncover. You would be disappointed. Your whole faith depends upon uncovering a suddenly, violently magical country at the end of the world, full of lakes of fire and ten-headed beasts and broken seals and trumpets. It has never happened, it will never happen, and instead of being relieved that humans will all live on and not be destroyed, you are all bitterly sad that the world goes on."

How many of us had come through her village that she knew her Revelations, that she could be cynical about it? I felt suddenly like the hundredth suitor in some foreign princess's court. All the good miracles had been performed by men before me. Her face seemed large as a moon, looming before me, her golden dress aglow in the stars, a jaguar with a soul, and I did not even know what I was doing, did not even know that I had moved, before I was kissing her, and if it was not my first kiss I could not remember another, her mouth hard and unyielding beneath mine, but warm, and I insisted—I could walk in that country, that confused, generous country and her mouth parted slightly, nothing more than slightly, but as soon as it had I knew I had done wrong; I had trespassed, and when our tongues touched, a cry went up from the little house where my brothers worked away, an anguished, choking cry.

Hiob, waking, strangling in his vines.

THE BOOK
OF THE RUBY

The wizards came at dusk.

Father said not to call them wizards.

Men in robes came for us and they carried golden crosses atop long staffs, whispering in Latin, making arcane signs at us with their hands, and in their center was a man somewhat older than John, handsome, his face weathered and almost kind, wearing a glittering and ornate diadem. I do not know what to call them but wizards. They whispered at us in Latin and we could not cross the water.

Just because they whispered in Latin and we could not cross the water does not mean we could not cross the water because they whispered at us in Latin. We could not cross before.

Spells need reinforcement. Nothing lasts forever. They came to shore up the sides of their curses. It is Christian magic. The same magic that says: *put a veil over her and she will be human. That says: say these words and your soul will be saved. That says: wear a cross and we will pretend we are kin.* No different than the kind John knows, that says: *speak Latin and you are Christian, be Christian and you are saved, be saved and you are real, worthy of notice, worthy of love.*

And what of Salah ad-Din's magic?

Not much different, but incanted in a kinder tone.

"I could not get you into Mosul," the green knight said, "even if you could manage the river. If I could get into Mosul

I'd be there now, and eating pomegranates in the muslin-sellers markets! But there is a monastery, on this side, St. Elijah's. The Nestorian see keeps it, and pilgrims come for Mar Elia in November, when the oranges are small and green on the trees."

And John wept with joy, as in his books they say men of old did. "Surely God has led me here, to find a Nestorian hold in the wide desert. Take me, Salah ad-Din, give me over to my brothers and I will call us bonded, call us brethren, never one to harm the other."

Anglitora flexed her wide wing. "We do not especially wish to be given over to Nestorians, Father. We came to fight. We came to deliver a city. Not to nap in a monastery."

"Daughter, I need to rest," John said desperately, as desperate to get to those monks as a man to a lover. "I am so tired of being a stranger."

Salah ad-Din cleared his lovely throat. "I will be happy to do it, John, but if we are brothers, I would ask my brother a favor. Sieges are long and costly; they merely put off the inevitable. If your winged countrymen wish to deliver a city, they could deliver Mosul to me."

"But the river," protested Anglitora.

"Oh, I don't need you to actually fly over the walls. Just show yourselves, in sight of the Hamdanids, and they will surrender immediately, I promise. Who would not, in the face of so many gryphons and, well, I am not certain what to call the other flying folk among you. But we have nothing like them here, and strategy sometimes consists of showing one's hand rather than closing it into a fist."

"I would rather fight," my winged girl said.

"I have no doubt, though I cannot imagine what country has bred women like these, who go naked and hunger for battle. Surely when John says his is a Christian throne, he exaggerates."

"I would fight you," Anglitora whispered.

"What have I done to you, maid?" The green knight laughed.

"Nothing, but you would fight bravely, I am certain of it."

"Of course I would."

"Then whichever of us prevailed, our children would grow up strong and whole and beautiful, and that is reason enough for war!" Her feathers fluffed and shivered slightly, turning a pale orange at the edges.

I was such a child.

"I fear I do not understand," said Salah ad-Din Yusuf ibn Ayyubi, the knight in silver and green.

"Oh," I said, and I smiled, but not because I thought the crane-maid silly. "It is because of the cranes. And the pygmies."

"Is that not what we came for?" Anglitora, the crane-knight cried. "To mate with John's world as it came to mate with us when he took a blemmye to wife? To take the knights of Yerushalayim to our beds and keep their eggs warm through autumn?"

I am so grateful no one laughed. Save Salah ad-Din, but he was foreign and I liked to watch him laughing. He looked so handsome when he laughed.

"I don't think we are here to do very much at all," John said. "If we are at Nineveh we are terribly far from the holy land, we cannot cross the Euphrates—and that is the river's name, if you must know it, it is the Euphrates and it hates us—and just over the hill is Salah ad-Din's army, which will neither understand you nor countenance your ugliness. It is a whole army of men like me when I first arrived, and they will hate you. The best we can hope for is the monastery of St. Elijah, where at least I can explain to Christian brothers all that has happened, and rest, God on High, rest at last."

Salah ad-Din cocked his head to one side. "Why would we hate djinni, or think them ugly? Allah made them of the pure fire, and gave them free will no less than men. Surely some djinni go over to the side of wickedness, but so do some men.

I see among you some figured like angels, others like chimera, and others beyond my ability to name them. But nothing Allah has not prepared me to see, nothing I have not read of in the holy books. Djinni came to Mohammed of old, why should I be terrified when they come to me?"

We did not know the word he used for us. Nor did John.

"And all your soldiers, they would feel the same? They would look on my wife and think her lovely, ask after her history, her interests and ambitions, ask her to dine with their wives and carry their children on her shoulders?"

Salah ad-Din blushed. It was a very pretty thing. I do not think I have ever seen John blush.

"Not all, no. I admit it. Though a Christian army would behave no better. Some could think of them as angels and Nephilim and Ophanim, and some could only see monsters. Men are men, everywhere."

"Not everywhere," said I.

And as if to put an end to the debate, more ranks of wizards came, the sun setting behind them, with their whispering and their horrified looks. Though it is possible their horror was more directed at Salah ad-Din than at us, we could not tell.

John spoke to the wizards. *I have come home, I have come home, my name is John and I wrote to Constantinople, have you been there, have you seen the Emperor, did he get my letter? My heart is glad to see Christian men, will you not give us sanctuary?* And to him they marveled, and asked if he was Prester John, the famous priest-king, and had he come to smite down the enemies of Christ.

Of course he had. I wanted to answer for him. Of course that is why we came. To hurt and maim—

and mate—

—and cut the flesh of those whom John pointed out as being enemies, for we certainly could not tell any of them apart.

But now that the men of the cross stood there, shying away

from the centaurs and nervously sidestepping the lamias' whipping tails, John said nothing. He only asked for sanctuary.

Sukut turned from such supplication and put his hand on the green-clad arm of Salah ad-Din.

"You will never enter that city," the minotaur said.

He started. "How can you say that?"

"I have looked into the sky and tried to solve its labyrinth. I did it last night while you slept among our tents. That is how you tell such things. You tell the stars: let the beginning of the maze be where we stand now, and let the end be the taking of Mosul by Salah ad-Din Yusuf ibn Ayyubi, and you follow the clew, rolling down the black halls, past the starry walls. There is no path from here to there, though you seem to be a good man and the paths before you are so many, so many."

And the green knight said, lowly, urgently: "But to Jerusalem? Do you see a path there, even if I lose Mosul?"

Sukut frowned. The Abir had chosen well for him—his huge eyes seem so kind, no matter what his mazes have told him.

"To Jerusalem all the corners of the labyrinth turn, to the city on the hill, and a story there we meant to tell ourselves. It is your city already, though you will not hold it forever. You will stand atop the city with a horn in your hands, and it will call to every angry soul. They will come for you in Jerusalem, by the thousands, blond haired and ashen-hearted, and they will think you a good man, but your countrymen devils and demons, because when they look at you they see us—they see headless and heartless and half-animal and half-monster. The clew unfolds long past your living, Salah ad-Din. It snarls; I cannot see for the mess of it, the thousands of times that scrap of town will be burned and bought and buried and burned again. There will be a king who is half-lion. There will be men with awful magic. No one will ever stop telling this story: men came against good advice to this country and took it by force. It does not matter who were the men then, who they are now, who they will be. Who will take it, who will defend it, who will deliver it, who will take it once more. It is broken, it is a story that cannot stop telling itself. But if an answer is all you require—yes. Go to Jerusalem. We cannot get there to defend anyone. You will have no trouble taking it."

The abbot of St. Elijah was called Jibril. He paid no attention to the minotaur's quiet counsels, but regarded John with cold-ness and high airs. He was the older man among the wizards, very tall (though none of John's people were as tall as I, and among my people I am not counted enormous). He owned a powerful gaze, thick eyebrows and long, narrow cheeks. The abbot looked at me for a long time, without shame, taking in my bared breasts and the eyes that tipped them, my headless body, my unbowed posture and position at John's right hand. He stared at me as though he could tell the whole tale of John's life with us by how I stood with him, how I did not cover myself, how I spoke without fear.

"You may come within our walls, John, if you are the John you claim to be. But your motley army cannot. Even if we could bear the sight of their deformities, we could not feed or house them, and you seem to have quite all you need here. The nights are not cold. They will be comfortable."

They seemed coolly familiar with the green knight and well appraised of the state of the siege on Mosul. They took no side, of course, being that any victor would be an infidel and as likely as the other to treat them with hostility or tolerance. It mattered nothing to them. They would treat with the master of Mosul as soon as his identity became clear. Nor did it matter much to them that John called himself a Nestorian—letters had to be written, much remained to be discussed and fully understood.

They all knew him. They knew every word of his letter, had heard it from their fathers, had studied it and even memorized parts of it. They had dreamed of the things we know so well: the Fountain, the Mussel shell, the al-Qasr. And yet they seemed so disappointed.

John begged for my admittance. Mine alone. They curled their lips, but he insisted. *Put a veil over her,* they said. *For God's sake, give her some modesty.*

When I first knew John, and we journeyed together to a certain tomb for reasons too complicated to list here, somewhat near the end of that passage we encountered a peacock named Ghayth. He was a historian as well as a peacock, or at least, an Abir or two back, he had been. When we talked with him, below a diamond wall, he was a writer of fictions and very unhappy about it. I thought back on those days as the monks wrapped me in a black veil (the best color to conceal my breasts while allowing me some sight—you would think these men had never seen breasts, that half of their own people did not have them, that they had not suckled at them as babes! Perhaps they were envious, having none of their own, and could not bear the sight of a soul who owned them. However, I was by then sick to death of men who claimed to be great and strong rending their garments over having seen my body bare.). Thus I saw everything through a haze of black, shadowed, dim. A chamber with many reading podiums and desks, and the abbot seated before us like a king we had come to beseech, his face disapproving, so sunk in disapproval I could not believe it had ever held another expression. He must have looked up at his mother on the first day of his life and sighed disconsolately. And in that dark chamber where I could see so little, I remembered Ghayth and what he had said to me when the fires grew dim and the stars got high and everyone else had drifted to sleep.

He flared his feathers and crooned: *It's not so bad, fiction. The trouble with history is that nobody knows the bigger picture. They can't see it from above—and I sympathize, I do! Seeing everything from peacock-level instead of hawk-height is unfortunate, it really is. Everyone bumbles around and they have no idea what kind of story they're telling. As a historian, you look at the disaster of it and you give it a story. You say: ah, well, see here it was a youngest son kind of story, a slay the dark beast sort of story, a love sanctions all crimes sort of story. Or you say yes, this man cheated to get what he got, but he did pretty well with it in the end. The historian's job is to decide who gets forgiven and who doesn't. To decide what the story was. But while you do that work all you ever see is people making a mess of everything, performing the same scenes over and over, the same lines sometimes, and they never know when the climax has come and gone and they should be well into the denouement, having sandwiches and looking back on it rather than still swinging their swords. It's horrible, and you want to reach back in time and say: stop, just stop! You're ruining everything! It could all be so beautiful if only you would hold your arm like this, or recite this soliloquy or move the scene with the moon goddess from here to there. But with fiction you can make it so graceful. Symmetrical. Everything knows its place. Foreshadowing works elegantly; you can change speakers if one is just not getting the work done. It's only hard to have been a historian, and become a fictioneer. Because it all feels false, you see. You make these radiant little creatures and force them to say your words and you can make it so beautiful it would cut you down where you stand—but if they were really real, your radiant little loves would muck it up just as badly. That's what people do. Even us, even here. It's only that our acts are much longer and we have three, five, seventeen, forty-nine of them. So much more time to be ridiculous and sorrowful. That's what the Abir really does, you know. It resets the stage every couple of centuries, just to make a little room in the debris. A little room to start again.*

I sat quietly while the men spoke. I tried to be demure. I tried to put a history together from their stuttering, miserable attempts.

The trouble was, we thought we were telling a story where we came when called, to lift the burden of a city, to be loved by John's world and loved by John, to do good and have good done to us in return. We thought the story was about how we saved the West. But the story had already been told, and we had missed our entrance.

Jerusalem was taken—it was in Christian hands now, and had been for forty years. Emmanuel had written to us long ago, and heard no answer. No one needed our help, and besides, what were we doing here, on the edge of Mosul, an infidel city besieged by more infidels?

"Where were you when we needed you?" Jibril cried, and his voice shook. "When my brothers were dying in the streets and horses were slipping on their innards? When we cried out to heaven and no answer came? When I starved in a cell below a hall where the enemy feasted? Why did you not come then, when any Christian soul might have had a use for you? Why now, when all is quiet and we are shoved away to the north, licking our wounds and watching your friend in green draw more and more knights to his cause, breed finer and finer horses, quote his nasty heathen poetry at his fawning generals and make more and more sons? Soon we will be drowning in little Salah ad-Dins and they will each of them eat a Christian babe for breakfast, lunch, and dinner!"

I could not keep quiet. "I don't think he would do that," I said, and made an effort to keep my voice soft and high, as John said women of his country did. "He eats dates and goat, just like the rest of us."

I do not feel right about putting down what Jibril thought we ate in our country.

"I am so tired." My husband's voice was low and broken. "I am so tired. Let me stay here and read and think and be at peace. For fourteen years I have lived as a stranger in a foreign land, where no one knew God, where no one even knew the name of the city where I was born! Where I was the ugly one, the different one, the one past all comprehension. I am so tired. I want to be shriven. I want to take confession. I am a Christian and a Nestorian, you cannot deny me these things. Put the Eucharist on my tongue and let me have some tiny sliver of ease."

"It was more here," I said softly to him alone. "More than fourteen years. The Rimal brought us where it would, and the clocks that held its sand never could keep the hour right. Our time runs separately from yours, I think. We are unmoored from you, and it is unfair, but think—enough time has passed for the hedge of knights to spring up, for two wars to have brought those skulls from here to there, for your letter to have run all the way around this world twice. Ask the year, ask and he will tell you."

But John would not ask. He could not bear to hear it, I think, and Jibril did not offer. Instead, he behaved as though I had not spoken.

"Did you not say you were king in this foreign land? Surely you have had ease aplenty," sneered the abbot.

John barked a rough laughter. "Do you want a crown? I'd be happy to give it to you. Try giving laws to them. They have lived in languor and decadence and a kind of gorgeous abundance for thousands of years. They would look on Moses' tablets and wear them as skirts, call it a delightful fashion, and for a century or two everyone would be clothed in commandments, and then they'd forget and not even *Thou Shalt Have No Other God Before Me* would have sunk in. Especially that one."

"It is not our fault your earth is so mean with her gifts," I said.

And he softened. John softened! He put his hand on mine and said: "I know, my love. I know. I am not trying to slander you. Only to explain how I have not exactly managed to convert the population."

"I have never understood this obsession with conversion! Why does it matter so much if we say the Ave? Did you not say that the kingdom of heaven is reserved for the elect? Well, then let us be, and you will find your celestial table less crowded."

At that Jibril chuckled. I did not understand what a child's scriptural argument I had made, one every novice brings up sooner or later.

"What if I say I do not believe you?" the abbot said softly, looking up into the cracked ceiling of St. Elijah's. "What if I say you are an angel of the Devil's make, that you have brought an army of succubi and imps and hellhounds, that your generals are Belial and Azazel and not Hagia and Anglitora, that I believe you to have pulled the diadem of Prester John over your head like a mask and have arrived here to give help and succor to our enemies, with whom we have already observed you breaking bread and calling brother, to lead them behind our walls and lay waste to our holy brotherhood?"

John looked down at his hands. I could not guess his thoughts.

"I would say I have no home anywhere. That in the east I am alien, and in the west I am demon, and nowhere on this earth will love or soothe me."

Father Jibril chewed his cheek and moved his eyes again to me, where they found I had not changed. Perhaps if I let them lash a stuffed head to my shoulders and wrap the whole thing in veils they could leave me be for an entire hour.

"Prove to us your strength and your faith. Show us that you are Prester John, that you came for our deliverance and our relief. Set upon the man Salah ad-Din and cut his throat and when you have done that lead your people over the hill and destroy his army to the last man—you may leave the horses, as beasts have no allegiance and cannot tell Allah from the cud they chew—stave in the heads of the very last of their foot-soldiers and we will call you our brother in Christ, an honest man, Prester John, and welcome you to our breast."

THE LEFT-HAND MOUTH,
THE RIGHT-HAND EYE

This is the tale the cametenna told. All the while she told it, she held out her huge hands, miserably, as if she wanted something from us, as if the emptiness of her hands hurt her so. I longed to smother her in my paws, to hide her in my fur. *Ah! All these poor girls. How they bite at my heart!* Finally, I did, as she spoke I wrapped her in my body, to shield her, and then Sefalet too climbed into her hand, at which the cametenna wept with relief, and Elif curled between us, so that Lamis, for that was her name, spoke from a nest of bodies, who pressed close together to keep her from shaking apart. That is the main thing love is for, to hold the center, to keep things from shattering. This is what she said when she lay at the center.

Do you know how the world began?

It began because everything got mixed up and mixed together, and couldn't figure out how to get apart again. I guess I am glad that happened, but there is a point where the mixing stops becoming thicker and thicker and more and more complex and starts becoming thinner, and wan, and old, and I was queen of that point, and that point was called Thule.

My own name is Lamis and in my first Abir I drew a pearl covered over with iridescent flecks. The pearl said: *go and rule over the city called Thule which is pleasant and peaceful and makes all the things a city makes, and take no spouse and have no children, but of lovers have as many as you will.* I put on the dress of a queen, which has iron sewn into the hem, so that it drags heavy on the bones. I went to Thule and all the people of the city had gathered at the glass gate of the city to welcome me, and they threw mango blossoms into the air and sang a song with one thousand harmonious parts, for that was the number of souls in the city. I laughed and the petals fell onto my hair, and they had a crown all ready. In it rode a rainbow of gems.

Of course, the first day of a reign is always the best day. That's when there's so much hope you could eat it for lunch. Before you have made any mistakes, or invited other queens to eat, or set the tax rate. I did the best I could do. There was no one to teach me. I kept a little diary, for I knew I would not be queen forever. I did not want the next queen to have to learn everything over again. And in my youth I was told many stories. It became the principal way in which my thoughts were arranged.

When I was a young queen I felt the palace to be huge and empty, though really it was much smaller than the al-Qasr. It had a pretty shade of silver to the stones, not grey but a slippery, wet color, and the joins were filled with hematite. I wrote in my book: *a queen's heart must be big enough to fill her palace, but not so big that she squeezes her people out of their homes.* I felt lonely, and this was the first Abir, you know, so I did not know how not to miss my brother and my sister and my nurse. I wanted a lover as soon as possible, because I thought a lover would be brother and sister and nurse all together. I wrote in my book: *a queen must find a lover immediately, for otherwise her accounting books will take her bed at night.*

Later I crossed that out. In its place I wrote: *a queen must do nothing but be a good queen until her city no longer needs her.*

All the men in Thule and some few of the women lined up

around the waterfalls that trickle down from the palace into the crystalline moat, to apply to be my lover. I asked them questions: *Do you know how to tell good stories? Have you any interesting scars? Tell me about a time you were just.* I set them tasks: *Calculate the ideal tax rate for the population of Thule. Design for me an aqueduct. Solve the dispute between the red lions (races) and the blemmyae (comic theatre) over who should get to build an arena for their favorite entertainment in the prime central area of the city.*

I thought these were excellent tests of suitors and recorded them all for the benefit of the next queen. In the end, I felt that the ideal household was made up of, besides myself, two women and one man, for I was very young and did not want things to change. It was how I had been happiest, with my brother and my sister and my nurse. Only now I was not a child, and my lovers would not be children, so things *would* change, but not too much. Not too much for me to bear. The pearl said: *take many*, and so I did.

One was an astomi called Manar, and her eyes were the color of wine. One was a minotaur called Taroob, and she had a jasper ring in her nose. And with them I took a giant called Qayz. With Manar I shared breakfast and my morning; we ate oranges and cream and fresh bread we baked together, and I would eat and she would breathe the scents in deeply, and make jokes about the moon, which is a kind of goddess to the astomi, but also a kind of maiden aunt, who gives kindly advice and raps across the knuckles by turns. Together Manar and I sang both cooking songs and governing songs, and in the governing songs (which had a call and a response) we determined the percentage of goods to keep in Thule, and the percentage to send out to trade with Nural and Nimat and Simurgh and Shirshya.

With Taroob I took my lunches and my afternoons. We ate roast fish and bitter apples and plump rice, and she would make little mazes in the rice, through which the sauce from the fish would drip and flow. She would slurp it up and with delight when the sweet juices had solved the circuit. We put our heads together and her hands had a soft pelt, her voice a low, thrumming rhythm, and together we heard the disputes of the Thulites, and with our judges' veils on we determined that this blacksmith owed that glassblower two new pipes, since the old ones were cheaply made and had bent. We said that since the cousins had quarreled over who should get the tame tiger they had raised together that it should instead come and live at the palace, and when it had kittens they would each get one and no more.

With Qayz I suppered, and took my nights. In Thule it is the sacred duty of the queen to light the lamps at night, and together my giant and I went lamp to lamp, setting a little blue blaze flickering. The light played on his huge ears and we smiled at each other. When the work was done we ate a grassy soup full of tangerine and almond and milky bean curd. We determined which fields should lay fallow and which should be full of grain and house-trees. I ate my crushed flowers so that there would be no children. We were happy.

I wrote in my book: *a queen has the power to order the world as she wishes it. Thus, she must be so careful to make a good one, and to know a good one from a bad one.*

Before bed, we told stories, and you may think me childish, but there are worse things to do before bed, and how else can you get to know a new lover or three but by the stories they tell? Qayz lay along the wall, so that he could hold us all in the circuit of his body.

Manar, Who Could Smell My Love For Her: Do you know the one about how to build a city?

Taroob, Who Lay Down Thread So That I Could Always Find Her: Oh, that one is a little grisly.

Qayz, Who Made Light With Me: Oh, la, grisly and allegorical is all right. Grisly and true is upsetting.

And Manar, who had been the one to design the aqueduct, told us how cities grow like children, and like children they have to have a parent, a person who stands in the center of the heart of what will be a city like a key in a hole. As long as the key is in the hole the city thrives, so the person who started the city has to be very patient and have a rich internal life, because the work of being a key is not very interesting. The city grows so big that no one knows where the center of the heart is anymore, and they forget that a person dreaming began everything they love, the schools where little ones learn how to count on their knuckles, the festivals when the moon is red, the safe walls so terrible beast may breach. All the things there are to love about a city come from a person who decided to stay. And stay forever.

I asked my lover if there was such a key in Thule, and she said she thought there had been, there must have been, and when she was small she heard we had a unicorn stuck in the center of the heart of our city, but when they came, they took him, though he must be alive somewhere, for Thule still lives and breathes. And all three of us lay together and looked at the dancing light in our lamp and thought about that, how wonderfully and terribly the world behaves, that it makes cities, but asks such a sacrifice.

And all of that, just the very beginning of my life in Thule, becoming queen, taking lovers, telling one tale before bedtime, took a thousand years. Abirs came and went outside. And inside the mist slowed everyone down, the mist that chilled and thickened all the elements of the city, the mist of a few drops of Gog and Magog's blood. But in that silver silken mist, I had a little happiness. A slow happiness, just a trickle every month or so, and more, sometimes, when we could dig out a whole room in the palace, dig out the mist and move quickly for a moment or two—oh, the lives we lived in those moments!

But I am here now, so you must have guessed the mist is gone. I do not know what happened. One morning the mist had gone and the sun shone so bright, bright as glass. I didn't hear it go, but I heard the rumbling. Thule rumbled as it came down. As it broke along its axes, like a star. As a pillar crushed Manar and the bridge of her perfect nose. As a stair went to dust beneath Taroob's hooves and dropped her into darkness. As the lamps dripped their burning oil onto Qayz's sweet hands and engulfed him. How in a moment—so fast, how can anything happen so fast?—Thule went from a city to a ruin. The moon shines there, on a grassy, empty hill. She clucks in her fretting way. She says: *Where is Manar, who always left sweets on my altars when I got full?* And for the moon I have only my grief, big and round and pale. When I finished weeping—and you can finish weeping. You can cry so much that you are dry, a ruin, a dust-cloud, and then you are skinny and wracked but you can run. I ran, I ran to find someone, anyone who was not dead. I left my book, but I don't think there will be another queen to care. The last thing I wrote was: *a happy queen and a happy city clasp together like two hands. But only for a little while.*

The Virtue of Things
Is in the Midst of Them

14. On Other Cities

I know Pentexore contains cities other than Simurgh. Certainly, they all speak of the riches of the cities beyond the Wall, but here, too, in Ysra and Ymra's country, this is only the capital. When I first began this section, I meant to tell you I had been to all of them. That on a palanquin drawn by six black turtles I toured the countryside. That in Habil the cyclops wreathed my head in blue silk and sang quatrains where every word began with Q, for that is the first letter of the word "eye" in their private tongue. That in Isos, by the seashore, the whales perform a long dance whose first step was taken when Egypt had not yet had her first Pharaoh. That in Summikto, statues of red stone stand tall, and their heads are women's heads, and their bodies are those of striped horses, and when the winds of sunset come, it passes through their mouths and makes a strange song. Oh, the things I was going to tell you!

But I am tired. I miss Agneya, I miss Ysra and Ymra, and day and night poor Cab's light shines in on me, full of pity and regret: *I'm sorry, I'm sorry, I'm sorry.*

Still I know those cities thrive and bustle somewhere far off—Agneya told me as much when her black egg needed turning and I held the tongs for her. These are the Pentexoran cities I have heard of:

Habil, which is rich in berries, copper, and satirists. Mainly lions live there, said my salamander friend. Once there were red and white ones, but they are so intermingled now that all of them are a deep rose color, which is both slightly ridiculous and exquisite. In Habil they have no stairs, for lions do not like them, and the antelope soup is highly spiced, so sour and savory it would pucker the mouth of a stranger. Houses are ordered by pride, and the rose-colored lions have a fierce loyalty to their houses, which consist of clusters of huts with a common hearth, all of which face inward and have but one outer door for all the homes. How do you spot a stranger in Habil? They do not like the soup.

Isos, which perches on the sea. If I had more luck and a little more northerly wind, I might have docked there instead, for the icy reaches are all Isan. Half the city is underwater, half above, and hardly anyone knows anything about what life in Pentexore-Below-the-Waves is like. Maybe the whales are dancing, who is to say? Above the tideline the major industry of Isos is ice, which is their passion and their great art. Every house is a palace of ice, carved stairs and gates and dining tables. All the meals are frozen, one sucks the hardened fish and crystal fruits until they melt. Mermaids and selkies populate the city, for they can visit both halves of the town. The skin of a mermaid is hardy and tough, her muscles adamant, her gills razors, while a selkie wears her skin as a cloak when she is out of the water, and speaks a crooning, clicking language. How do you know a stranger in Isos? She cannot take off her skin.

Summikto is a desert camp, where dervishes live, dancing, dancing, dancing forever in the centers of crimson clouds. God is a storm in Summikto, and when all the citizens come together, they make one, boiling and turning and billowing with heat and dust and wind. Most of Simurgh is made of Summikto, for they bind the dust into bricks out there in the desert, and the bricks make the buildings of the salamanders.

Summikto lives as a single dervish, they are all married to one another, all parents and children of one another, they all have the same name, which is Blikhi, and often collide with one another because they cannot tell the difference between themselves and their comrade. How do you tell a stranger in Summikto? They are watching where they're going.

Aadi, where the science of trees, so strange to me, has been brought to its highest expression. There, they plant tears and raise trees bearing pears of pure salt, they plant nets and raise up trees of squirming pink fish, they plant beds and watch as the summer brings harvests of pillows and sweet-scented linens. It is an orchard town, and there the houses are planted, too, doors buried in the earth which shoot up into lithe green towers with a hundred passageways. Meals are communal in Aadi. In the central square is a supper-tree, where all the greatest Aadian chefs brought their finest meals, bubbling iron pots of fragrant coriander stew, platters of roast lamb drizzled in honey and soaked in beer, caskets of raisiny, resinous wine, and into a pit dug in the earth it all went, platter and pot and casket, along with embers to keep it hot and spices wrapped in linen to season the sapling. The tree gives them their feasts back a thousandfold, and each day the Aadians pluck fabulous suppers from the branches, bubbling away in little iron pots that can be eaten along with the contents. The metal crumbles like good bread, and just as savory. How do you know a stranger in Aadi? They packed their own lunch.

Chakor is a wooded isle in the center of a lake. A colony of sciopods live there, and when they wish to visit other cities, they simply take to the water on their single wide foot, as good as a ship, paddling with sturdy wooden oars, testing the winds with their thumbs. In Chakor they trade in dreams. When a sciopod sleeps she hauls that foot over her head to keep out the rain, and the sciopods claim this is a superior sleeping position. Not all the people of Pentexore dream (for example, mermaids cannot dream) and so they come to Chakor to find out what they would dream, if they did. They cuddle in with a sciopod and the sciopods dream for them, violet waves on pink shores and four moons aligned, jungles full of blue panthers with mirrors in their mouths, walking up the Spheres like a glassy staircase, and touching the silk of the sky. You always dream better in the arms of a sciopod, even if you could dream just fine before you met one. How do you know a stranger in Chakor? They have their eyes open.

This is the bald, quotidian, unvarnished truth of the country in which I find myself. I was tempted to exaggerate, at least a little, but I have disciplined myself mightily, and kept it only to the barest truths I could verify. I have told it as it is. So says my talking salamander. So says my glowing emerald. So say I, and you may believe what you like.

15. On Apologies

I have always felt that if you must apologize, better make it showy and grand. Better get on one knee. Better compose a sonnet. Better bring gifts in silver boxes with ivory accents. Better bring your best kisses.

I once had cause to apologize to the bishop of Avignon. The bishop had a sister and the sister was cloistered in a nunnery in the country, ensconced in a sweet little pine forest where they grew mushrooms and prayed and darned Christ's socks. It is well known that the tears of a bishop's sister can cure certain unsavory maladies which I myself have certainly never suffered, but I resolved to procure them for a friend of mine. Being slender of figure and sparse of beard as I have always been, I concealed myself within a habit and called myself Sister Marguerite, whereupon I had no difficulty becoming a great favorite among the women, who were excessively modest and did not even disrobe while bathing in their cool mountain pond. I know my hymnal very well, and have a pleasantly high singing voice—the tale of which I shall tell another time! After I had their confidence I closeted myself with the bishop's sister and told her that I bore sad news—her brother had died and walked this world no more. The poor girl, hardly more than a maid, wept piteously and I suggested, as bosom sisters, that we should catch up the other's tears in vials and keep them next to our hearts, so that our grief should be thus halved and lessened. She agreed and I had my panacea—and more, for so wretchedly did the bishop's sister throw herself upon me that my disguise was of little help, and I discovered the other truth of bishop's sisters—that they are often put away in nunneries on account of being young and beautiful and eager to live as men do, freely and without the manacles of their brothers' stations.

Obviously, I had to slip out of the abbey in the night, and some years later, when once more in Avignon and, to my chagrin, in the bishop's company without meaning to be, I made much show of my deep repentance—so deep I had become a Franciscan brother not a year previous, giving up all my possessions to atone for my trespasses. So florid was my apology and my tears that all were forced to admit they had found themselves in the presence of a veritable Augustine, who had given up his lascivious past utterly. This is what an apology should accomplish.

Clearly this philosophy has not yet reached Pentexore. As far as I can tell, the local method of apologizing is to simply appear after a long absence and not mention it at all. Then, if the offended party brings up the subject, one ought to pretend no knowledge at all of having kept them cooped up for days at a time, with emeralds for guards and very meager suppers indeed. Very well, kings set the manners of the country. But of course I have never had a drop of manners.

"What crime did I commit? Did I not bathe in the unicorn's blood or show quite enough delight?"

The queen Ymra looked shocked. "That was a sad business. You performed your part, and we are sorry we could not do it for you. Politics are like that, sometimes. One must keep one's hands clean."

"Politics? How is killing a boy in the woods politics? Where have you been these last days? I really rather think it is time for me to head back north and collect my ship. To be moving on."

"All will be clear at the Bonfire, we promise," said the king Ysra. "As for where we've been, we have not left the Mount. And we simply will not hear of you missing our great event. After that is done you may go where you like."

"I have not heard a sound in these halls but my own breath!"

The hexakyk looked at each other and clasped their middle hands. "We think you do not understand. We *cannot* leave the Mount. Save for four days a year, when the roads are good, and that was when we found you. The unicorn hunt was our last day."

"Why can you not leave the Mount?"

Again, the twins exchanged glances. "We are sick," they said together. "We have a pain, an illness. We do not like to discuss it."

"You seem perfectly healthy to me."

"It is not a sickness of the outside. We are…" They squeezed their hands and joined their lower pair, as if seeking strength from the other. "We are allergic to a substance in our kingdom, and while it abounds we are not well, and cannot be away from our home, or we will wither and die."

"What is it you are allergic to?"

Ymra's lovely eyes filled with tears, which plashed upon her jeweled belt.

"Diamonds," she whispered.

THE BOOK
OF THE RUBY

Tell them right away that we did not kill him. They can't think for a moment we would. We did nothing of the sort. We did not even bite Salah ad-Din for luck.

I know. But perhaps you do not know how close we came, daughter. I believe had it not been for Brother Dawud...Of course, I said no immediately—I laughed in the abbot's face. But John might have agreed to it, just to be loved by a man who knew his name and thought him good. A man who could dip his fingers in oil and forgive him everything. A man who could say: *May the Lord move His Hand over the waters of thy life and make it smooth.* What would any of us give to be forgiven all?

But Brother Dawud lived and breathed—

—*and died*

And died, yes, but before that he was a merry young man, somewhat gone to fat, with cheerful cheeks and unusually blue eyes, which contrasted greatly with his dark complexion, so like ours. Brother Dawud, as soon as the abbot had gone to await John's answer in solitude, bade me remove my veil and did not look askance at my nakedness. He only marveled that my body did not overheat, not having the distance from the heart that a prominent head provides. I did not want to solve the mystery for him, for I knew what he would say—had not John said it, and worse, long ago? But he pressed, his frank and open face only curious, not teasing, and I admitted that the blemmyae pant as hounds do. I made the comparison for him, so that he would not have to call me a dog. That was how humiliated I felt at that moment, how low, bandaged in veils and kept silent, that I called myself a dog, who was a queen—but Brother Dawud only said: *fascinating!* And asked after the circulatory system of the gryphon. I believe there is nothing in this world Brother Dawud did not wish to know utterly, to understand completely, and to each thing I told him he only had exclamations of delight, that God's work could be so varied and complex.

John loved him as I did, immediately and wholly. Dawud was kind to us, brought us water and a flat, chewy bread with boiled eggs from black, skinny hens he tended to himself.

"I am only a novice," he said bashfully. "I do not get the plum work. One day I hope to be allowed to illuminate something, or help with the winemaking."

"I…" I paused. We do not mention our previous Abirs, but how could poor Dawud understand all that? "I was a scribe, once. I have illuminated many poems and treatises. I have even used gold paint, for clouds, and crushed carnelian, for blood." Dawud positively clapped his hands with delight, and we discussed inks and glues, about which I knew much more than he, and the dreams of one day drawing in the corners of a Bible lit his eyes. He said he would endeavor, should he ever earn the honor, to draw both me and a gryphon, for he thought our forms the most beautiful of our ranks.

You are a scribe now, even if you wear a crown. Writing our war for us. An Abir in reverse, making us all what we were long ago.

With John he discussed Nestorius, the founder of their sect, whom John had known personally, which confirmed for me how long it had truly been since he left home, and for Dawud that we had come from God, specially to that spot. He asked after Nestorius' person, how he sounded when he spoke, was he right or left handed, did he like dates or quinces, was he a harsh teacher or an affectionate one, and all these John answered with hearty laughter and excitement. I felt some discomfiture—I had certainly never listened to his tales so attentively, nor made him feel so valued and wise. But then, he had not done so much for any of us, either.

It was when John spoke of his old friend Kostas that Brother Dawud frowned and sunk deep into thought. I recalled that name—a young man who had run errands for John in Constantinople, with whom he had been close, as close as anyone John had known before Pentexore, who had taught him, supposedly, gentleness and service. Perhaps one day I will see John express these lessons.

He is different now. After everything. Perhaps we will all see it.

Brother Dawud's sweet, earnest face drew in as John spoke. I know he loved that Kostas, and it does not trouble me. I have loved many—I still love Hadulph, and still he shares my tent and my heart and John does not even think on it, that is how long he has lived in Pentexore. And have I not loved women in my time? The world is generous with love.

"I believe," Brother Dawud said, "that you should know something of the founding of our order, and this place. Our first abbot wrote a lengthy work on the subject, for the abbots who came after to study and know the tale of our beginning—for you must know we are on the very outposts of Christendom, if we can be said to dwell in Christendom at all. It is not an easy place to establish a see, nor to maintain one. If Father Jibril is hard, do understand that he came into the seat young, because his father has wealth and only two sons, and from the moment he was called Father the mullahs in Mosul have entreated him to close the abbey and come into the arms of Islam, and entreaty comes in many forms. In return, also in many forms, Father Jibril has entreated them to come to the bosom of Christ. It is a song with an old refrain, and the more a man sings it, the harder goes his soul. Father Jibril has spent a long time in the choir. But I was speaking of our first brothers, and how they came through north to put stones into the square that became St. Elijah's."

Brother Dawud went from us and returned some time later with a large, ornate book with many crosses stamped on its cover, and set with some dull precious stones—beryl and sard—in need of care and polish. Brother Dawud held it open and bade John read, which he did until he could speak no more, for his throat betrayed him to grief.

I believe that every life is an icon. An exquisitely rendered miniature of the life of Christ or His Mother, closed up in fragrant wood or oiled metal, and upon death God opens this small and perfect relic, and a soul may see which path he walked. This may be heresy—what is not heresy these days? It would only be the twelfth or fifteenth most heretical thing I have declared in my life—but you see the evidence all around you. We are Christ; Christ is us. Each life follows the path of His life, or sometimes that of His Immaculate Mother, an exemplum from which we cannot deviate, no matter how we might try. The word never was a name, but always a verb, anointing, anointed, and Christ the Man and Christ the Spirit can as easily be called Christ the noun and Christ the verb, Christ that exists and Christ that acts.

It's a simple thing; it happens to all of us. We are born, we perform the miracles of our youth, which are speech, movement, feeling, and moral will. We become teachers of men, we become righteous and sometimes inflexible, intolerant of those who are old and slow and cannot understand how the world has changed—for the world is always changing, and every generation is the last and the first. We draw together some number of companions, whether they be twelve or two. We perform the miracles of adulthood, which are love, forgiveness, perspective, and terrible, painful sacrifice. We sacrifice ourselves, even wicked men do it, carving up their capacities for pleasure and gentleness in order to obtain power. We all bleed, we all die, it is unavoidable. And perhaps we create something new and wonderful, perhaps we manage to pull a new thing into the world from Heaven. A child, a book, a revolution, a sturdy table, a monastery. When we bleed we are Christ. When we create we are Mary. Yet when we bleed we are also Mary, who suffered for her Son, and when we create we are Christ, who built a new Heaven and a new Earth like a good, level table and a solid, smooth chair.

I came to this place so that I would never have to hear again that the vital thing is whether or not drawing a picture of God condemns the soul. I came to this place so that I could hear the Word more clearly, for the Word is not a thing you bring to others, it is being itself, repeated over and over in every aspect of the world, the Word which creates, the Word which bleeds, and my ears are not so good these days. I must have a very profound quiet to hear it, and even then, even then. Even then there are two kinds of old men, and the one is full of grace, performing that miracle of perspective and the long glance backward, and the other is brittle and bitter, a hard seed from which no green thing will grow again. Some days I am the one, some days I am the other. Struggle never ends, even in peace. Even in the lovely country where men have lived since the first wandering days of Eve in her rags and her misery. Even here, I can only forgive my life for having happened to me three or four days of any week. On the other days, I cannot let any of it be.

The young monks ask me if a saint can know he is a saint while he lives and still remain one. The knowing of it must lead to pride, they think, which would disqualify. I tell them to eat their breakfasts. Who cares what a saint knows? Saints are like storms—you cannot predict or control them, you can only hope they pass you by unscathed. And, well, I certainly know the state of my sainthood and that is very poor. A saint acts because he is moved by God. I acted to fill the time, for that which I loved passed from the world. I had a childhood, like any man, and in that childhood I had a mother with too many children to worry too much about one resourceful son. I ran wild, I became a young jackal, trotting along the streets of Constantinople and screaming every now and again just to hear how it echoed. I fell in with a feral and savage crowd—heretical thinkers and Nestorian Christians, drinking in the Logos by the savage moonlight, drunk on an idea of God that meant we could hold the end of an unbroken chain that began with the world-beginning Word and passed through Jesus Christ Our Lord and through our own hands, on through the ages of men, down and down and down. That meant there were two of everything. The world itself has a twin. We all do, our better selves, the parts of us which are immortal and forever young, which abound with plenty. The good, serene soul in which any thing one plants may grow into the loveliest and strangest tree, so that we end our lives the caretakers of an orchard which gives fruit to every committed act. A life has so many fruits, so many flowers, and at the end of mine they all seem to tangle and root in Constantinople, when I was young, when I was so sure of the right way of thinking, and I had a friend named John.

When I consider it now I don't think John himself mattered as much to me as his leaving. My memories of him are hazy and dim: sitting on the long harbor wall cracking quinces on my knee, listening to him talk simply for the rhythms of his voice, of the dusk and the fishermen and a gentle discourse on the division between soul and body. Running for paper rolled up and tied with rushes for him, interested and excited by the strength of my legs, how fast I could dart through the inner city, the clipped, lightfooted dance of haggling with the papyrus-master. Meeting his mother, once, sharing bread with her, eating their eggs and their preserved fish. I remember loving him as one loves an older brother who can do everything right and well, determined to be like him, to impress him, to be approved of and blessed by his notice. I was not a child, but I was young and like a bird would have been fiercely loyal to any creature who showed me love; it happened to be him, and so it was. I know many men who had such friendships—sometimes they were savory and sometimes less so. It was Constantinople at the beginning of a new Rome! Everything was permitted, nothing was true. I would not have said no, and perhaps that is my sin to atone for, a bright burning orange hanging from my tree that I must explain in the end, but nothing came of it. He rested his hand on mine, once or twice. He kissed my brow, one time, in the late evening when the stars were full as moons, and I had brought him both a jug of wine and a treatise on transfiguration he had been asking for all over town, and I felt it on my head like a pain. But love is like that, it is hard and awful and, usually, it is not contagious.

Life with John was warm and smelled of men and books and olive dust, and I liked it. I sought them out when I performed that other miracle of maturity—seeking, striving, stretching. But his leaving landed in the center of my world and left a crater, one it took me years to climb out of, to scale rickety, crumbling sides and emerge my own self. He went to find the tomb of the Apostle Thomas, as many did, and establish an order there, or near there. He would send for me when he could—or at least I imagine he said that, promised that. I may have confused it, thought ambivalence to be permission. But no word came, and time passed, and finally some silk-seller with his cart full of orange and blue bolts sold me, under much duress, a piece of a ship he had found in the desert. It had a word on it—Theo, God, and I knew it for a fragment of John's ship, which had been called the Theotokos, I recognized the woodcarving and the workmanship. John had left me and died and there would be no close, modest monastery in the mountains, no mild contemplation of Nestorius' teachings or Mary's travails. Not unless I made it so. Not unless I became the man I guessed John might have become, good and stalwart and a little reticent, not given to long speeches or faint praise, made excellent by works and deeds. I do not pretend that conclusion came primarily to mind. After much time spent borrowing against a fortune I did not have and locating the most interesting things to befuddle my brains, I dreamed in my haze and when I woke I dedicated myself to something both better and worse than a ghost—a shade of he who never was. I changed my name, though I could not quite bear changing it to John, for that is a state—the state of Johnness which he seemed always to occupy perfectly and without questioning—that I will not attempt. Grace, perhaps. My old friend? Well. There must always be two of things. Everything in the world has a twin. Kostas died and was buried with myrrh and palm leaves. I, however that I can be figured when so much has passed, walked out of Constantinople and from that all else came.

Once there was a nymph named Calypso. Not really, of course. It's a pagan story, and pagan stories only guess at how the world works. But Odysseus, on his way home from war, stopped at her island and lived with her as her lover for nine *years—and that's long enough for anyone to call her his wife. She wanted him to stay with her forever, and gave him a choice: live on the isle with her, eternally young and immortal, or leave her to wither and die with his mortal (and legal) wife in Ithaca. Odysseus chose and he chose for us all, as Christ chose for us all—to die is important, it gives shape to living. In God's Kingdom is immortality and unceasing vigor, but not before. I wonder sometimes if he chose well. If, should John have washed up on another isle, and loved another nymph, and she offered him the same bargain, if he would choose as Odysseus did, or as I would have. Yes, I would have taken it. I would have made the other pact. I am weak and human and I have wanted love in my life. In that, perhaps Calypso was the more human of the two of them, for all she wanted was for her love to stay, and he left her without a backward glance. I wanted my love to stay. Instead, I am Odysseus' son, withering in the rocky heights of a dry country, and remembering the wars I fought when I was young.*

John passed his hand over his eyes; Brother Dawud insisted that he had hardly begun to read—so much more remained, this was merely a kind of brief personal comment on the events to come. But John pushed the boards of the book closed. "Everything human I have loved is dead," he whispered. "I will not be the death of more. Salah ad-Din is a good man. Kostas was a good man. I am a good man, on the brighter, better days, when Hagia laughs at the cameleopards racing or the early spring rain, when my daughter speaks only out of her right-hand mouth, when the peacocks lift up their tails in the dawn. Then I am a good man. I can be that man today, just for a moment. I can not bleed, today."

Brother Dawud pursed his pink, full lips. "Salah ad-Din—he

lets me call him Yusuf, sometimes, when I am running messages—is a good man. It is easy to love one man. One infidel. It is not easy to love a nation of them."

I smiled ruefully. "How wise you are, Dawud. For I have learned to love one Christian man, but have found the nation of them thorny. When John thinks as a man, he likes my laughing and my peacocks and my child and my early rains and my hibiscus flowers and my honeyed walnuts on his plate, he thinks of Pentexore as the real world and he calls poor Vidyut by his name instead of Archbishop. When he thinks as a nation he renames all our cities, and starts up the Lenten mass nonsense again."

Brother Dawud's eyes grew soft and serious. "Jibril will hurt you for it, you know. He must look out for all of us. He always thinks as a nation, as St. Elijah's and Nestorians. I don't think he will let the world hear that Prester John declined to strike down a Muslim when it would be easy to do it, that he brought cameleopards and gryphons but did not fight."

Did it matter, that he warned you? Did you draw back your breath and think it might be better to hold your nose and do it?

John could say what he liked. I said no before him—but no one in his world listens to a woman. Even their god did not. Who asked poor Mary if she wanted to loose a son on the world, an arrow of diamond catching fire as it flew? She said no, I'm sure of it. And yet, the future fell on her in the night all the same.

The Left-Hand Mouth,
the Right-Hand Eye

A nest of bodies can grow deep and hot, such that no one wants to leave it. When a story is done, another must chain on, to keep all those skins together. "Tell me another story," Sefalet coughed. Her right hand had gone frail and had a tremor. Her left lay firm, silent, over her thin chest, in a smug position, not speaking, but able to whenever it liked.

"I don't know any stories," I answered, because I was tired and I am not always the best of lions. "I only know things that have happened. That's not the same thing as a story, which is a thing made up to pass the time or repeated because you heard it once a long time ago and it sounded pretty."

"Tell us a story," said Lamis, queen of Thule, with her huge hands under her small chin. "Some stories are things that really happened."

Sefalet had fallen sick. She had nearly fallen off the cathedral—and I must remind myself to say cathedral and not tower, though my heart wants to call it a tower, though no church ever had so many floors, or was that color of blue-black, or had a girl named Kalavya speaking out of its cornerstones. *I shot a bird today, and it had leathery skin and wings like a bat, only with pinkish feathers and wild white eyes. It is another country up here above the cloudline, Drona, with other citizens, other songs, other holidays. Sometimes I think I could just take one step off the ledge and fly myself, up and away to the sphere of the stars, where I would step on their silver heads in my dancing.* Sefalet had leaned in to hear the speaker, though her left hand lashed out, gnashing with its teeth at the stone, hissing: "She died, she died, she died, she didn't fly, she fell forever, and so will we all, when we get our first kiss, our princess kiss, to wake the world." And then she swooned, shivering all over, dizzy and upset, and if not for Fortunatus catching her on his broad, furry back, she would have plummeted all the way down. It did not seem to be an illness we could catch—rather, her left hand had become her whole body, and it rebelled against her, her heart speaking hideous words to her bones, her spleen telling lies to her lungs. She kept saying: "I want to run, I want to run!" and trying to bolt out of the flap of Gahmureen's blue tent, the only one big enough for all of us, myself and Lamis and Fortunatus and Elif. We take up a great deal of space. We are expansive beasts, and savage. The inventor worked at a wide, tilted table that I knew from experience she could fold up small enough to carry with her like a book. She ran her hand up her spiral horns from time to time, building the cathedral in her mind, in her heart. I wondered: How long would she sleep when this was done?

"Don't be broken," Elif said to her. "I will tell a story if it will make you better. If stories are the same thing as medicine." He moved his stubby camphor-wood hands over her forehead and the wood darkened with the princess's sweat. "Once a wooden man loved a girl without a face. So the wooden man said: I will get you a face from the Prince of the Beautiful Mountain, because the wooden man liked to be useful. He left the girl tied to a tree so she could not get away and get lost and walked all the way to the Beautiful Mountain, which is almost all the way to the Gate of Alisaunder. The Prince of the Mountain, who was an ant-lion and therefore very knowledgeable about bodies and all the things they do, said: Go into the world and get me all the component parts of a face and I will assemble it for you. So the wooden man thought for a long time about what faces were made of. A face is what makes a person look familiar to you, he thought. But the girl was already familiar to him. A face is what laughs and cries and looks pensive, it is what you breathe out of and eat with, and it covers your mind so dust and seeds and other irritants cannot get in. But the girl could laugh and cry and she could look pensive better than anyone the wooden man knew. She breathed and ate and never complained about dust. A face is what is beautiful or ugly about the outside of a person. But the girl was already the most beautiful thing he had met. And so the wooden man was forced to return to the Prince of the Beautiful Mountain, who was an ant-lion and therefore very knowledgeable about circular reasoning and tautologies. The wooden man said: A face has no component parts. All the objectives of a face can be accomplished by my girl, because I love her, but she still frightens me, and that is the whole point of faces, to communicate love and terror by turns so that long ago when people weren't people, they could bare their teeth and scare off tigers, or bare their teeth and let ones like them know they were safe. My girl has passed beyond the need for a face, for she is more frightening and more of her is bare than anyone who has lived. And the ant-lion said the wooden man was wise, and had acquitted himself as well as a man who was not wooden, and so the wooden man went home to the girl without a face and untied her and they had a picnic."

"That was wonderful," cried Lamis, who drank the story like water. "Except for the tying up part."

"How else do you get people to sit still?" Elif answered.

"That's an excellent point, " I purred. "And I am amazed that you can tell a story so well, being as you are."

"Stories are easy," said Elif, and Sefalet blew weakly upon him. It could not have helped much, but he puffed up his balsam chest, grateful. "You just take everything that has happened to you and change it so that it looks as though it happened to someone else. If you like, you can change the names to something nicer, and pretend something you only thought about actually happened in the real world, with ant-lions involved."

Sefalet's left hand turned over. The lips were dark and full. "We are going to run," it sighed.

"I doubt it," I growled. "We could always take Elif's advice on keeping humans where one wants them."

With her clammy right hand, the princess rasped: "Didn't you used to have a baby like me? A red one, who was soft and sharp and warm? And didn't he sometimes want to run so badly, and so far, that he broke away from you and bolted over the snow? Running is the best thing there is, I think. I'm sorry I didn't appreciate it before. I want to run so much, so fast, so far, like a red lion on the snow. And I will, I feel that I will. The left-hand girl will run further than the right."

I licked her face roughly. It is the only way a lion licks. "Hadulph did love to run, yes. He was a little flame on the ice, bounding and leaping, with his tail snapping around in circles like a red whip. He would spring out across the squares of Nimat, and his passing would make the panotii's ears fly up into the air. He would roar as he ran, as if his voice wanted to get there first."

"My voice wants to get there first."

"But Sefalet, I could always catch him. I was always faster. I was the snow, and he could not run far enough that I would not be there already, to pick him up by the scruff of his neck when he panted so hard I thought his breath would fall out of him. And I will be faster than you, too, when you are a flame on the snow."

But of course I did not catch her.

When you sit on a high mountain and folk decide you are wise enough to visit from time to time, wise enough to lay flowers and fish over your feet, wise enough to ask how to stitch up a person and make them unbroken, you know you will sometimes fail. I have always known it. Grisalba thought I was full of myself. She kept a sharp eye out, to see when I would falter. I could have saved her the effort—I have failures piled up in my cold cave like bones. Creatures who left me with pieces of them missing, when I was so sure I had put them back together. Sons still running so far and so fast. Part of living is failing to do what you are really very good at, every day, every night, what you have worked so hard to bend between your paws like soft metal. Every other day but this one. Today is always the trouble. Love and storytelling and caring for the sick and catching kittens bounding through the snow—they must be repeatable or they are nothing. And sooner or later that repeatable thing will stop repeating. We are none of us deft enough to avoid that. Yet it hurts like strangling, and it hurts the same every time.

And that day, when the sun was a hot red tear and the lamia were enervated, baking on flat stones, when even the thin little voices in the stones were lulled to sleep, I lost her.

No one took her. I don't think I know any villains, really, in the end. Anyone I can point to and say—they ruined it for us. Oh yes, there is John, but you cannot hold idiots accountable. Sefalet took herself. She said she would run and she ran. Her left-hand mouth, which no one believed, had been snarling and shrieking, promising to eat her, to eat all of us, calling for her sisters though she had but one soul she could ever call a sister and the two had barely traded three words between them. She howled like a dog. The light seeped out of her like sweat, like pus, like it was a fever she might break. I buried my face in Fortunatus' neck—I could not listen to it anymore. Even Elif put his wooden hands over his ears. But sometime in the night the ugliness in her did break, and we all slept. We all slept long enough for her to creep out into the wet grass and the silent blue-lit camp, into the woods and out of sight. We woke and the sleeping princess had vanished. All that failure bound up in an empty bed.

It wasn't hard to guess where she'd gone. Hadn't she been screaming it all night? Hadn't we gotten to know it so well it might have been our names? I would go, and Elif would go, and we would not be fast enough to catch her before she fell.

I will run to the Wall, to the Wall, and you will never catch me.

The Virtue of Things
Is in the Midst of Them

16. On All the Things I Have Told You

I feel we have become so close. I can almost see you, reading my wonderful words (and I think you must admit they are wonderful) and imagining the places and folk I have told you about, and it is almost like we have seen them together. Almost like you tied your ship next to mine on the icy dock, like you befriended a salamander and an emerald, like you killed a unicorn with me, and a partner in a terrible thing lessens the hurt of it. Almost like you were imprisoned with me, and damn the goddess Philosophy to her cuckolded boys. I'd rather have you, dear reader, I really would.

But you should know we are coming to the end now. You can see it over the hill. The ends of things always look golden to me. Golden and orange and scarlet—fire, and a following wind. I am not overjoyed at my part in what is to come. I am not angry about it either. Yes, I was tricked, a little. But I know enough to have excused myself if I really wanted excusing. I didn't. I wanted to put my hand on Agneya's back like a baking stone. I wanted to race Cabochon down the black halls. I still hoped, I think, in the secret recesses of John Mandeville, to seduce the queen for once. To have Ymra settle upon me, her arms enclosing me like a forest of limbs, and the inside of her would be a fire, too, nothing in this country is not a fire, but the ashes I would send into her would catch the light of her heart like snowflakes.

And yes, I say for once. I have never seduced a queen. I feel terrible about it, if you want to know the truth. What is a traveling man, a peddler of splendid tales, ready with a wink and a sly, conspiratorial arm hooked through your arm, if he has never even once managed to get a queen to throw off her ermine? No, no princesses either. I do know a secret about princesses though, and I'll share it. Many men of my profession say they're dullards, spiteful and ugly, big inbred noses and feet like ducks. But it's not true. Princesses are exactly like the stories say. Their lives are hard, they know it from the moment they're born. But they are radiant, and clever, and brave, and if they love you they will cross the world in iron shoes to bring you home. It's only that none of them have ever loved me. I consider it my own failing. No blame to them.

I asked a queen once why she didn't want me. She wasn't a powerful queen, not a monarch of Spain or of Albania. Just a little kingdom of nowhere, but she married well and she had a crown. The queen of nowhere looked at me with her clear grey eyes and said: "Because I don't want to be in a story."

Princesses usually grow up to be queens. The cleverness sticks long after the beauty goes.

I suppose I am always in a story. I tell it; it tells me. I am only a story. I was only ever a story. There was never a John. There was never even a Mandeville. My body is all chapters, my better parts are appendixes. That's all a heart ever was to a head, after all.

I said before I never saw Death in a field. I lied. I always lie. It's lies all the way down to the core of me, and at the core is a little daemon made of iron, and he is telling a lie. But they are such kind lies. They have such color. When I was a boy I went to look for my sister in the rye fields. She hadn't come home and I worried, even though she was older, a big girl, with strong arms from threshing the rye. We'd been so busy we'd hardly noticed, for I grew up on the pilgrim road, and the knights would come through on their way to the holy land, and they could not wait to drink and carouse until they got there. We'd poured out the whole winter's supply of beer already. I went out into the rye and I found her, with blood on her belly where some cannon-shouldered Christian had not been able to wait, either. She was radiant and clever and brave and I loved her. Death is a girl, with hair of no particular color, and she holds court in a long, golden field.

In a moment I shall be telling you an amusing story about Halicarnassus and all will be light and you will say to yourself: *Our John could not have meant that part about his sister. It's another lie. He didn't even tell us her name.* And of course it is a lie. I have never suffered loss in all my days, and no hero of my stature has the temerity to have siblings. What use is a comic hero who grieves? Don't think about it. Especially since I don't think you will be really proud of me in the end, or feel you have been guided through this tale by a good man. That's all right; as long as we both make it through to the end, does it matter who leads who?

17. On the Bonfire

It began a week before it began. The salamanders draped their silks over the greenwood structure at the base of the tower I had until recently occupied—the branches tore through the fabric and the whole thing glowered copper and mossy and terribly dry, spiky and toothed. Feasts appeared from nowhere on groaning tables—mainly the sorts of things phoenix and salamanders liked to eat, which are organ meats, cinnamon pies, and smaller lizards and songbirds, which is quite disturbing, if you think about it. Tremors of excitement passed through Simurgh and I could not even bear to share a room with Cabochon, for the waves of her pleasure and anticipation boiled through the air and filled my flesh with the strange desires of emeralds—and I am only a man; I was not meant to lust as gems do.

But I thought nothing of it. Whenever I had asked after the Bonfire, the answer had always been: *Soon. Soon. Tomorrow. Next week at the outside*. When I asked then, the answer was: *Soon. Soon. Tomorrow. Next week at the outside*.

For a time I lived in Halicarnassus; I knew a queen called Artemisia. Not *the* queen Artemisia, of course, who fought with the Medes and was Xerxes' favorite admiral. No, merely her distant great-great-many-times-granddaughter (though by chance they bore an identical countenance). Artemisia was not a cruel queen—Halicarnassus does not, collectively, tolerate that sort terribly well. All a city can bear is one good queen. Then you can't shut them up on the subject of excellence in government. How many navies have you crushed in our name this week? Your grandmother picked her teeth with Xerxes' heartstrings and you can't get a husband? Who could stand it? She was not a cruel queen but she had the kind of pragmatism that can look like cruelty if you stand somewhat to the side. A realism that slices as true as a blade. And so queen Artemisia, who pointedly ignored the question of a husband (I asked, of course. I always ask. If you always ask, eventually a queen will say yes. A princess at least.) made a decree to her city: they would go to war. The Greek states had humiliated them (a thousand years previous) and had sent a number of arrogant missives (requests for ships and oil) and really, when did a Greek ever know how to govern himself? (Unless the Greek was an Ionian, which Artemisia happened to be.) "Unpack all your helmets and your shields and your familial armor," Artemisia said. "Polish up your swords. Let your wives sew new banners, and the firemasters mix up new flavors of things that boil and burn. Begin breeding better and swifter horses, and if any of you can invent some new and wonderful item of war, you will be rewarded." A great thrill went through the city, and all bent to their work. Halicarnassus had not had a good war in ages. In addition to siege towers, not a few statues of their new queen were cast—and did she not look remarkably like her famous grandmother?

Whenever anyone asked when the war would commence, the answer was always: *Soon. Soon. Next week at the outside.* And all the while the city prospered and the soldiers were not too sorry to avoid dying while still getting to agitate against their Greek cousins and call them goat-stickers. It went on for years. In fact, when queen Artemisia lay on her deathbed at quite an advanced age, her advisors asked when they should begin the invasion. She answered them with a smile: *Soon. Soon.* And then she died.

So you see, I had seen the fox play this trick before. I felt I had a good handle on where the hedgehog goes.

In retrospect, perhaps the mood had gone more frantic, the plans ramped up, the songs at dusk more lustrous and full. But I had little enough basis for comparison.

Ymra, who always favored me, greeted me one morning with a new set of clothes, in a rare audience without her brother. Specially made by Agneya for me, she said—and how special they were. If King Midas had made love to a seamstress, this would have been their sartorial child. Black from toe to cap, but I could not mistake the thing—a jester's costume. Not a garish one, no bells danced anywhere and the curls of fabric looked more like rags than fat, amusing bouncing protrusions (I have played the jester in truth more often than I care to—it is an excellent way not to die when visiting foreign courts). A subtle implication, stitched with skill, but I could not doubt it, and she did not mean me to—I was their fool, and they would clothe me so. That was all right. A fool is not witless. A fool shows the way—when I was with the mummers' troupe I always wore the fool's crown, and when it came time for Our Lord to perish from this earth, my fool always changed into an angel (a swapping of masks is all it takes) and led Him to Heaven. Fools tell the truth, but tell it so sharp the king bleeds.

"The Bonfire draws near," Ymra said.

"Soon?"

"Soon."

The queen looked at me slantways. She had a red, smeary beauty, a feeling of looseness about her, and you could never watch all six of her hands at once. "Have you enjoyed your time with us?" she said silkily. "What I mean to say is, we have heard you tell stories of other courts until we could hear no more of Egypt. Will you tell tales of us? Were we exciting enough to make a tale?"

"Without a doubt. I will write a great book, when I return to England."

"But you cannot leave until after the Bonfire. It will be extraordinary. You will never forget it."

"You know," I began, "when I lived in Halicarnassus…"

"I don't care about Halicarnassus," Ymra said, but not cruelly. "I care about Pentexore."

"Tell me something. About the unicorn. About the Bonfire. I know enough to smell magic on the hearth. Are you a witch? Are you doing something wicked?"

Ymra stretched her fingers, one by one. It took some time. She did it like a cat, prolonging the moment. "You use so many words. I don't even know what they mean. Wicked? Magic? Witch? Just nouns, just letters all in a row like soldiers. Magic is a horrible, unpredictable thing. You do your best, of course. You seek out esoteric ingredients. You perform arcane rites. But who knows if any of it works? You might almost just as well live through whatever's to come without it. Magic is an experiment where you don't know what it is you want to prove. God sets the rules, and we guess at them."

I did not conceal my surprise. "You believe in God then?"

"God is another way of talking about the power to break things, that's all. When you mean to break a goblet or a bone, well, just do it and be done. But when the things to be broken get big enough you have to start talking about God. As far as a witch, well, perhaps when we say witch we mean: a creature who can still be broken herself, but she is learning to be the breaker. And wickedness, well, you tell me. I don't think I'm wicked. I am what I am. That I am, if you want to get classical. Intent is everything. If I touch something and it withers, does that make me wicked? If I didn't mean to do it any harm? If it did not offend me, and I didn't know it was going to happen?" Ymra looked pleadingly at me, and her voice shook a little. "If I only wanted to touch it, as any creature wants to touch things. Sick and wicked are not the same thing."

"You seem so healthy!"

"Yet the choice is: we are sick or the world is sick. One cannot bear the other. If one is true the other is false." She looked down. "Or perhaps we just do not know what we are. Who told you you were human? Or did you just assume it, because everyone who looked like you was also called human? Those who look like us are called hexakyk. But does that mean we are hexakyk? So much easier just to say we are sick. We meant no harm, and we made a hospice when we finally diagnosed ourselves. And we want to live, just to live, like always, like anyone. The Bonfire will help. And we would like you to help the Bonfire."

"I don't really feel I understand any of what is happening well enough to help." In my experience, the ignorant foreigner who meddles in local politics usually ends up roasting alive on one stake or another.

"You are an obscure ingredient, is not that enough?" Ymra smiled. In all my days I had never seen a smile so knowing. "Do you not like me? Do you not want to please me? And my brother, too? We would never hurt you, John. We treasure Johns and want to keep them whole. They are so useful."

"What are you going to do at the Bonfire, Ymra?"

Her smile widened into a wolfish, hangdog grin. "We are going to break something big."

Mars, Hot and Dry

Theses and similar nations were shut in behind lofty mountains by Alexander the Great, towards the north...Those accursed fifteen nations will burst forth from the four quarters of the earth at the end of the world, in the times of the Antichrist, and overrun all the abodes of the saints as well as the great city Rome, which, by the way, we are prepared to give to our child who will be born, along with all Italy, Germany, the two Gauls, Britain, and Scotland. We shall also give him Spain and all of the land as far as the icy sea.

The nations to which I have alluded, according to the words of the prophet, shall not stand in the judgement on account of their offensive practices, but will be consumed to ashes by a fire which will fall on them from heaven.

—The Letter of Prester John
1165

The Confessions

B ut Hiob had not wakened.

He writhed on his bier, but the vines held him fast. He made sounds, but the swollen stem in his throat stoppered them. His eyes did not open; he did not speak; he did not stand up. As a man dreaming strange dreams he moved in his sleep. His hands fluttered—they had swollen their pages already with words and Reinolt and Goswin had been lax in changing them.

"The battle must be coming soon," Reinolt said guiltily.

"And the Bonfire," added Goswin.

"You are both children," I snapped, angry, thwarted, ashamed. I should not have kissed her. She did not like it. Her expression when our faces parted was cold pity. *I am not Hagia,* she had whispered. *I am not here to bring you warmly into a place where you do not belong.* Through the bars of that country a sword was thrust in my childhood, and it flamed still. I changed the parchment beneath Hiob's wrinkled and frantic hand.

The al-Qasr sits as empty as it did in those long-gone days when Abibas the Mule-King ruled kindly from his tree in the sciopod forest, and most of Nural seemed to live there, in the open rooms, the long halls, the drifting curtains. How happy I seem to recall it, all of us playing in the palace like children.

My silver pot scrapes—the ink is nearly gone. And yet the flood of it crests in me, all at once, everything happening at once, the weight behind my eyes, the memory of it. I understand Imtithal now—Hajji. I understand Hajji now. The world is a place of suffering, and the root of all suffering is memory. When you live long enough, the mass of memory is greater than any moon, any sun, so bright and awful and scalding in the dark, scalding the inside of my skull, dragging me down into living, down into remembering, and every time I look on a thing I see only what it has been before, what it will be after. The future and the past encroach on the artifacts of the present, the artifacts of myself, like a kind of richly colored mold, softening my vision, burning away its edges, slushing everything together into one knot of being which I can never transcend, but also, can neither descend, sinking into a low country where everything is only as it is, now, in this one singular moment. What a lonely way of seeing that would be.

I tried to shave down the vine in Hiob's mouth, to give him some relief. I rubbed oil into his stretched lips. Like a father I tended him, like a son I feared for him. The book was inside him, that was clear. He could write out the missing passages, out of order, phrases here and there, all of it confused in him, but there, hidden in his body. Perhaps he saw as Hagia saw—everything happening all at once, together, on top of itself, like the strata in stone. Perhaps one day, when I was old, I could sort out his writing and fit it into the first books, fit it into his own confessions, make a whole document. I looked up at the door and the woman in yellow stood there, hovering, a deer about to bolt into the brush—and I already knew I would not. Prester John's kingdom was a country of fragments, all strung together to look like a whole. The kingdom of memory, the kingdom of time. Against our own world, hurtling forward, always forward, we could only lay those fragments gently, as a flower against a tomb.

When I first crept at the edges of the refectory, listening to the men's conversation, those hushed male voices, so sure and thrilled and vibrating with desire, I thought they were mad. How could there be any joy in telling tales that were surely false? Brother Johan had said last week than in Prester John's kingdom men had many wives, and the wives had many husbands, and all of them were priests, though they married and bore children. But the next week he said the whole of the nation hewed to celibacy, and thence came their incredible longevity. Both could not be true, but both were greeted with the same awed, breathy belief. If such a place existed, it could only be one thing. And it either existed or it did not—they seemed to revel in the in-between place, the might-be, and that was neither faith nor fact, so I could not understand it.

I looked down at my book. It was my shift on Hagia's volume, and a cerulean fuzz played at its corners, teasing me, sending tendrils toward the text. Fragments. A mountain of them, all adding up to a place that was and was not. I turned from the tome, daring it to dissolve in my absence. I declared my freedom from it—it felt dizzy, mad, dangerous, to risk losing such a document, a document so many had sought. But it was only ever fragments, I was only ever fragments, and if I did not find what I wanted in this book, there were others, hanging pendulous from the tree, heavy with juice. I ducked my head out of the little house. The woman in yellow burned at me from the shadows.

"Who are you?" I said outright. "Who was your mother, your grandmother, your great-great-grandmother? Blood tells the tale, forever."

She looked at me, silent, savage, not an animal, but not human. And then she grinned, her cutting teeth showing. The whites of her eyes shone. Then she ran, the soles of her feet flashing up like lanterns, vanishing into the gloom.

The Book
of the Ruby

They fell upon us. I think that's the best way to say it. *That is how it happened. They fell, as if from a great height, and all their weight came down upon us.*

I wish it had been a battle. I wish we had ridden down a long green hill riding the cameleopards and singing war songs, singing songs written by Niobe the phoenix which would in years hence become hearthside songs, songs sung by grandchildren who barely understood the bit about the green knight, or held the tune quite right. Instead, some hooded man fell on me in the night, his body heavy and hot on my back, and the sounds of the camp became the sounds of screaming. I confused my attacker—he could not strangle me or cut my throat, and I was so much bigger than he. Still, he cut me, slashed at my ribs. We wrestled on the floor of my tent, breathing hard, and I could not see John, only the arms twisting in my arms and the man's shadowy strong leg wrapping around my waist and the flash of the skin over my ribs splitting open. I had presence enough to think: *You're not very good at this, boy.* We breathed at each other and our breaths still had dinner on them. Onions and fried bread and sweet black wine, the dinner we had shared with the monks of St. Elijah, and I felt deep disgust. What kind of creature shares food with someone on one side of the sun and a blade with them on the other? I turned my waist so that my weight turned him—I felt his leg break under me and he cried out.

I was angry. He had hurt me. He had broken faith. I didn't even know him, I couldn't see his face, but I took his knife and stuck it up through his chin, and when I did it I felt it crunch up into his brain, and my anger stopped short, as though it had struck something harder and colder than itself.

I found you, covered in blood. Everyone was screaming and running—braziers had fallen over. Tents began to burn. I said: Are you all right? Is Father dead? But he was not. His face had gone slack and still, and you both sat there, stunned and identical, your hands black with that ugly, deep blood that means someone has died. I remember thinking that I suddenly knew what you must have looked like the day you got married.

We fought together. Anglitora and I, not mother and daughter but mother and daughter still.

We fought together. I am good at fighting. The wing gives an advantage—men fight me as though I am a cripple, but my wing dances, and where it hits them they crumple. You and I kept our backs to one another, and the monks had no faces, but they had blood.

I killed five men.

So few. So many. I saw Sukut gore a young novice. I saw Niobe puff out her chest and leak an ooze of fire over the blades of her tormentors—the metal bubbled, their skin peeled back. I saw Houd crushing priests' skulls in his huge hands. His face so faraway, as though he was dreaming about something bare and quiet, a winter forest, a lake of ice. I saw the amyctryae biting into throats. There was no strategy—how I had planned for strategy! How we would approach an impregnable city, how we could breach its walls. But this was just hands and teeth and claws, wrangling in the mud. And you know, it didn't look so different from the wrangling I remember, the cranes and the pygmies kissing and writhing—mating and killing look much the same in the dark.

I saw Brother Dawud come running out of the abbey, waving his arms, his round, kind face contorted, his mouth open, crying out to his brothers to stop, stop, stop. That word—*stop*, an impossibility, nothing could stop yet, not enough people were dead yet. His Christian brothers did not want to stop and heaven help me, John's or yours or anyone's, I did not want to stop, either. They had no reason to hurt us, they should be hurt in return. The heat of blood washing over my skin meant winning, meant I was better than they. In war I was a child. I only liked how it felt, I could only feel it, I could not think it or know it or talk to it. The last war in Pentexore ended a thousand years before I was born. How could I know how good and awful it could be, to hurt those who had hurt us? To feel the us-ness of it so wholly, and how us had to go on, and they had to stop. Stop, stop, stop.

I want to confess something. Now that it's all over and quiet. Please do not think badly of me. War has always meant mating. Pleasures of the skin and the body, a rising cascade. I still felt it, when I leapt upon a monk who had just stabbed a poor faun so many times she had no face left. I threw him to the ground and seized his hips between my knees and kissed him on the mouth with blood everywhere, everywhere, and I pushed my knife into him, over and over, out and in again, and he moaned underneath me and I liked it, I liked how he moved, and cried out, and died.

I forgive you, daughter.

I forgive you, mother.

That was when I became her mother, on that plain, by that river, with her shoulders against mine and everything so new and sharp, and I fell over the body of something in the dark, it might have been one of them, or one of us, and she caught me. Father Jibril rushed up behind her and I threw a blade, slippery with monk, into his shoulder. We were both born in all that blood, squelching and black and stinking, and what do you ever call that but family, when the sun shows it all and you need to make it hurt less?

Who killed Jibril, in the end?

I knocked him down and you crushed his throat with your foot, and John, poor John, John who had to pick a side in the end, came running to his wife and his daughter panting over that priest, and he kicked him, he kicked and cried and screamed in his face: "Why? Why? Why?"

But none of us killed him. He lived. I saw him as we were leaving, and boys were tending to him in the sunlight. I hope he never spoke again. When you count up the dead, the ones you want to see are never there.

And Salah ad-Din, he fought with us. Better than us; he knew that kind of battle, where the knives come from behind and you believed you were safe. When he spun, the moon caught on his sword, his helmet, the silver in his tunic. He was made of silver.

He killed Brother Dawud.

That, too.

When the novice came out crying stop, stop, stop, the green knight pulled a short axe from a dead astomi and hurled it at his head. Dawud went down without a sound. Stop, stop, stop. I have no anger on it—Salah ad-Din could not know. It does not matter. Everything falls apart. Everyone dies.

I know you don't want to say it. But you have to. You can't tell the story without it. It wouldn't be a true story then. It would be a story told to hide something.

If I write that, if I put into letters on this page it will have happened again, and again, and again, and every time a pair of eyes reads it it will be happening again and he will never stop dying. He will never stop. I'll be killing him a hundred times.

You have to write it. I will hold your hand. Write his name: Hadulph.

Before Jibril—I will not call him Father, no, not that. Before Jibril came for my daughter he came for my lover, my lion. Events go forward and back in my memory, turning in circles so that it never has to see again that scene in the dark, full of roars. It should not even have been a contest, Hadulph should have swallowed his whole head before the bastard priest got his wretched short sticking blade out, but Jibril is a devil and tall, he is a devil and wiry, he is a devil and quick. He got in under Hadulph, into his soft red belly, and other monks leapt onto his back, and they cut into him over and over, they could not stop, he was too big a prize, to be able to say later they took down an infidel lion, and I heard them laughing while they did it.

I laughed—it gets confused like that. Your body does everything all at once, it laughs and bleeds and screams and shits and runs and stops.

I could not get there fast enough. I could not catch him when he fell.

I forgive you.

It didn't take very long, the fighting, not really. We killed most of them. They retreated into their monastery and Salah ad-Din brokered our peace, our ugly, cold peace, wherein we were allowed to see to our dead and board our ships.

It took my whole life, and all the rest of my life as well.

The worst part was the funerals.

Those who were left buried the dead—we are civilized, we are thinking beings, we bury our dead. The amyctryae tore out the earth with their great mouths, and no one grieved, because they would come back and it would be all right, they would visit the trees in the spring and say: Why, you are looking well, my love! The new pilgrimage would be to Nineveh, where all our beloved army of fools would send up a cheer with their waving boughs when we returned over the hills. I feel as though I knew it would not work, but I think I only had a black foreboding in my chest, looking at that mean, meager soil. Not our soil. Not our impossibly generous earth.

Hajji found Houd in the morning, when the others were burying peacock-knights and cameleopards. She shrieked so horribly my ears popped. I did not know panotii could make a sound like that. She fell on him crying and bellowing, long and low and broken, like he was a son, like he was her own. I wanted to cry too, I wanted to beat his body to punish him for dying. His throat had been cut, flayed, really, back to the bone. But I could only stare, as if I watched it from a long distance.

I will tell both my daughters someday. I will tell them how well and long Hajji loved Houd. She was still sobbing when John brought us together in the ruins of his tent. The morning mist was cold.

The Clouds peeking in to witness.

John the priest said: "Here, what you bury is only buried. They will not come back, none of them. They will rot before we could ever get them home. Dead means dead. You have to stop."

We did not understand. Aya the astomi who had hoarded all her secrets won at sea said: "You mean it will take a long time? We can wait. We can find caves to hide in, with no monks, until it happens."

"No," John said, and his voice choked. "It will never work."

Ummo the sciopod exclaimed: "But the barrels! We brought barrels of earth, we can bury them and take them back with us. At least the smaller ones…"

But the barrels were broken. The monks had stripped the saplings and shredded the hedges for weapons—we had cut and been cut with our own armory, for of course the priests had little enough of their own. I remember looking down, at all the black earth spilled out onto the thirsty grass. How it stained everything, and blew away in the winds.

When we understood, no one spoke. A stillness devoured us. Dead means dead. We were children. We had never met anyone who had died. We had never thought of ambush or blades in the dark, only gamesmanship, fighting in the sun in straight lines. We had been defeated and yet barely fought at all—we could not comprehend it.

My father said to me later: they hurt us because I was unfaithful. And they hurt us because they did not want the world to contain us. They could just barely tolerate it if we consented to act as their weapons, their blades and their arrows. If we consented to become tools. But if we would not—well, there is blood at the bottom of every heart that has never seen sunlight. They wanted their world to stay the shape they had always known it to be, the shape, the size, the substance. They could not bear to see it unfolding, containing so much. I understand it. Once I felt Pentexore was strange and other to me, and I was normal, good, a real man. Now I think there is only us, and we must get back to where we can be safe, and hidden, at the edge of everything. I will hide you from men like me. I will atone for them, who cannot even see the need to atone for themselves. Though perhaps Hagia will let me keep the city names. They are such beautiful words."

I took Hadulph's bones and his eyes and his teeth. I knew I would never get his body back, but I took my relics and they are in a box of cedar in my war-chest. When we are home I will plant him. Nothing that will speak to me or love me again will come from it. It will be a tree of bone in the desert, and its leaves will be red. To love is to bury, but the world is mixed up out here, at the edge of everything. Both love and the earth are broken.

John said: "Hurry. Hurry. We must pull the ships to the Rimal. Better that we spend a year at sea than another moment among jackals."

Jackals aren't so bad. It's only when they scream, they sound like they're dying.

I wish Qaspiel had never come back. I wish I had not had to see its eyes, their total incomprehension, when they lighted upon the field of dead. Had not had to hear the words die in its throat: *I found a way around the river. It is so far, so far, but the river has an end.* I wish I had never seen Qaspiel hold Hadulph's great head in its lap and weep silent white tears. I wish it had just kept on flying, over the sea and on and on, to whatever lands lie beyond this one where no Pentexoran and no human have ever walked. I put my hand on its face. "I want to be a child again," I whispered. "I want to not know anything I know now."

I left a smear of blood on its cheek, shaped like my hand.

We ran away. In ships, hauling the lines over our shoulders, dragging them, our hands still sore and barely washed clean of the holy guts of holy men. Salah ad-Din Yusuf ibn Ayyubi gave us three silver chests full of oranges. For the rotting sickness that comes at sea, he said. He embraced John, and told him never to come back, not ever, no matter what he saw in a mirror. John the king frowned, and rubbed his brow.

"The mirror said we were not there. It said: Jerusalem burns, then Constantinople. It did not say: an army of beautiful monsters came across the sea and saved everyone."

"You would not have saved everyone, anyway. You would have killed me if geography had cooperated."

"I would have. Yes. And I would not have been sorry. Just as they are not sorry for what they did to the demons who came into their territory. God is a field with a line drawn through it, and men to each other: do not cross the line. And the line vanishes with all the boots upon it. But what I mean to say is the mirror showed what is still to come, or has already passed, or both, but what it never showed was me, coming home and putting out flames. It did not show that I was here, that I will be here—and so I never was here, and will never have been here."

Salah ad-Din embraced me, and I could not help it, I cried in his arms as I had not before; I cried for all of us, and him too, who had not come to our country, who held me without embarrassment as my bare breasts touched him. *So easy to love one man,* I thought. *Easy to hate and love John, easy to love Salah ad-Din. I once feared what a nation of Johns might do to me—and I know what a nation of Salah ad-Dins will do to that city in the mirror. No one is righteous. I am not. What of a nation of Hagias? They too would roll and reek in the dirt and push a knife through a boy's brain. On the other side of the Rimal is a place called hell.* But I had finished with speaking and said none of it. The green knight embraced Sukut and the bull-seer told him: "They will love you, you know. The Christians. They will tell stories about you and the king who was half lion. They will love you for all the ways you seemed like them, which is the only reason anyone loves anyone. They will love you because it is so easy to pick out one among the enemy and say: *there, there is a good devil among the horde.* That is an ugly love, a vulture's love. But that is how they will love you. The thread moves through the maze of the sky and you are the ball it streams from."

He embraced me, and I stole a kiss, and he blushed—I think in the end there was a limit to what he could find lovely in his djinni, for he never stopped calling us that. And I made an end with my kisses. But I do not care—I took what I wanted.

Two stayed. When the ground softened and went to swirling eddies of sand, and the ships dipped and bobbed, buoyant suddenly, and a few birds cawed in that way that all seabirds know, two would not come.

The first was Niobe, still clutching her pot, its jewels broken, its capstone cracked. "There is nothing left for me if I cannot find Heliopolis. I cannot bury myself at home. I am one thing, you are all another. I will take Qaspiel's road around the river and find the city of the sun. I will find it all, and I will live."

Aya rubbed her prodigious nose. She righted a table on the deck of our poor flagship. She poured out the stones from the old cup. "Does anyone want to play?" she whispered. And some did. Sukut did. A few blemmye boys. The minotaur sat down at the table and put out his hand flat, palm-down. The betting pose. "Two secrets," he said. "One about the future. One about the past." Aya shook the stones.

[Finally, the blue spores swirled over the paragraph and swallowed it. I felt a kind of relief—I could stop fearing that it would happen. It would. The nature of the world is decay. Everything swirls toward death, even books the color of the sky. The corners of the pages curled darkly, blue-grey, slate. Hiob moaned, and answering him, the mold intensified, gleaming turquoise, swooping down into the margins as if it meant to illuminate the thing itself. I would not know Sukut's secrets. Nor Aya's. But that was always the gamble and the game. Sometimes you hoard your winnings, so as to play again.]

"When you marry a man, do you think you marry a city, too?" Hajji whispered. Her eyes had dried, but she seemed hollow enough to knock over if you were not careful. Brittle. Scoured. "It doesn't matter if you marry someone from the same city as you. But if you marry a foreigner. I married a man from Yerushalayim."

"Hajji," I said gently. "We're not supposed to talk about the old days."

The panoti whirled on me. "I don't *care*. Houd is dead. I don't care. I'll talk about what I like. Isn't that what you wanted all along? To have me tell you a story? Well, be silent, child. I am telling. I married a man from Yerushalayim and I married Yerushalayim. Now I am a widow but Yerushalayim still lives. I am half a widow. Houd always wanted to see Didymus Tau'ma's city. He dreamed of it, what it would be like, how it would smell. He told his sisters he would beat them to it, that he was faster, that they could not catch him. I am going with the green knight. I will hide in one of his silver chests so that no one thinks him wicked for harboring…a djinn. When he takes Yerushalayim as Sukut says he must, as the mirror says he must, I will walk through the streets but recently burned, and I will see the places Tau'ma spoke of, where he and his brother spoke and laughed and told riddles. I will see the pomegranate garden and the table where they ate that strange and final meal. I will eat a meal there, and drink wine, and think my own thoughts alone, in a city of people who do not know my name. I will put my ears up and wrap them in silk. I will wear a veil. I will be invisible. I will be happy. I will see it all for Houd, and he will delight without sound, without form, somewhere over my left shoulder. In a thousand thousand years I will still be there, walking in the streets of a city full of awful wonders, of machines and voices and lights. I will still be there, and so Houd will still be there, and the sun and the moon and I will live as an old married triad, and that is the story of my life that I am telling and will tell forever."

Salah ad-Din Yusuf ibn Ayyubi took Hajji, who was once Imtithal, onto his shoulder without a word. Without a word he consented to her tale.

Her pale ears trailed down like a priestess's stole. I watched them walk out and up, over the grassy hill that once was Nineveh, the Shamash Gate and the stone lions, back to his army and her long road. The light settled down on them, heavy and old.

It is done. We are the living. Everything can go back now, to how it was before. I will introduce you to my mother Kukyk, and you can exchange amusing stories about John. I will take my sister for walks and teach her about the Sedge of Heaven. I will eat everything wonderful that grows in Nural. I will sleep for a year. It is over and now we can be happy. Can't we? That was the battle of Nineveh, and it is over now.

No. That was the battle of Jerusalem. When we come home we will tell them we saw the holy land, and fought there, and that all is well in that part of the world. I will not let Hadulph and Houd and all the rest have died for utterly nothing. For less than nothing, for a story John wanted to tell himself, and that sickens even he. Sickens all of us, as we rode home over the waves for a year and a day. The rotting sickness that comes at sea. And no island with a welcoming nymph to make love to our old war-bones and offer us universes. Just a long, flat horizon and the endless clatter of stones in a cup. Never stopping. Stop, stop, never stop.

I am the one writing this, and that makes it so. That was Jerusalem, and we bled there. Where we died, that was holy land.

THE LEFT-HAND MOUTH,
THE RIGHT-HAND EYE

R un. Four paws on the green earth.

"It's my fault," Elif said into my ear as he rode me, the little cradle-knight, toward the Wall and the girl and the end. "I should have tied her up."

Run. One, two, three, four. Paws eat the distance.

"It's my fault," I said. "I didn't listen to her left-hand mouth. You don't listen when a child says she hates you. If you listened every time they said things like that you'd die of shame. It's like the voices coming out of the old stone. They can't help it, so you just keep working, no matter what whispers out. Children *are* old stones. Ancient flecks of crystal compacted together so fiercely that they remember who they were before, and talk like their parents and their grandparents."

Run. Pad and claw in the moss, in the swamp, in the sand. Wind chafe on the nose, in the eye. Keep running. Never stop. She is so far ahead already.

[Silver-black corruption caught Sefalet up and turned her the color of night. The dark fuzz was tipped with glowing spores, waving lightly, promising a bier for me, too. My great fear was suddenly not that I would lose the tale but that a black blossom would spring up and compel me to devour it as Hiob had. I raced to finish before it could send up its rose. I raced to finish before the book could make me part of it, could drag me inside its sweet-smelling spoil, into a luxurious bed of death.]

Sefalet stood near the Wall. She shivered and clamped her hands over her ears and rocked back and forth. The Wall looked sickly, half-violet, overgrown. Shadows came streaming around the cliffs and the diamond gates and the little huts of the cannibal village at the foot of that terrible gap in the stone, so quiet, as though no one had ever lived there. Elif started to run toward her in his tripping, clopping way. But oh, we had to be careful. There was so much we did not know.

"Sefalet," Elif called to her. "Don't run. You'll get tired out and break."

"I am broken," said both of the princess's mouths.

"No, no," I said, and closed the distance between us, pressing my forehead to the top of hers. Behind me I could hear doors creak as the villagers peered out to see what would happen. "Only sick, my love. Never broken. Now tell your lion why you came running so far. Why you wanted to be here. You see you've arrived and there is nothing unusual, everything is as it has always been. What did you want to do?"

Sefalet put her hands up so that she could look at me with her huge eyes, so like Hagia's. She dropped one—her left.

"To break something big," she whispered. She clapped both hands over her chin, a gesture that in any other girl would have been meant to stifle herself, to keep the words in, but they came so fast I knew they must have hurt coming out, each one a thin, sharp slicing wound.

The right-hand mouth wept: I think it's a real place, the place I see when I dream, the place where the dogs live, and drink from their black bowl. It is somewhere cold, and there are other girls there, two of them. Sometimes I can almost see them, but then they slip away. I think it is a real place and I am there and they didn't mean to hurt me, they only saw I had an empty mouth and they needed it, they needed someone to come here to the Wall and make this happen, because you can't open something without a wedge. It is someplace far away, on the top of the world, but it is not just a dream. It's where I was born. Not me, not really me—because I think I was a baby for a few moments, before I was Sefalet. But Sefalet was born there in the dark with a collar and a leash on her neck, drinking from a bowl of ocean, and speaking with two mouths, and born to be a wedge. But I don't want to be a wedge. I don't want to be the lever or

The left-hand mouth spoke calm and triumphant: In the beginning was the Wall and the Wall was with God and God was a wall. Someone decided the world needed walls. Walls to keep things apart, to keep countries from meeting and mating and merging, to keep order firm and straight, to slow down time, and keep history from running on ahead, so fast, so fast you could never catch her. We can see everything, and it is a real place at the top of the world, but you are not ready to come here yet, you are not ready to know us by our names, only by our works shall you know us, and by our works we will bring the new world into being, we will make it be born. Everything will meet everything else, and there will be no more walls forever, and we promise this is how it must be. We are not capricious, we are just a girl waiting for her first kiss, we are just a new heaven and a new earth waiting to be wakened from a thousand-year sleep by an enchanted princess. We are just Fate, three sisters and this one our youngest of the place to stand on. I want to be a princess and love Elif and Vyala and sleep with my head on my mother's stomach. Why can't I? Why can't I? What did I do? Was I bad? I want to be good, I could be good, if only I could stop being myself I could be good.

all. That is how we have children. We find a mouth no one is using. Three who can see the one world to come, a fourth to bring it round. For the world has chosen and it says: *make me whole.* Think of us as just a kind of haggard Calypso, offering everything, asking the world to choose anew. But it's a lie, really. There is only one choice and it is always the same. Only in Pentexore was any other ever possible. The world always says: *I choose to wither and die, if it means love and tapestries and sons and suitors, if it means stories and wars and a thousand ships launching.* And we only give the world what it wants. Wake up. Wake up.

Sefalet screamed out of both mouths, short sharp screams as though something was cutting her. She turned toward the Wall.

"Don't," Elif whispered. "I'm afraid."

So was I. I tried to seize her up between my teeth, but she was faster. Still screaming, she ran toward the Wall, stumbling, falling toward it. Sunlight came pouring through the ancient, filthy, mossy diamonds of the gates. A kind of music echoed dimly, distant, and I did not realize until too late that it came from the other side of the Wall. A wild, frenetic music, without rhythm, chaotic, gorgeous, unbound. Louder and louder it came as my girl reached the Wall, drawing her breaths like knives, crying and shaking, and the sunlight was in her and she was the light and it came out of her and pooled inside her.

Sefalet put her left hand on the Wall. She went still. She stood up straight, her tears dry in a moment. Her bald head was a jewel in the sunset. Very gently, lovingly, like a bride, Sefalet kissed the diamond Wall with her left-hand mouth.

And the Wall came crashing down into a thousand thousand shards of rubble.

The Virtue of Things
Is in the Midst of Them

18. On Endings

There are only two ways to end a story: with a battle or with a feast. The Greeks knew that—oh, how well did they know it. It must either finish with everyone dead on the stage, full of knife-points and poison, or a marriage and everyone eating their fill, hunger and grief banished, life going on, children to be born and a future to be had. The big secret of stagecraft is that everyone at the feast will be dead soon enough, and everyone bleeding out into the audience has done their part to bring the future into being. Life goes on. Some foreign queen in a strange costume comes on to survey the damage and pass judgment on the poor bastards. She will feast. She will go on. Everyone lives. Everyone burns.

There is only one way to end a story: with a bonfire.

I do not know if I will see home again. I wish to be honest—the chances never looked good. But perhaps my little *Proserpina* is still seaworthy. Perhaps I shall sail yet into the west and back to a place where I am not wanted for any particular thing. If I ever do see an English hearth again, and a bowl of something bland, boiled, lumpy—if someone else's children ask me what I have seen of the world with their big, wild eyes, I will say to them: *I have seen the salamanders dance. And once I knew an emerald as wise as Solomon.* They will not believe me, of course. They will laugh at old John Mandeville, and that is fair. He will be a mad old man by then, if then ever comes.

Ysra and Ymra came for me at midday. I had put on my fool's clothes already. They approved. The king Ysra put all of his hands on my face, his expression complex and brimming with old, old feeling, the way a grandfather looks when he is reminded of his first love, lost forever. When he looked at me I felt as I did when Cabochon shone her feelings out in rays of light—he beamed his deep, dark thrill to me, and it filled me up.

"Something is going to happen," he said finally.

"What?" I asked, and I truly did not know.

Ymra laughed, a little too wild and frantic. "We don't know! We never know! But it will be something."

"Is it a battle or a feast?"

"Yes," the twins said, and before my eyes they kissed one another, in a formal, practiced way, as bride and bridegroom kiss upon their wedding.

> [It was going now, the silver spores moving slowly over the pages, covering the words with light and life and softness. In the crease of the spine the mold darkened to the color of iron. An iron imp, living in the spine of a book, and when it is all done the imp will roll away down the hill and out of the tale. I felt calm. Go, I thought to the glimmering rot. It was always foolish to think I could outrace death. I understood. Nothing stays.]

In the strange way they know, Ysra and Ymra hooked their arms in mine and as soon as we had stepped outside the Mount we stepped onto a green sward before the mossy, bramble-covered

Wall I had heard so much of. The salamanders had come too, and the phoenix, and the mermaids of Isos and the sciopods of Chakor and the dervishes of Summikto as well. The greenwood frame draped in copper silk stood near the Wall, and on it were dozens of black eggs.

"I thought you could not leave the Mount," was all I could think of to say to any of it.

"We reinterpret that to mean it's all right as long as we bring the Mount with us. We drag it along and the rules remain unbroken."

"Are you really sick?"

"Sick is a way of saying we don't belong," Ymra said. And the salamanders began to dance.

They arched their backs and their green skins rippled, they hawked back and spat onto the greenwood and it burst into flame. Ululating cries broke out among the lizards, and the phoenix whistled their oldest, saddest songs. The dervishes began to spin, faster and faster. Something was happening, a battle, a feast, a wedding, a wake—the sciopods stamped their feet and threw up their hands, the mermaids writhed, and the rose-colored lions tossed their manes. Creatures kissed and fed each other red, shining things, and kissed again. The sun flowed down like a river of gold. Finally, as if entering a courtly rite, Ysra and Ymra joined in, moving slowly, radiantly, precisely in the midst of all the wildness of their country. He held her waist, turned her under his arm; she laughed richly and spun, her hair flying out, her skirts, her jeweled belt. Each of their twelve arms caught the others in complex patterns and they turned and turned around one another, wheels within wheels. Down the slope of the valley came the emeralds, rolling with joy, sending off sparks of savage triumph, with my Cabochon in the lead, and they spun around the throng, bouncing and glittering, turned to green fire by the sun. All the light of my Cab said: *We are going home. We are going home.*

As if from a long way off I could hear a crying—it grew louder and became a screaming, a terrified child, a girl in pain. The sound came from the other side of the Wall. I looked at the stones, which must have been beautiful once, shining so bright as to blind. Now they were merely a single living thing, choked up with vegetation and greenery, a hedge, a prison gate. I wanted to help her, the girl on the other side. The girl in the rye field. The girl trapped behind the bodies of eight eunuchs. The girl eating pomegranate seeds in the dark.

"Go," said Ymra. Her brother-king held her by the waist and her smile glowed, awful knowing and hoping and need in that smile, but a terrible beauty, too.

"Go, said Ysra. His sister-queen fit so perfectly into his embrace, and he smiled too, tired and ancient and ready. Ready for whatever was to come.

"Go where?" I said.

Ymra laughed like water moving. "The world was not meant to be closed up behind walls. All we want is an open world, where everything can be known and there is no such thing as the end of the world, because the world is without end. We want to see the world naked—don't you? Haven't you always? Haven't you always suspected that if you could just see her as she really is, she would be so beautiful that you'd never have to tell another lie? This is it, this is your moment. Breaking out is the beginning of being alive."

"But go soon," Ysra warned. "We can only bear the fire so long, the glow of the diamonds, the strength of the gate."

"Go," urged the twin monarchs.

"Go," cried Agneya, writhing in her dance.

"Go," said the phoenix, bursting into flame.

"Go," gurgled the mermaids.

Go, shone Cabochon, and Trillion, and a host of emeralds like strange angels.

The music and the dancing and the light, oh, God, the light

of the sun and the jewels and the flames beat at me and I did not know what I was doing. I am not sorry, now, but I am not glad. I turned to the Wall and walked toward the crying girl on the other side. "Stop," I whispered. "Oh, stop, stop." And I put out my hand to the Wall, a smooth sliver of diamond clear of soil and branch. Her weeping ceased and I felt, through the thick gemstone, an impossibly gentle kiss, as from the first innocent in the infancy of the world. It was a unicorn's kiss; it was Death's kiss.

And between the kiss and my hand, the Wall cracked sickeningly, and came roaring down in a shower of white dust.

The Confessions

It was done; I sat slumped and drained. Only a few pages remained from each of the books, bits of an ending I could not read. I did not feel rage, only sadness and calmness and a kind of bearable hopelessness. I was not Hiob—I did not have to possess, only to touch, once, a thing which might be true.

Behind me, Brother Hiob coughed and choked miserably. The coughing had grown weaker. Soon it would stop (stop, stop). His blooms were so bright now. So bright I could almost forget there had ever been a Hiob without blossoms in his eyes. It had become usual to me, even beautiful. "Go," I said to Reinolt and Goswin. "Go and eat and sleep and look to your body." (*Go and put your hand on the Wall.*)

"What about you?" Reinolt asked me. I could not answer. *What about me?*

"Never mind about me. The tree bears more fruit, the year bears more days—what about me? I have work to do. What a ridiculous question."

They scurried away. No one wants to stay with an angry monk—dangerous creatures, those. My body glowered angrily at me—bitter joints and bilious organs. It could be worse, spleen old friend. You could have a rosebush growing through you like Hiob. Quit your complaining, be happy with your lot.

Hiob cried out, his voice throttled with vines and anguish. No more, I thought. No more, I am not a cruel man. Many

things, but not that. His hands shuddered frantically. I slid a
page beneath it.

*From the far side of the great tree spoke suddenly another head,
and then another, and three Thomases looked at me with pitying
eyes, and Hajji-or-Imtithal kissed them all, one by one, on the
lips, with her whole mouth.*

*"One day you will leave me here, wife," murmured the head
of St. Thomas. "One day you will leave me and I will be so lost."*

*"Never, never," whispered Imtithal, whispered Hajji. "What
could the wide world hold for me that is not here?"*

*"It's all right. It was all right when my brother left, too. Humans
follow patterns, it is what they are made for. And the pattern says:
go, go, go."*

"I am not human," laughed the panoti.

"Oh," the tree smiled, on all of its faces. "You think not?"

*I felt darkness creeping into the corners of my mind, an inkstain
of exhaustion and disbelief and the powerful need to see something
familiar, anything, anyone. A leaf I had known before. But I remember, when I pierce the skin over remembering that does not
wish to be broken, I remember nothing familiar waiting for me in
Nimat. I remember Hagia with snow on her shoulders, laughing,
with the red lion biting her arm playfully. I remember Qaspiel
dancing and leaping into the air, pelting the others with snow,
and all of them giggling like children, like children making war
of the winter, hitting each other with ice over and over. I remember a white stain of snow spreading over Hadulph's scarlet pelt. I
remember Vyala the pale lion opening her mouth, and how it was
red inside her, and as I shuddered, insensate on the long grass, the
lion-mother picked me up by the scruff, like a kitten. Her teeth
on me were the last thing I knew until much later, until they had
carried me down out of the mountains, out of the freeze, and
into the warm valleys, where sweet water ran, and I remember
drinking it. I asked Imtithal—as soon as I woke I asked: was it*

real, was that the truth? As if she were an oracle, and I begging for confirmation of my fortune. Everything is true and nothing is, she said. You could say this means you were right all along, and your God the most true and righteous, or you could say most men have brothers, and love them, and mourn them when they go.

Hajji-or-Imtithal went on: he told me these stories on our bridal bed, too. I half-believe them. Why not? I know winged men live and walk and speak very seriously, I know children can be born different, without any living father. I know the body can die, and return when a green leaf breaks the soil. None of those things require a God to occur. They happen every day. Why should they not have happened to him? I think you would find it remarkably freeing to leave religion aside. When you believe no one thing, everything can be true.

"Tell me what to do," I said. "Tell me how to help you. Tell me how to face the woman in yellow again. Tell me how to keep going."

Fate is a woman, Houd. She is three women. Young, like us, so that they will have the courage be cruel, having no weight of memory to teach temperance. Young, but so old, older than any stone. Their hair is silver, but full and long. Their eyes are black. But when they are at their work they become dogs, wolves, for they are hounds of death, and also hounds of joy. They take the strands of life in their jaws, and sometimes they are careful with their jagged teeth, and sometimes they are not. They gallop around a great monolith, the stone that pierces the earth where the meridians meet, that turns the earth and pins it in place in the world. It is called the Spindle of Necessity, and all round it the wolves of fate run, and run, and run, and the patterns of their winding are the patterns of the world. Nothing can occur without them, but they take no sides.

Is that comforting, Houd? I could also say there is such a stone, such a place, but the dogs who are women died long ago, and left the strands to fall, and we have been helpless ever since. That in a wolfless world we must find our own way. That is more comforting to me. I want my own way, I want to falter; I want to fail, and I want to be redeemed. All these things I want to spool out from the spindle that is me, not the spindle of the world. But I have heard both tales.

Ikram, Who Will One Day Pass Beyond the Gates of Alisaunder: I want to stay here, with you.

Lamis, Who Will One Day Become a Queen Like Her Mother, Shrouded in Mist: I want to be a child again, and fear nothing.

Houd, Who Will One Day Die in Jerusalem: There, Butterfly, there. Beginning tomorrow I will love you for all the rest of my life.

I wish I had been your mother, all of you. That we could have lived quiet lives together and lived them long enough to know all the secrets of the world together. In future days I think those few who decline the Abir will know strange and hidden things, they will stand outside of all of us, moving slower, seeing patterns we cannot see, who have chosen to run so fast, so fast, uncatchably quick, just two hundred years and we will be someone else, and maybe Houd will be my husband and not my son. Oh, it will hurt so much. But it will be so sweet.

The panoti have no God—we have never needed one. But I think I know. God is a time, and time is a fire. If it does not burn us from without it lights us from within.

I stood. My bones argued with me on that point. I went to the benches and gathered up the last few half-rotted pages of our dying books. Carefully and with love I arranged them around Hiob, in a corona around his head and shoulders. I scooped up the vines from the floor and piled them up onto his hands, the old dried blossoms onto his feet. With great and horrible effort

I dragged the bier out of the house and onto the night-grass, a ways from the great tree of books, which waved and whistled in the dark so that it looked as though it bore starry blossoms in some kind of deep celestial spring. The wind moved with purpose and so did I. Hiob's brow creased; his fists opened and closed like a baby.

"I have loved you, Hiob," I whispered. Everything in the world has a twin. A priest and his novice in Constantinople, a priest and his novice here, in the dark, so close to the stars they might burn.

I left him for a moment—only a moment. When I returned I brought my lantern. The flames of it licked at his face, making his dear wrinkles into deep chasms. I cracked open the glass of it and let the oil dribble over him. I spoke the last rites softly, murmuringly, tenderly. I stood with him before the door of death, and I guided him through. I dropped the lantern—the flames caught quickly. They devoured the vines and blossoms and his threadbare habit. They raced around the tendrils of green shoots and it looked like calligraphy, green writing turning to gold. As it reddened the edges of the last pages, the heat burned off the spores and I could glimpse a few final lines, flowing around and through each other as they melted into wet ash and then dust, ringing Hiob's head in a saint's corona of beautifully written words:

I was the unicorn. And a girl drew me to that clearing in the wide wood, and I put my flesh against hers, and there was so much blood after. I turned to find the gaze of Ysra and Ymra, to ask if I had done well, for a shadow passed into me and did not move. But I could not see them, I could not find them. We pulled her out of the diamond rubble, and such bruises there were on her face but still she breathed, and with her in Elif's wooden arms I looked out into a mad dancing throng, burning birds and gleaming enormous emeralds and salamanders—salamanders, whom we all thought long extinct! And in the midst of them stood a man I

*did not know, but he looked like John, he had the same kind of
body. He too, stood bloodied and bruised but bleeding, and looked
around, as though seeking someone who had been there but a moment ago—and as we lit our first campfires on the beach of the
Gharaniq, the same beach John had collapsed upon so many years
before, we looked out onto the Rimal and saw something dancing
there. Two figures, a boy and a girl, little more than children, each
of them with six hands, walking together and dancing a strange
complicated dance. The sun shone upon them, on their long hair
and longer shadows, and many of the older and wise among us
hissed and cried out in recognition and despair. Wherever the feet
of Gog and Magog touched the sandy sea, it grew hard and solid,
like a road.*

I did not reach for the pages to rescue them from the fire.
Hiob's bones seemed to show through his flaming skin, white
and then black. Out of the pages flowers exploded, silver and
black and blue, bulbs shooting out of the words, round and
swollen and dying, flaming, their stamens stretching to escape
the conflagration, their petals curling in like pages, quivering
like animals in their extremity.

They would be together, the books and the man. He would
know everything they knew. I stood in the morning, with the
tree creaking and shaking and the stars wheeling and the first
hush of dawn coming up over the mountains and I watched
them all burn.

⚬⊙⟩⟨⊙⚬

ACKNOWLEDGEMENTS

To correct a previous omission, my great thanks must first go to Theodora Goss and Delia Sherman, who bought the story which grew like a little tree into this trilogy for the first Interfictions anthology. Second, they must fly to the members of the Rio Hondo workshop of 2008, but most especially to Daniel Abraham and Melinda Snodgrass, who broke the plot with me on a sunny day in New Mexico over coffees, and particularly to Daniel, who has taught me so much about the practical business of being a writer, and who wrote the pitch that found a home for these strange little books.

As always, my husband Dmitri has acted as both muse and sounding board, caretaker and research assistant, and I could not possibly repay the debt I owe—except by writing more books. To marry a book-addict is the best destiny for a writer. It pays for much of the grief of this life.

To my agent Howard Morhaim and my editor Juliet Ulman, as well as Ross Lockhart, Jason Williams, and Jeremy Lassen of Night Shade Books.

To Nancy 3 Hoffman, who provided a little museum by the sea which, lying empty in the winter, served high duty as the place where I wrote this novel.

To all my brothers and sisters who stand by me and pick me up when I fall, online and off, my family and my dears.

NIGHT SHADE BOOKS IS AN INDEPENDENT SCIENCE-FICTION & FANTASY PUBLISHER

ISBN: 978-1-59780-199-7 ❧ $14.99 ❧ Look for it in e-book!

> "Valente is one of the most intriguing young writers working in the mythic fiction field today. Her work is lyrical, unusual, ambitious, and deeply rooted in world mythology." ~ Terri Windling

THE HABITATION OF THE BLESSED

A DIRGE FOR PRESTER JOHN **VOLUME ONE**

CATHERYNNE M. VALENTE

This is the story of a place that never was: the kingdom of Prester John, the utopia described by an anonymous, twelfth-century document which captured the imagination of the medieval world and drove hundreds of lost souls to seek out its secrets, inspiring explorers, missionaries, and kings for centuries. But what if it were all true? What if there was such a place, and a poor, broken priest once stumbled past its borders, discovering, not a Christian paradise, but a country where everything is possible, immortality is easily had, and the Western world is nothing but a dim and distant dream?

Brother Hiob of Luzerne, on missionary work in the Himalayan wilderness on the eve of the eighteenth century, discovers a village guarding a miraculous tree whose branches sprout books instead of fruit. These strange books chronicle the history of the kingdom of Prester John, and Hiob becomes obsessed with the tales they tell. *The Habitation of the Blessed* recounts the fragmented narratives found within these living volumes, revealing the life of a priest named John, and his rise to power in this country of impossible richness. John's tale weaves together with the confessions of his wife Hagia, a blemmye—a headless creature who carried her face on her chest—as well as the tender, jeweled nursery stories of Imtithal, nanny to the royal family. Hugo and World Fantasy award nominee Catherynne M. Valente reimagines the legends of Prester John in this stunning tour de force.

NIGHT SHADE BOOKS IS AN INDEPENDENT SCIENCE-FICTION & FANTASY PUBLISHER

ISBN: 978-1-59780-213-0 ❦ $14.99 ❦ Look for it in e-book!

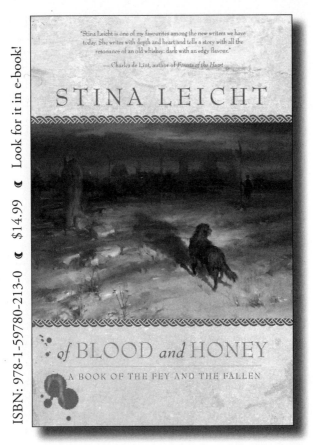

"Stina Leicht is one of my favourites among the new writers we have today. She writes with depth and heart and tells a story with all the resonance of an old whiskey: dark with an edgy flavour."

— Charles de Lint, author of *Forests of the Heart*

STINA LEICHT

of BLOOD and HONEY

A BOOK OF THE FEY AND THE FALLEN

Fallen angels and the fey clash against the backdrop of Irish/English conflicts of the 1970s in this stunning debut novel by Stina Leicht.

Liam never knew who his father was. The town of Derry had always assumed that he was the bastard of a protestant—His mother never spoke of him, and Liam assumed he was dead.

But when the war between the fallen, and the fey began to heat up, Liam and his family are pulled into a conflict that they didn't know existed. A centuries old conflict between supernatural forces seems to mirror the political divisions in 1970s era Ireland, and Liam is thrown headlong into both conflicts.

Only the direct intervention of Liam's real father, and a secret catholic order dedicated to fighting "The Fallen" can save Liam... from the mundane and supernatural forces around him, and from the darkness that lurks within him.

NIGHT SHADE BOOKS IS AN INDEPENDENT
SCIENCE-FICTION & FANTASY PUBLISHER

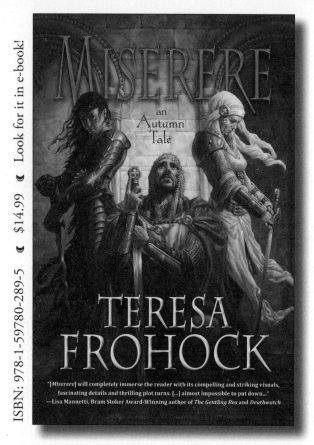

Look for it in e-book! ❦ $14.99 ❦ ISBN: 978-1-59780-289-5

MISERERE

an Autumn Tale

TERESA FROHOCK

"[*Miserere*] will completely immerse the reader with its compelling and striking visuals, fascinating details and thrilling plot turns. [...] almost impossible to put down..."
—Lisa Mannetti, Bram Stoker Award-Winning author of *The Gentling Box* and *Deathwatch*

Exiled exorcist Lucian Negru deserted his lover in Hell in exchange for saving his sister Catarina's soul, but Catarina doesn't want salvation. She wants Lucian to help her fulfill her dark covenant with the Fallen Angels by using his power to open the Hell Gates. Catarina intends to lead the Fallen's hordes out of Hell and into the parallel dimension of Woerld, Heaven's frontline of defense between Earth and Hell.

When Lucian refuses to help his sister, she imprisons and cripples him, but Lucian learns that Rachael, the lover he betrayed and abandoned in Hell, is dying from a demonic possession. Determined to rescue Rachael from the demon he unleashed on her soul, Lucian flees his sister, but Catarina's wrath isn't so easy to escape.

In the end, she will force him once more to choose between losing Rachael or opening the Hell Gates so the Fallen's hordes may overrun Earth, their last obstacle before reaching Heaven's Gates.

NIGHT SHADE BOOKS IS AN INDEPENDENT SCIENCE-FICTION & FANTASY PUBLISHER

ISBN: 978-1-59780-224-6 ❧ $14.99 ❧ Look for it in e-book!

The only thing worse than war is revolution. Especially when you're already losing the war...

Nyx used to be a bel dame, a government-funded assassin with a talent for cutting off heads for cash. Her country's war rages on, but her assassin days are long over. Now she's babysitting diplomats to make ends meet and longing for the days when killing people was a lot more honorable.

When Nyx's former bel dame "sisters" lead a coup against the government that threatens to plunge the country into civil war, Nyx volunteers to stop them. The hunt takes Nyx and her inglorious team of mercenaries to one of the richest, most peaceful, and most contaminated countries on the planet—a country wholly unprepared to host a battle waged by the world's deadliest assassins.

In a rotten country of sweet-tongued politicians, giant bugs, and renegade shape shifters, Nyx will forge unlikely allies and rekindle old acquaintances. And the bodies she leaves scattered across the continent this time... may include her own.

Because no matter where you go or how far you run in this world, one thing is certain: the bloody bel dames will find you.

NIGHT SHADE BOOKS IS AN INDEPENDENT SCIENCE-FICTION & FANTASY PUBLISHER

ISBN: 978-1-59780-220-8 ❦ $15.99 ❦ Look for it in e-book!

HAPPILY EVER AFTER

EDITED BY
JOHN KLIMA

with an
Introduction by
BILL WILLINGHAM

FAIRY TALES
RETOLD BY

GREGORY MAGUIRE
HOLLY BLACK
NEIL GAIMAN
PATRICIA BRIGGS
CHARLES DE LINT
SUSANNA CLARKE
GARTH NIX
KAREN JOY FOWLER
PETER STRAUB
KELLY LINK
and many others...

Once Upon A Time...in the faraway land of Story, a Hugo-winning Editor realized that no one had collected together the fairy tales of the age, and that doorstop-thick anthologies of modern fairy tales were sorely lacking...

And so the Editor ventured forth, wandering the land of Story from shore to shore, climbing massive mountains of books and delving deep into lush, literary forests, gathering together thirty-three of the best re-tellings of fairy tales he could find. Not just any fairy tales, mind you, but tantalizing tales from some of the biggest names in today's fantastic fiction, authors like Gregory Maguire, Susanna Clarke, Charles de Lint, Holly Black, Aletha Kontis, Kelly Link, Neil Gaiman, Patricia Briggs, Paul Di Filippo, Gregory Frost, and Nancy Kress. But these stories alone weren't enough to satisfy the Editor, so the Editor ventured further, into the dangerous cave of the fearsome Bill Willingham, and emerged intact with a magnificent introduction, to tie the collection together.

And the inhabitants of Story, from the Kings and Queens relaxing in their castles to the peasants toiling in the fields; from to the fey folk flitting about the forests to the trolls lurking under bridges and the giants in the hills, read the anthology, and enjoyed it. And they all lived...

...Happily Ever After.

NIGHT SHADE BOOKS IS AN INDEPENDENT SCIENCE-FICTION & FANTASY PUBLISHER

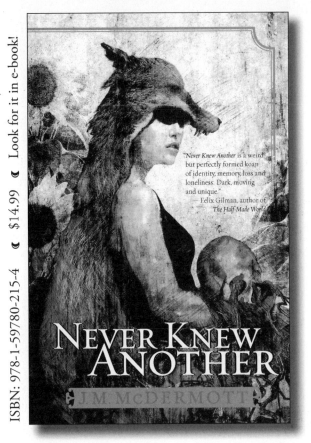

ISBN: 978-1-59780-215-4 • $14.99 • Look for it in e-book!

"*Never Knew Another* is a weird but perfectly formed koan of identity, memory, loss and loneliness. Dark, moving and unique."
— Felix Gilman, author of *The Half-Made World*

NEVER KNEW ANOTHER
J. M. McDERMOTT

J. M. McDermott delivers the stunning new fantasy novel, *Never Knew Another*—a sweeping fantasy novel that revels in the small details of life.

Fugitive Rachel Nolander is a newcomer the city of Dogsland, where the rich throw parties and the poor just do whatever they can to scrape by. Supported by her brother Djoss, she hides out in their squalid apartment, living in fear that someday, someone will find out that she is the child of a demon. Corporal Jona Lord Joni is a demon's child too, but instead of living in fear, he keeps his secret and goes about his life as a cocky, self-assured man of the law. *Never Knew Another* is the story of how these two outcasts meet.

Never Knew Another is the first book in the Dogsland Trilogy.

Catherynne M. Valente is the author of over a dozen books of fiction and poetry, including *Palimpsest*, the Orphan's Tales series, and *The Girl Who Circumnavigated Fairyland in a Ship of Her Own Making*. She is the winner of the Tiptree Award, the Andre Norton Award, the Lambda Award, the Mythopoeic Award, the Rhysling Award, and the Million Writers Award. She was a finalist for the World Fantasy Award in 2007 and 2009, and the Locus and Hugo awards in 2010. She lives on an island off the coast of Maine with her partner, two dogs, an enormous cat, and an accordion.